OXFORD WORLI

THE GIRL WITH TI

AND OTHER STORIES

HONORÉ DE BALZAC was born in 1799 at Tours, the son of a civil servant. Put out to nurse and sent later to boarding-school, he had, except between the ages of four and eight, little contact with home. In 1814 the family moved to Paris, where Honoré continued his boarding-school education for two years and then studied law at the Sorbonne. From 1816 to 1819 he worked in a lawyer's office, but having completed his legal training he knew he wanted to be a writer. While his family gave meagre financial support he wrote a play, *Cromwell*, but it was a complete failure. He also collaborated with other writers to produce popular novels. During the 1820s he dabbled in journalism, and tried to make money in printing and publishing ventures, whose lack of success laid the foundation for debts that plagued him for the rest of his life.

In 1829 Balzac published his first novel under his own name, *Le Dernier Chouan* (later *Les Chouans*), and *La Physiologie du mariage*. In 1830 came a collection of six stories called *Scènes de la vie privée*. Self-styled 'de Balzac', he became fashionable in the literary and social world of Paris, and over the next twenty years, as well as plays and articles, wrote more than ninety novels and stories. In 1842 many of these were published in seventeen volumes as *La Comédie humaine*. Important works were still to come, but ill-health interfered with his creativity and marred the last years of his life.

In 1832, in his extensive fan-mail, Balzac received a letter from the Polish Countess Hanska, whose elderly husband owned a vast estate in the Ukraine. The next year he met Madame Hanska in Switzerland, and in 1835 the couple agreed to marry after Count Hanska's death. For seventeen years, with intermissions, they conducted a voluminous correspondence, until their marriage finally took place in March 1850. Balzac died three months later in Paris.

PETER COLLIER is Emeritus Fellow in Modern and Medieval Languages at Sidney Sussex College, Cambridge, where he was University Senior Lecturer in French. He has translated Zola's *Germinal* for Oxford World's Classics, and Proust's *The Fugitive*. He is the author of *Proust and Venice*.

PATRICK COLEMAN is Professor of French at the University of Los Angeles, California. He has edited Rousseau's *Confessions* and *Discourse on Inequality*, Constant's *Adolphe*, and Balzac's *The Wild Ass's Skin* for Oxford World's Classics. His most recent book is *Anger, Gratitude, and the Enlightenment Writer* (OUP, 2011).

OXFORD WORLD'S CLASSICS

HONORÉ DE BALZAC

The Girl with the Golden Eyes and Other Stories

Translated with Notes by
PETER COLLIER

With an Introduction by
PATRICK COLEMAN

OXFORD
UNIVERSITY PRESS

Great Clarendon Street, Oxford, OX2 6DP,
United Kingdom

Oxford University Press is a department of the University of Oxford.
It furthers the University's objective of excellence in research, scholarship,
and education by publishing worldwide. Oxford is a registered trade mark of
Oxford University Press in the UK and in certain other countries

First published as an Oxford World's Classics paperback 2012
Impression: 10

British Library Cataloguing in Publication Data
Data available

Library of Congress Cataloging in Publication Data
Data available

ISBN 978–0–19–957128–4

Printed in Great Britain by
Clays Ltd, Elcograf S.p.A.

CONTENTS

INTRODUCTION

BALZAC is a writer eager to provide his readers with answers to questions, with solutions to mysteries. Do you want to know how a Restoration banker makes his money, how a Romantic dandy spends his days, what schemes may be concealed behind a lady's veil or a thief's disguise? Balzac will give you even the information you didn't know you wanted, and more. This generosity with information, which befits the capacious genre of the realist novel, is also found in Balzac's shorter fictions, where one expects a more concentrated action and a more focused selection of detail. In *The Girl with the Golden Eyes*, one of the three stories gathered here, the plot doesn't even get going until Balzac has given the reader a virtuoso description of a day in the life of typical Parisians of almost every social class. This wealth of information seems to be included more to dazzle the reader with a display of knowledge than to provide a context for the action, but one of Balzac's aims is to make us wonder whether there is ever such a thing as an irrelevant detail. Anything and everything may contribute something vital to our understanding of reality. The novelist Henry James, a great admirer of Balzac, put the point well: 'nothing appealed to him more than to show *how* we all are, and how we are placed and built-in for being so. What befalls us is but another name for the way our circumstances press upon us—so that an account of what befalls us is an account of our circumstances.'[1]

Indeed, the events in the story sometimes amount to a brief episode in a longer chain of events whose links extend far into the past. Do you wonder how it comes about that someone of routine habits suddenly explodes with passion, or how an apparently flourishing business falls so swiftly into bankruptcy? Balzac is ready to link effects with their hidden causes, often introducing his analysis with the simple 'Here is why...'. Where the narrator gets his knowledge, however, is less clear. On one level, of course,

[1] Henry James, 'Honoré de Balzac' (1902), in Henry James, *Literary Criticism: French Writers, Other European Writers, the Prefaces to the New York Edition* (New York: The Library of America, 1984), 135.

the knowledge the novelist claims must be taken for granted, at least provisionally. Only after we have taken our bearings under the author's guidance and explored this fictional world for ourselves can we get a sense of whether or when it makes sense to question what we are told about that world. Yet, in Balzac's fiction authoritative explanation is so insistent that it draws attention to itself from the start. It unsettles the conventions of what knowledge can or should be taken for granted just as much as Balzac's copiousness of information disturbs our conventional sense of the balance between description and plot. The two other stories in this volume illustrate the point. In *Sarrasine* many of the guests at Madame de Lanty's ball wonder how the family acquired its fortune. Only the narrator knows, yet he is himself one of the characters in the story, and he never tells us how he came to know the answer. The more he underscores his special access to a hidden truth—the better to seduce his curious female companion—the more the reader wonders about his privileged status.

In *The Unknown Masterpiece* we have the ironic situation of a fictional artist named Frenhofer explaining why a painting done by an artist who actually existed, François Porbus, doesn't really 'live'. The reader gets a vivid image of that painting (which itself exists only in Balzac's story), not from a description of what Frenhofer sees, but rather from his explanation of what he *doesn't* see because Porbus failed to execute the painting properly. The critic Roland Barthes has pointed out that an ugly face is easier to describe in concrete detail than a beautiful one, since it is easier to visualize something flawed than something perfect, but Balzac gives the idea a new twist. We derive our image of the painting from a technical analysis of Porbus's failure to use lines and colours properly; the content of the painting, the scene Porbus depicts, is hardly described at all. Frenhofer goes on to correct the painting with a few quick strokes, to the admiration of his audience. Yet, if the explanation of how the painting is constructed becomes the focus of attention, then the public is more likely to question the artist's authority than if it were simply given a finished painting to admire. Trained artists and connoisseurs have of course always argued about technique, but here these matters of craft are brought out into the open and turned into a discussion about the basis of artistic power. One definition of 'modern' art might be precisely that it accepts, even invites, investigation of the process behind the product, but Balzac is perhaps the first writer to present the issue so explicitly, and with the intention of increasing rather than diminishing our reverence for the artist.

It was only to be expected that Balzac's free way with information and explanation would itself come to be scrutinized. In the last two generations especially, critics have double-checked the accuracy of Balzac's information about the society of his time, debated the persuasiveness of his explanations, and deconstructed the authority with which Balzac offers them. A great writer, it is now generally assumed, must be wary of conclusive answers. For the *nouveau roman* writers of the 1950s and the structuralist critics of the 1960s 'Balzacian' became the label for a literary attitude of over-confident certainty in the truth of artistic representation, an illusion best consigned to the dustbin of discredited ideologies. Roland Barthes's study of *Sarrasine*, published under the enigmatic title *S/Z* (1970), has become a classic of this kind of criticism. The very strength of the argument has prompted more recent critics to push back against it, and it is now agreed that in some ways Balzac is a less assertive writer than may appear at first sight. A categorical pronouncement he makes in one place is often contradicted by another one offered elsewhere, a clash of perspectives of which the author was well aware as he juxtaposed them in the collected works he called *La Comédie humaine*.

Yet, one should beware of turning Balzac too quickly into the postmodern ironist he is not. If his fiction is less tidy in its resolutions than he sometimes boasts, it is not because Balzac finds himself unable to provide a solution to the questions he raises. In a fictional œuvre as ambitious as the (unfinished) *Comédie humaine* some loose ends will never be tied up, simply for lack of time and space. It is more faithful to Balzac to think of him as someone determined to provide the reader with answers, but to recognize that information and explanation are not the only kinds of answer he offers. Alongside what might be called the provisional mysteries of how and why something happens, there is also the deeper, more enduring mystery 'that' something just is. Here, the answer takes the form not of information or explanation, but of an invitation to receptive contemplation. A novel such as *Eugénie Grandet*, rich in explanatory detail at the start, ends with such an invitation: to see the heroine as the person she has become, in a manner that leaves off searching for further knowledge, not because we have no further questions about her past or future, but rather because those questions gradually lose their point as we allow ourselves simply to take in the picture of the woman with which Balzac leaves us. After reading a novel like this one, we understand how Henry James, who at first sight appears so much more preoccupied with literary aesthetics than Balzac, could speak of an 'inscrutable perfection' in his predecessor that transcends the mass of all-too-scrutable details.

One should not, however, exaggerate Balzac's idealism. In other novels, *Père Goriot* being a good example, this kind of contemplation is dramatized within the story as only a moment within the life of a hero who quickly returns to more practical concerns. As he contemplates the dying Goriot, the young Rastignac is so deeply impressed by the spectacle of the old man who has foolishly but unstintingly sacrificed everything for his children that for a moment he sets his self-interest aside. Yet, although Rastignac is forced to recognize the mixed nature of his own motives, his eagerness to put the answers to his questions about Goriot's daughters to practical use is ultimately unaffected. What he discovers gives him pause, but it does not reach the core of his identity. The stories in this volume present their heroes with this more radical kind of test, an image of themselves and their desires not so easily integrated among the others that together compose the necessarily plural or divided identity with which the modern self learns more or less comfortably to live. The outcome in each case is different, but it is important to recognize that whatever the result, it cannot easily be judged by reference to an agreed-upon standard of success. One reason why these stories are unsettling is that the severity of the test is not matched by a clear notion of what would constitute a heroic response.

Each of the three stories dramatizes what happens when a

question vital to the erotic and aesthetic desires of the hero (in each case the central character is a man) is answered, not just by information gained or explanation found, but by an object or image which, when finally seen, forces the character to confront a difficult truth about those desires. Not only is the female figure who represents both a sexual and an artistic ideal not who the hero thought she was—a common enough mistake—but the desires themselves suddenly appear in a new, unwelcome light, such that the hero's most cherished image of himself is redrawn. It is the kind of answer that cannot be put to immediate use. First and foremost, it needs to be faced, and the self-contemplation involved is no easy matter. What is particularly intriguing about these stories is the way Balzac embeds this drama within another one. In each case, the central character's quest is an object of discussion by or with other characters, and in different ways the answers revealed about the questing character reveal something in turn about the curiosity of these other characters. Because of their peculiar double structure, which highlights the unexpected existential and moral stakes involved in dealing with discoveries of meaning, these stories may be said to belong to what one critic has called Balzac's 'hermeneutical narratives'.[2] One should add that this hermeneutical focus extends to the way Balzac structures the reader's relationship to the texts. In contrast to a novel like *Père Goriot*, the stories do not tell us what happens afterwards, when the surviving characters return (if they can) to their normal lives. The author leaves us at the point where the drama of discovery turns back on itself. What readers are supposed to make of what they have learned is an issue Balzac also leaves open.

It is likely that Balzac's narrative strategy in these stories owes something to his experience in journalism. In 1830, after the commercial failure of his historical novel *The Chouans*, Balzac turned to the new weekly and monthly magazines that sprang up just before and just after the July Revolution which toppled the restored Bourbon monarchy and put Louis-Philippe on the throne. For several years, he earned much of his living from the

[2] Chantal Massol, *Une poétique de l'énigme: le récit herméneutique balzacien* (Geneva: Droz, 2006).

sketches, stories, reviews, and polemical essays he contributed to them. The first two stories in this volume date from this period. *Sarrasine* (1830) appeared in the *Revue de Paris*, a general-interest magazine launched the year before, while *The Unknown Masterpiece* (1831) came out in *L'Artiste*, a weekly paper focused on the arts. Each was published in two instalments. *The Girl with the Golden Eyes* (1834–5) was written when Balzac had achieved some measure of success and was beginning to publish again directly in book form, adding new works to old in an ongoing series of volumes of 'scenes' and 'tales'. As in some of the other new works, however, Balzac incorporated into this longer story a bit of his journalistic writing, a humorous profile of 'The Little Haberdasher' (1830), a sketch of a contemporary social 'type' he had published in the satirical paper *La Caricature*.

The first decades of the nineteenth century had seen the significant expansion of a reading public eager to keep up with topics of current interest, from the latest trends in art and fashion to the exotic customs discovered in foreign lands—not just those of the 'Orient' France was exploring and conquering at this time, but those of the hidden corners of the ever-expanding and diversely stratified metropolis that Paris had become. Clever entrepreneurs such as Émile de Girardin, with whom Balzac was acquainted, attracted subscribers with new magazines designed both to satisfy and to cultivate what today we call the 'aspirational' desires of cultural consumers. These were not yet the cheap mass-circulation newspapers of the 1840s, in which Balzac, like Eugène Sue and Victor Hugo, would publish long novels in serial form. The production techniques for these were not yet in place. Rather, these smaller publications of 1830 aimed at various 'niche' markets, and sought to give their relatively prosperous readers a flattering sense of being 'in the know'. Their contributors, including Balzac, tackled such topics as the unwritten and supposedly mysterious rules of behaviour that marked one as belonging to, or a suitable candidate for, a prestigious elite group, or labelled one unwittingly as an illustration of a particular social type. In these articles the boundary between investigation and imagination is often hard to draw, just as it would be difficult to determine to what extent readers were seeking practical information or merely a model for the witty conversation that itself constituted an asset in Paris society. The fact that Restoration censorship did not allow for explicitly political debate in these papers presented an additional occasion for writers to display their ingenuity by forcing them to find clever ways to elude a constraint they could not openly challenge, just as they needed to find a balance between conforming to the expectations of the paper's subscribers and providing them with the surprise revelations they also craved. Balzac, for one, made no secret of his discomfort with a creative servitude he felt all the more keenly because of the contrast with his own ideal of the unfettered artist inspiring the people to think great thoughts. At the very least, he could make his readers aware of how conscious he was of their curiosity, thereby infusing his writing with a further dimension of knowing irony, an irony directed at the author as much as at his readers, but which he sometimes turned into an occasion for more biting reflection.

Sarrasine

We see this most clearly in *Sarrasine*, the earliest of the stories gathered here. The unnamed narrator is presented as a liminal figure standing on the threshold of a lavish party given by the Lanty family. He has brought with him a young woman who seems not quite to belong in this exalted milieu. Although in the final version published here she is called Madame de Rochefide, the name of a character who appears elsewhere in the *Comédie humaine* (Balzac adopted this device of 'recurring characters' to give his work greater unity and depth), she is identified as a dancer, hardly the occupation of a genuine lady. There is the suggestion that the narrator hopes to gain her favours by offering her a glimpse of high society and initiating her into some of its secrets. One wonders, though, if the narrator would have volunteered to tell the sexually scandalous story of Sarrasine if he had not been provoked into doing so by an unexpected turn of events. After an unsettling encounter with a strange old man who plays a mysteriously important role in the Lantys' family life, the narrator and his companion take refuge in a room decorated with a painting of Adonis, with which Madame de Rochefide becomes so smitten as to arouse the narrator's jealousy. To break the spell, he will reveal the identity of the person who served as the ultimate model for a figure Madame de Rochefide says is more beautiful than any ordinary man. The narrator can't compete on the level of erotic attractiveness, nor can he paint, but he is in possession of a secret known only to a very few, and he counts on this knowledge to triumph over the competition. What he fails to anticipate, however, is that his revelations will turn against him. Madame de Rochefide will find in them an unwelcome answer about her effort to legitimize the fulfilment of sexual desire by attaching it to a transcendent ideal that lifts it above the level of material transaction.

The disconcerting effect of this framing narrative echoes that of the events the narrator goes on to relate, and which took place in the mid-eighteenth century, that is, in a pre-revolutionary past recent enough to lie within living memory yet psychologically remote. An impetuous young sculptor named Sarrasine leaves Paris for Rome in order to complete his artistic education. For reasons Balzac only hints at, Sarrasine's teacher has kept him in the dark about some of 'the realities of life', notably about what kind of singers at that time played the female operatic roles in the Papal States. Yet Sarrasine's failure to take the many hints given him by the diva known as La Zambinella, with whom he becomes infatuated, suggests a stubborn insistence stemming from something more complicated than simple naivety. In a story actually written in the eighteenth century (the autobiography of Casanova, for example, which Balzac may have used as a source), the hero's eventual discovery that 'she' is really a castrato would have been the occasion for a comic or rueful comeuppance, or for a display of compassionate sensibility. Sarrasine, however, is neither a picaresque hero nor an enlightened man of feeling. His reaction is rage, a rage that is directed more against himself than at anyone else, and at his artistic just as much as at his masculine identity. The 'truth' about the beauty he has captured in his sculpture of Zambinella, the iconographic source of the painting contemplated by Madame de Rochefide, appears to undermine the integrity of the artwork as much as it exposes an unacknowledged dimension of the artist's desires.

The revelations Balzac so complexly orchestrates in *Sarrasine* certainly reflect a general mood of disenchantment with literary idealism, as well as his resentment at having to cater to the prurient yet jaded curiosity of magazine readers. But they do more than make a point about the writer's powerlessness and prostitution in the cultural marketplace. The lurid excess of the drama combined with the inarticulateness of the characters' reaction to it point to a deeper unease, one which can be illustrated but not explained. In this respect, *Sarrasine* belongs to a tradition of French Romantic fictions about men suffering from a disturbance in the conventional pattern of erotic and gender relations. In Chateaubriand's *René* (1802), the hero's life is blasted by the revelation of his sister's incestuous love for him. The hero of Stendhal's *Armance* (1827) refuses to marry the woman of the title because of an impediment that is never revealed in the novel itself. In a letter he wrote to his friend and fellow author Prosper Mérimée, Stendhal claimed the problem is impotence, the subject of the unpublished novel which inspired him, Madame de Duras's *Olivier*, but it has been argued on textual and other evidence that homosexuality is also a possible explanation. The most immediate influence on *Sarrasine*, however, was Henri de Latouche's *Fragoletta, or Naples in 1799* (1829), which Balzac reviewed upon publication as a favour to an author who was also a literary friend. Like Sarrasine, Latouche's hero is a Frenchman in Italy, in this case an officer of the revolutionary army fighting on behalf of the short-lived Neapolitan republic, who falls in love with a tomboyish girl who eludes his pursuit. Back in Paris on leave, he discovers his sister enchanted by Fragoletta's delicately handsome brother, who likewise flees when the subject of marriage is broached. Early in the book the hero is taken to see a Roman statue of a hermaphrodite in a Naples museum (the description fits the Borghese hermaphrodite purchased by Napoleon in 1807 and exhibited in the Louvre). The end of the novel reveals, though in discreetly veiled terms, that Fragoletta is such an in-between creature, admired in art as combining the beauty of both sexes, yet prevented in life from enjoying full sexual partnership with either man or woman. As in *Sarrasine*, the tension between artistic fullness and sexual lack is also illustrated by the figure of the castrato singer. We are told that a sign on a Naples building advertises that castrati singers are produced there. Although many French readers would be able to understand the Italian phrase in the text, Latouche offers a translation in a footnote, taking the opportunity, however, to change 'castrated' to 'perfected'.

Latouche's irony is connected to the political events of the novel. The sign is being repainted as a corrupt and despotic monarchy is returning in triumph to Naples, and as Napoleon's *coup d'état* draws the curtain on a French republic already weakened by the feckless leaders of the Directory. Latouche's republicanism was not shared by Chateaubriand or Stendhal, or by Balzac, who at the time he wrote *Sarrasine* was moving from a youthful liberalism similar to Stendhal's to an allegiance to the exiled Bourbon monarchy as idiosyncratic in its way as that of Chateaubriand. Yet, common to all these writers is a sensitivity to the emotional turmoil caused by the dislocations of political and moral order that began with the Revolution and the execution of the king, the symbolic father of the nation, and continued through further violent changes of regime and ideology: the militaristic virility of Napoleon's empire, the reactionary efforts of the Bourbons to restore the prestige of throne, altar, and age, and the complacently bourgeois monarchy of Louis-Philippe, with his cloying image as the model family man. For sensitive young men especially, these changes seem to have affected the most intimate dimensions of personal identity, such as the integrity of bodily self-image and sexual difference, and the deep cultural taboos that underpin that identity by demarcating familial bonds from those of marriage and other sexual, emotional, and social relationships. That the connections were more intuited than explained is understandable, since such disturbances do not lend themselves to clear theoretical understanding on the part of those who experience them. The kind of 'answer' *Sarrasine* offers seems designed to make one wonder how the question might rightly be phrased. One might call it a symptomatic fiction.

One further feature of *Sarrasine* is worth remarking, and may serve as a transition to the next two stories. This is Balzac's ambivalent presentation of the various father-figures in the story: Sarrasine's biological father, the Jesuits, and the painter Bouchardon. None of them is entirely bad; indeed, they are all quite indulgent in various ways, at times surprisingly so, given the turbulence of Sarrasine's character. Their authority is not really disputed, yet the young sculptor does not find in any of them the guidance he really needs. There is a failure in the transmission of a crucial structuring viewpoint, one that would enable Sarrasine, by working through or against it, to define himself clearly in relation to the world and his own desires. What that something is is not defined, but its absence seems to be related to the violent but obscure disorder in Sarrasine's character that drives his first mistress away, as if it were something she, as a woman of Sarrasine's own generation, could not remedy. (It is noteworthy that the crucial relationship of Balzac's own early manhood was with a considerably older woman, Madame de Berny, who was both his lover and a substitute mother, and that with the gruesome exception of Paquita's mother in *The Girl with the Golden Eyes*, maternal figures are notably absent from all three of the stories here.) When confronted with full knowledge of the 'realities of life', Sarrasine is unable to handle it. A father-figure's failure to transmit identity-structuring guidance to the younger man, a failure manifested in the latter's morally and aesthetically polarized conceptions of womanhood, is also found in *The Unknown Masterpiece* and *The Girl with the Golden Eyes*, but in a more elaborated, reflective form that suggests that if Balzac has not found a resolving insight, he has at least gained some perspective on the problem.

In these stories the disruption of genealogical and gender structures that in *Sarrasine* short-circuits the narrator's communication of desire and triggers in his listeners an inchoate and melancholy pensiveness becomes the starting-point for a less paralysing contemplation of unconventional forms of desire. Enabling this exploration is Balzac's belief in the process of aesthetic reflection, modelled not by ordinary father-figures but by artists devoted to the authority of art itself, as an alternative means of structuring the identity of the self and integrating its chaotic and conflicting desires into a larger whole. This shift in perspective is already apparent in *A Passion in the Desert*, a short tale Balzac published the same year as *Sarrasine*. A soldier on campaign in Egypt with Napoleon meets a female panther in a cave. A strange intimacy develops between them—one might even call it an affair, given the sexual overtones of the narrative. As in *Sarrasine*, the relationship ends in violence, but when the soldier tells his story, many years later, to a woman he meets at the zoo, his tone is more wistful than seductive, for his desire is transformed into a painterly appreciation of the desert landscape that was the setting for his experience. The rhetoric of sublimity into which the disquieting elements of the tale are absorbed may sound hackneyed to the sceptical reader, but through it Balzac is sincerely reaching for some kind of aesthetic transcendence.

The Unknown Masterpiece

The Unknown Masterpiece offers both a more explicit and extreme example of the aesthetic redemption of questionable desires by art, and a sharp critique of such attempts. Again we find two connected plots, and as the story was revised over several different versions, Balzac seems to have hesitated as to which should serve as a frame for the other. At the centre of the tale is Nicolas Poussin, one of the great artists of seventeenth-century French classicism, portrayed here at the start of his career. Newly arrived in Paris, he encounters two older artists: François Porbus, a real painter associated with the court of Henri IV and Marie de Medici, and an invented character named Frenhofer (no first name is given), whose career is said to have begun well back into the sixteenth century as the pupil of Jan Mabuse (d. 1532). The historical setting provides Balzac with a convenient way of treating the long-standing debate over the relative priority of line and colour in painting, which in the Italian Renaissance had opposed the painters of Florence and Rome to those of Venice, and which had been revived in new form in French Romanticism in the quarrel between the partisans of Ingres and Delacroix. As the dedication of *The*

Girl with the Golden Eyes to Delacroix indicates, not to mention the frequent use of 'red', 'yellow', and 'white' in the story, Balzac leant toward colour, but he was even more interested in the possibility of transcending this opposition in a higher, more totalizing conception of art, and the development of this concern is reflected in the composition history of *The Unknown Masterpiece*. The information about Mabuse, Porbus, and Poussin in the 1831 magazine version of the story is drawn almost entirely from accounts of the painters' lives in Michaud's *Biographie universelle*, a widely distributed reference work of the day.[3] Frenhofer's detailed critique of Porbus's painting was added in 1837, by which time Balzac had become personally acquainted with leading members of the Paris art world and had gained a greater familiarity with its technical vocabulary. At the same time, this display of critical mastery will make Frenhofer's fate appear all the more poignant. If *his* reach exceeds his grasp, then what chance do others have? Unless, that is, Balzac is saying that the writer can succeed where painters have failed.[4]

In addition to providing Balzac with art-historical perspective, his decision to set the story in an earlier period of French culture had other advantages. One was to insert his tale into a broader current of reflection among painters of the Restoration period about the past as at once a source of renewed inspiration and an obstacle to it. This reflection on their historical condition was also a way for artists to think about their relationship to reality in general. They realized they had to define themselves in opposition to reality in order to achieve the creative independence they needed to represent it. One product of the ironic perspective to which such reflections led offers a particularly interesting analogue to Balzac's preoccupations in *The Unknown Masterpiece*. Ingres's *Raphael and La Fornarina* (1814) depicts the artist Balzac admired above any other sitting in his studio with his mistress Margherita Luti on his lap (she was called 'La Fornarina' because she was a

[3] See Adrien Goetz, 'Frenhofer et les maîtres d'autrefois', *L'Année balzacienne*, NS 15 (1994), 69–89.

[4] This is the case argued by Alexandra Wettlaufer in *Pen vs. Paintbrush: Girodet, Balzac, and the Myth of Pygmalion in Postrevolutionary France* (New York: Palgrave, 2001).

baker by trade). His arm is around her waist, but his brush is still in his hand, and his gaze is directed at the portrait of Margherita on which he had been working when she came in, not at the woman herself. Nor is she looking at Raphael, but rather at the spectators, as if inviting them to ponder the artist's ambivalent position, caught between the real and the painted woman.

Casting the artist's dilemma in terms of a love divided between the real and the ideal is a time-honoured conceit. But in a post-revolutionary world, in which traditional religious or philosophical world-views no longer offered a plausible imaginative context in which that dilemma could be resolved, the use of real-life models as a means to aesthetic transcendence could be seen as morally troublesome. Ingres's painting reflects this disquiet, but it also seeks to contain it by locating his scene in the historical past, just as other artists have used the resources of mythology or a mythified history to provide a mediating context for the treatment of problematic issues in the relation between art and sexual desire. 'La Fornarina' is in a sense already a figure of art, already at one remove from any living woman. In Balzac's story the notion of prostitution becomes increasingly problematic as we move from Porbus's (fictitious) portrait of *Mary of Egypt*, a saint of the early church, to Frenhofer's 'contemporary' portrait of the courtesan Catherine Lescault, nicknamed 'La Belle Noiseuse' (and who may or may not be Frenhofer's invention), and finally to Poussin's attitude toward his real-life model, Gillette. Even so, Balzac can write more freely, without moralizing precautions and justifications, about the relationship between a seventeenth-century painter and his mistress than he could do about a similar couple living in the Paris of his own day. The world of his story is still fairly close to the pre-modern France of medieval farces and Rabelais. Balzac could set his ribald *Contes drolatiques* in that period without fear of reproach, because the earthy tolerance for sexual licence associated with that past had been legitimized as a component of a 'French' national character.

At the same time, Poussin was revered as the inaugurator of the more severe outlook of an even more prized component of French tradition: the classicism of the seventeenth century. When the

Poussin of the story asks Gillette to pose nude for Frenhofer so that he may get a glimpse of the old man's jealously guarded masterpiece, his request is morally more fraught than the light-hearted, almost picaresque opening of the story led us to expect. In his own discourse about painting, Frenhofer endowed art with a value that transcends other considerations, and yet, instead of exemplifying a nobly sublimated desire, the old master speaks of the erotic satisfaction he derives from his work in terms that, to the astonishment of the other painters, seem to abolish the very distinction between the empirically real and the ideal that redeems what might be problematic in their artistic activity. It is interesting that the first version of the story ended with Gillette's indignant outburst against Poussin, and not with Frenhofer's reaction to the destruction of his illusions, and that the very last version of *The Unknown Masterpiece*, published by Balzac in 1847 after its insertion in the collected edition of his *Comédie humaine*, is called *Gillette*, the subtitle of the first section of the story.[5]

The other versions of the story, however, including the one included in the *Comédie humaine*, focus more on Frenhofer and on his reaction to Poussin's dismay at his inability to see anything more than a mess of lines and colours in the portrait of 'La Belle Noiseuse'. Balzac leaves some slight uncertainty about the reliability of Poussin's verdict, and there are readers, looking back from the perspective of modernism, who have wanted to see in Frenhofer an artist ahead of his time.[6] This was certainly not Balzac's conscious intention. He wrote in a letter that *The Unknown Masterpiece* was one of a group of 'philosophical studies' whose focus was how the execution of a work of art could be spoiled by 'an overabundance of the creative principle'.[7] Yet, while the tale may be intended as a cautionary one, Balzac draws no moral from it about how the artist should negotiate the conflicting demands of art and life. On the contrary, the revelation he arranges for Poussin,

[5] See also the explanatory note to this subtitle.

[6] Cézanne, for example, identified strongly with Frenhofer, and Picasso produced a set of drawings based on the story. See Dore Ashton, *A Fable of Modern Art* (New York: Thames & Hudson, 1980).

[7] Balzac, *Lettres à Madame Hanska*, ed. Roger Pierrot (Paris: Laffont, 1990), ii. 382 (24 May 1837).

whose puzzlement and disorientation he leaves the reader to contemplate, resists easy summing-up in moral terms. Frenhofer may have been misguided in his determination to have sexual and aesthetic desire converge on a single, undifferentiated object. Yet, in judging her service as a model to anyone other than her lover to be a form of prostitution, it is possible that Gillette may be guilty of the same confusion. When Poussin looks at her with his artist's eye, focusing on lines and colours, is that gaze incompatible with that of a lover? The scrupulous balance of moral and aesthetic qualities in Poussin's later work suggests that he found a way beyond the dilemmas dramatized in the story—at least in his artistic life. Yet, Balzac does not provide a lesson in how to get from here to there. The answers he does give, Frenhofer's and Gillette's, seem rather to deny the possibility of compromise or mediation between their polarized viewpoints. It may be that the very terms of the problem need to be rethought.

The Girl with the Golden Eyes

The Girl with the Golden Eyes was conceived as the final episode of a trilogy Balzac called *History of the Thirteen*, which also includes *Ferragus* and *The Duchesse de Langeais*. Its first publication was in book form, being added to the first stories in an ongoing series of volumes titled *Scenes of Parisian Life* (1834–5). The relationship between the story and the framing device of the trilogy is fairly loose. In the preface to *Ferragus* Balzac speaks of a secret society of thirteen powerful men who have sworn to support each other in whatever enterprises each of them might undertake, without regard for the political differences between them or for the moral judgements of ordinary people. Secret societies such as the Freemasons and shadowy political groups of the throne-and-altar Right or the republican-revolutionary Left were a much-discussed phenomenon in Balzac's France. In Balzac's stories, however, the apparently all-powerful Thirteen devote their energies not to matters of state, but to issues of merely personal concern. Moreover, in *The Girl with the Golden Eyes* there is an almost comical disproportion between the resources supposedly available to Henri de

Marsay to overcome the obstacles to his conquest of Paquita and the actual reasons for his success in gaining access to her. It is clear Balzac is using the Thirteen mostly for melodramatic effect. Yet, Balzac's use of the device is not entirely ironic. The notion of a secret society or conspiracy exerting a hidden influence on events may be fantastical, but the experience that generates such notions, the feeling of helpless passivity, of being caught in a web of causes and effects that escape one's grasp, can be all too real, especially in a world where traditional frameworks of understanding and social cohesion have broken down. In the later nineteenth and the twentieth centuries such anxiety would provide fertile ground for paranoid political movements of various, and often vicious, stripes.

In *History of the Thirteen*, however, Balzac is not concerned with this potential for mass mobilization, a theme that never interested him. He focuses instead on the tension between passivity and power within a single person, a tension all the more extreme in that the character belongs to society's elite. Each successive instalment tightens the focus of that tension. In *Ferragus* a respectable army officer and a wealthy stockbroker, both clever men, find themselves helpless to prevent disaster when they unwittingly upset the plans of a member of the Thirteen. In *The Duchesse de Langeais* the protagonist is a member of the group itself, whose elaborate plot to punish the woman who spurned him only demonstrates his continued enthralment. The devices employed are spectacular, but the premise itself is finally a rather conventional one, and so in *The Girl with the Golden Eyes* Balzac gives it an original twist. The challenge to Henri de Marsay's power will extend to what Balzac calls the 'core of his being', his masculine sexual identity, and he will be robbed of his revenge by another woman.

De Marsay does not consider that identity simply as a given, although his social prestige is based on his seemingly effortless possession of it. His identity is an ongoing aesthetic project he places above any immediate satisfaction of his sexual desire, although in the end it is undertaken in the service of that desire, and in this respect there is a certain affinity between the dandy and the artist figures in the two preceding stories. De Marsay can spend two hours getting dressed, to the wonderment of his acolyte Paul de Manerville, but his air of self-sufficient detachment, the lack of any sense of urgency in his pursuit of women, is a strategy by which he gains the admiration and envy of his friends and makes himself irresistible to women. De Marsay's narcissism explains in part the way the drama of the story is framed. As in the two other stories in this book, the hero's decisive aesthetic and erotic encounter with a mysterious female figure is preceded by conversation and speculation. In this case, however, that conversation does not involve a personal relationship between the conversation partners, one which will be affected by what the story reveals. This is less because de Marsay's dealings with Paul do not have an erotic component (there is clearly a mild homosocial, if not homoerotic undercurrent) than because de Marsay will refuse to involve Paul in his story or discuss its aftermath with him. From his point of view, the only discussion worth having about the meaning of that story has already occurred within the story itself, with his own sexual mirror-image. This brief narcissistic communion aside, de Marsay's relationship to other people is in reality an essentially impersonal one.

This attitude is the key to his social superiority, but as the story progresses what appears to be a form of aesthetic transcendence reveals itself to be a different kind of detachment. His enjoyment of a cigar as he walks home after his first ecstatic lovemaking with the girl with the golden eyes is an expression, not of a truly aesthetic distance from his desires, but of a coarseness of sensibility epitomized in Kipling's poem 'The Betrothed': 'a woman is only a woman, but a good cigar is a smoke'. De Marsay's mechanical gait reminds us of the Parisian characters Balzac depicts in the first pages of the story. Many readers have considered this introductory section to be a gratuitous, if dazzling, display of Balzac's powers of description, yet its presentation of Paris life as a Dantesque series of circles or spheres in fact provides an impersonal framing device most appropriate to de Marsay's story. Although they may think of themselves as free agents, the inhabitants of each circle are defined by their repetitive behaviours, even when they are striving to rise from one social circle to another. In

Balzac's disenchanted view of the French capital, the artists are no exception to the general rule, since they 'seek in vain to reconcile polite society with artistic fame, money with art'. De Marsay's ingenuity may have secured him entry into the privileged space of Paquita's room (one end of which, containing the bed, forms a semicircle), but he reduces the erotic discoveries of his encounter with the mysterious girl to orientalist clichés. Henri himself, we are reminded, is not as original a creation as he thinks. In an odd turn of phrase, he is described near the beginning of the story as one of a number of 'copies' his father, the dissolute Lord Dudley, made of himself through his own narcissistic couplings with a series of women across Europe. What seems at that point to be merely a joke takes on a more deeply ironic resonance as the story progresses.

De Marsay's reaction to a subsequent encounter with Paquita is initially very different. The jaded de Marsay does not mind being dressed in women's clothing by a girl he has discovered to be 'far from innocent', but he is insulted by the implication that he might be a stand-in for someone else. Whatever costume he may don or pseudonym he may adopt, he holds to the uniqueness of his self-constructed identity of desired, envied, and feared masculinity. When Paquita calls him 'Mariquita', his suspicions are confirmed. He flies into a rage, all the more bitter in that he had himself for a moment 'forgotten everything', including that very identity, in an ecstasy of erotic fusion with his lover. 'Mariquita' is often taken as a reference to Paquita's other lover, but this identification is problematic, since it is a diminutive for 'Maria', not for 'Margarita'. It is also likely that Balzac wants the reader to hear an echo of the slang term 'marica', meaning 'queer'.[8] If de Marsay is insulted to 'the core of his being', it is because the answer to his question about the image of himself reflected in Paquita's golden eyes evokes a possibility even more unacceptable than the first one: an actual other person for whom he might be substituting is less threatening than the other he may harbour unwittingly within himself.

[8] See Catherine Perry, '*La Fille aux yeux d'or* et la quête paradoxale de l'infini', *L'Année balzacienne*, NS 14 (1993), 261–84.

De Marsay's rage recalls that of Sarrasine, and it is also linked to murderous violence, but in this case the protagonist is neither perpetrator nor struggling victim, but a spectator robbed of any agency at all. The self-questioning or search for compensatory validation that might have resulted from this second insult is forestalled, however, by the discovery that his rival is his own half-sister, and that the unfaithful Paquita has at least 'kept it in the family' (literally, has been 'faithful to the blood'). The threatening ambiguity of sexuality is absorbed into the odd but unexpectedly reassuring complementarity between two different 'copies' of Lord Dudley. In coming face to face, the cuckolded siblings recover the sense of uniqueness and control they value so highly, and so neither partner needs to explore the matter further. One wonders whether the incest taboo that seems to matter so little to de Marsay still operates on a different level, providing a psychologically useful structure in a most unexpected way. In the end, de Marsay will keep his discovery 'within the family' as well, refusing to relay what is revealed to him to anyone else. Whereas the other two stories were open-ended, this one concludes with a circle closed in on itself, even though de Marsay seems still to have a fine worldly career ahead of him. When asked by Paul de Manerville what became of the girl with golden eyes, de Marsay responds with a pun, a figure of speech which plays with multiple meanings only to collapse them into a conversation-stopper. Paul is not even aware it is a pun, and the reader can do no more than grimace. De Marsay's parting word is the linguistic equivalent of the cigar he smokes with his hands in his pockets, a sign of willed nonchalance. This most disenchanted of Balzac's tales may be suggesting that a pun may be the only kind of answer befitting a Paris where everything, even art, is 'reduced to these terms: gold and pleasure'. On the other hand, since Balzac would go on to create some of the most expansive and multi-layered novels of the city in French literature, we need not take this reductive irony as the author's final answer.

NOTE ON THE TEXTS

Sarrasine first appeared in two instalments in the *Revue de Paris* on 21 and 28 November 1830, and was included in the *Romans et contes philosophiques* (along with *The Wild Ass's Skin* and a number of shorter tales) published by Gosselin in September 1831. Later Balzac removed the story from the category of 'philosophical' tales, placing it instead among the *Scènes de la vie parisienne*, a section within the *Études de moeurs au XIXe siècle*, published by Béchet in May 1835. It was reprinted in 1844 as part of the Furne edition of *La Comédie humaine* (begun in 1842). Balzac's own copy of that edition, on which he made a number of final revisions and which is called the 'Furne corrigé', provides the basis for most editions of *La Comédie humaine*, including the standard Pléiade edition published by Gallimard, where *Sarrasine* appears in volume 6. The translation follows this text, as edited by Pierre Citron.

The Unknown Masterpiece (*Le Chef-d'œuvre inconnu*), was originally published as a 'conte fantastique' in two parts in *l'Artiste*: 'Maître Frenhofer' on 31 July and 'Catherine Lescault' on 3 August 1831. It was reprinted in the same edition of the *Romans et contes philosophiques* that included 'Sarrasine'. A revised form of the story, with a much-expanded discussion of artistic technique and a new ending (see the Introduction), was published in 1837 by Delloye & Lecou as part of the *Études philosophiques*, and then in the Furne edition of Balzac's *Comédie humaine* in 1846. The text translated here again follows the 'Furne corrigé'. In this case, however, the text edited by Pierre Citron for volume 10 of the Pléiade edition departs from the usual practice and adopts the slightly different version of the story published by Balzac in a collection titled *Le Provincial à Paris* (1847), under the title *Gillette*. It is not clear which version should be considered definitive. Since the key differences involve the identity of the woman in the painting of the title, these are recorded in the Explanatory Notes.

The Girl with the Golden Eyes (*La Fille aux yeux d'or*), the third part of a trilogy entitled *Histoire des Treize*, following *Ferragus* and *La Duchesse de Langeais*, was first published in three chapters, 'Physionomies parisiennes', 'Singulière bonne fortune', and 'La Force du sang' (the last followed by a short ironic coda about a possible real-life Paquita), as one of the *Scènes de la vie parisienne* in the Béchet edition of the *Études de moeurs au XIXe siècle* (1834–5). The story was included, minus the coda, in the Furne *Comédie humaine* in 1843. The text translated is that of the 'Furne corrigé', edited by Rose Fortassier and published in volume 5 of the Pléiade edition.

NOTE ON THE TRANSLATION

In translating three of Balzac's most glamorous and extravagant novellas, I have been very conscious of the variety of stylistic registers involved. Balzac can be by turns tender or violent, mythological or realistic, sarcastic or laconic, decorative or descriptive, emotional or philosophical. As the material of these three masterpieces of short fiction shifts from painting, sculpture, and music to social display, sexual compulsion, creative panic, family passion, and violence, so Balzac's styles range from the metaphorical to the metaphysical, from the realistic to the dramatic. We move from Dante's *Inferno* to 1830s Paris, from meditation to reflection, from dramatic narrative to introspective afterthought, from social critique to psychological analysis.

In my attempt to capture and translate the tone and tenor of Balzac's prose, I have been greatly helped by my colleagues. My friends and research assistants Michèle Lester, specialist in French drama, and Ann Kennedy Smith, author of a study of Charles Baudelaire and painting, have lent me their eagle eyes, their literary nous, their editorial expertise, and their linguistic flair. Patrick Coleman, writing the Introduction and checking the notes of this volume, has gone beyond the call of duty and helped me resolve problems of textual sources, interpretation, and annotation. His meticulous reading of my drafts and his invaluable editorial suggestions are much appreciated. My most sincere thanks to Ann, Michèle, and Patrick. With their help, I dare hope and trust that this publication presents a set of dramatic short stories couched in an English where Balzac, were he writing today, might recognize his original.

P. J. C.

SELECT BIBLIOGRAPHY

French Editions

Balzac, Honoré de, *La Comédie humaine*, ed. P.-G. Castex, 12 vols. (Paris, 1976–81).

Biography

Carter, David R., *Brief Lives: Honoré de Balzac* (London: Hesperus, 2008).

Hunt, H. J., *Honoré de Balzac: A Biography* (London: Athlone Press, 1957; repr. with corrections New York: Greenwood, 1969).

Pritchett, V. S., *Balzac* (London: Chatto & Windus, 1973).

Robb, Graham, *Balzac: A biography* (London: Picador, 1994).

Historical and Cultural Background

Hemmings, F. W. J., *Culture and Society in France 1789–1848* (Leicester: University of Leicester Press, 1987).

Mansel, Philip, *Paris between Empires: Monarchy and Revolution 1814–1852* (London: John Murray, 2001).

Nineteenth-Century Art: Painting, Robert Rosenblum; *Sculpture*, H. W. Janson, revised and updated edn. (Upper Saddle River, NJ: Prentice–Hall, 2005).

General

Farrant, Tim, *Balzac's Shorter Fiction: Genesis and Genre* (Oxford, 2002).

Hemmings, F. W. J., *Balzac: An interpretation of 'La Comédie humaine'* (New York: Random House, 1967).

Hunt, H. J., *Balzac's 'Comédie humaine'* (London: Athlone Press, 1959). A chronological rather than a thematic account.

McCormick, Diana Festa, *Honoré de Balzac* (Boston: Twayne, 1979).

Collections of Essays

Bloom, Harold (ed.), *Honoré de Balzac* (Philadelphia: Chelsea House, 2003).

Kanes, Martin (ed.), *Critical Essays on Honoré de Balzac* (Boston: G. K. Hall, 1990).

Tilby, Michael (ed.), *Balzac* (London: Longman, 1995).

Individual Studies

Where the specific story or stories discussed is not immediately apparent from the title of the work, this information is provided at the end of the entry (G = 'The Girl with the Golden Eyes', S = 'Sarrasine', U = 'The Unknown Masterpiece').

Ashton, Dore, *A Fable of Modern Art* (London: Thames & Hudson, 1980). U

Barthes, Roland, *S/Z*, trans. Richard Miller (New York: Hill & Wang, 1974). S

Berg, William J., *Imagery and Ideology: Fiction and Painting in Nineteenth-Century France* (Newark: University of Delaware Press, 2007). U

Chambers, Ross, *Story and Situation: Narrative Seduction and the Power of Fiction* (Minneapolis: University of Minnesota Press, 1984). S

Creech, James, 'Castration and Desire in *Sarrasine* and *The Girl with the Golden Eyes*: A Gay Perspective', in Martine Antle and Dominique Fisher (eds.), *The Nature of the Other: Lesbian and Gay Strategies of Resistance in French and Francophone Contexts* (New Orleans: University Press of the South, 2002), 45–64.

Crow, Thomas, 'B/G', in Stephen Melville and Bill Readings (eds.), *Vision and Textuality* (Durham, NC: Duke University Press, 1995), 296–314. S

—— *Emulation: David, Drouais, and Girodet in the Art of Revolutionary France* (rev. edn., New Haven: Yale University Press, 2006). S (a shorter version of 'B/G')

Donoghue, Emma, *Inseparable: Desire Between Women in Literature* (New York: Knopf, 2010). G

Felman, Shoshana, *What Does A Woman Want? Writing and Sexual Difference* (Baltimore: Johns Hopkins University Press, 1983). G

Heathcote, Owen, 'The Engendering of Violence and Violation of Gender in Honoré de Balzac's *La Fille aux yeux d'or*', *Romance Studies*, no. 22 (1993), 99–112.

Kelly, Dorothy, *Fictional Genders: Role and Representation in Nineteenth-Century French Narrative* (Lincoln, Nebr.: University of Nebraska Press, 1989). S

—— *Telling Glances: Voyeurism in the French Novel* (New Brunswick, NJ: Rutgers University Press, 1992). G

Knight, Diana, *Balzac and the Model of Painting: Artist Stories in 'La Comédie humaine'* (London: Legenda, 2007). U

Kolb, Katherine, 'The Tenor of "Sarrasine"', *PMLA* 120 (2005), 1560–75.

Lucey, Michael, *The Misfit of the Family: Balzac and the Social Forms of Sexuality* (Durham, NC: Duke University Press, 2003). G, S

Paglia, Camille, *Sexual Personae: Art and Decadence from Nefertiti to Emily Dickinson* (New Haven: Yale University Press, 1990). S, G

Prendergast, Christopher, *Paris and the Nineteenth Century* (Oxford: Blackwell, 1992). G

—— *Balzac: Fiction and Melodrama* (London: E. Arnold, 1978). G

Schehr, Lawrence R., *Subversions of Verisimilitude: Reading Narrative from Balzac to Sartre* (New York: Fordham University Press, 2009). S, G

Sprenger, Scott, 'Balzac, Painting, and the Problem of Romanticism', in Larry Peer (ed.), *Romanticism Across the Disciplines* (Lanham, Md.: University Press of America, 1998), 155–84. U

Waelti-Walters, Jennifer, *Damned Women: Lesbians in French Novels, 1796–1996* (Montreal: McGill-Queen's University Press, 2000). G

Weil Kari, *Androgyny and the Denial of Difference* (Charlottesville, Va.: University of Virginia Press, 1992). G

Wettlaufer, Alexandra, *Pen vs. Paintbrush: Girodet, Balzac, and the Myth of Pygmalion in Postrevolutionary France* (New York: Palgrave, 2001). S, U

Wing, Nathaniel, *Between Genders: Narrating Difference in Early French Modernism* (Newark, Del.: University of Delaware Press, 2004). G

Two notable film versions are:

La Fille aux yeux d'or, directed by Jean Gabriel Albicocco (1961), with Marie Laforet.

La Belle Noiseuse (= *Le Chef-d'œuvre inconnu*), directed by Jacques Rivette (1991; Grand Prix, Cannes Film Festival), with Michel Piccoli and Emmanuelle Béart.

Further Reading in Oxford World's Classics

Balzac, Honoré de, *Cousin Bette,* trans. Sylvia Raphael, introduction by David Bellos.

——*Eugénie Grandet,* trans. Sylvia Raphael, ed. Christopher Prendergast.

——*Père Goriot*, trans. and ed. A. J. Krailsheimer.

——*The Wild Ass's Skin*, trans. Helen Constantine, ed. Patrick Coleman.

A CHRONOLOGY OF HONORÉ DE BALZAC

1799 Born at Tours, the son of Bernard-François Balzac and his wife Anne-Charlotte-Laure Sallambier. Put out to nurse till he is four.

1804 Sent as a boarder to the Pension Le Guay, Tours.

1807–13 A boarder at the Oratorian college in Vendôme.

1814 Restoration of the Bourbon monarchy in France with the accession of Louis XVIII. The Balzac family moves to Paris, where Honoré continues his education.

1815 Flight of Louis XVIII on Napoleon's escape from Elba, but second Restoration of the Bourbons after Napoleon's defeat at Waterloo.

1816 Honoré becomes a law student and works in a lawyer's office.

1819 Becomes a Bachelor of Law. The family moves to Villeparisis on the retirement of Bernard-François Balzac. Honoré stays in Paris, living frugally at the Rue Lesdiguières, in an effort to start a career as a writer. He writes a tragedy, *Cromwell*, which is a failure.

1820–5 Writes various novels, some in collaboration, none of which he signs with his own name.

1822 Beginning of his liaison with forty-five-year-old Laure de Berny, who remains devoted to him till her death in 1836.

1825–8 Tries to make money by printing and publishing ventures, which fail and saddle him with debt.

1829 Publication of *Le Dernier Chouan*, the first novel he signs with his own name and the first of those to be incorporated in the *Comédie humaine*. Publication of the *Physiologie du mariage*.

1830 Publication of *Scènes de la vie privée*. Revolution in France resulting in the abdication of Charles X and the accession of Louis-Philippe.

1831 Works hard as a writer and adopts a luxurious, society life-style which increases his debts. Publication of *La Peau de chagrin* and some of the *Contes philosophiques*.

1832 Beginning of correspondence with Madame Hanska. Publication of more 'Scènes de la vie privée' and of *Louis Lambert*. Adds 'de' to his name and becomes 'de Balzac'.

1833 Meets Madame Hanska for the first time in Neuchâtel, Switzerland, and then in Geneva. Signs a contract for *Études de mœurs au XIXe siècle*, which appears in twelve volumes between 1833 and 1837, and is divided into 'Scènes de la vie privée', 'Scènes de la vie de province', and 'Scènes de la vie parisienne'. Publication of *Le Médecin de campagne* and the first 'Scènes de la vie de province', which include *Eugénie Grandet.*

1834 Publication of *La Recherche de l'absolu* and the first 'Scènes de la vie parisienne'.

1834–5 Publication of *Le Père Goriot.*

1835 Publication of collected *Études philosophiques* (1835–40). Meets Madame Hanska in Vienna, the last time for eight years.

1836 Publication of *Le Lys dans la vallée* and other works. Starts a journal, *La Chronique de Paris,* which ends in failure.

1837 Journey to Italy. Publication of *La Vieille Fille,* the first part of *Illusions perdues,* and *César Birotteau.*

1838 Publication of *La Femme supérieure* (*Les Employés*) and *La Torpille,* which becomes the first part of *Splendeurs et misères des courtisanes.*

1839 Becomes president of the Société des Gens de Lettres. Publication of six more works, including *Le Cabinet des antiques* and *Béatrix.*

1840 Publication of more works, including *Pierrette.*

1841 Makes an agreement with his publisher, Furne, and booksellers for the publication of the *Comédie humaine.* Publication of more works, including *Le Curé de village.*

1842 Publication of the *Comédie humaine,* with its important introduction, in seventeen volumes (1842–8); one posthumous volume is published in 1855. Publication of other works, including *Mémoires de deux jeunes mariées, Ursule Mirouet,* and *La Rabouilleuse.*

1843 More publications, including *La Muse du département,* and the completion in three parts of *Illusions perdues.* Visits Madame Hanska (widowed since 1841) in St Petersburg.

1844 Publication of *Modeste Mignon,* of the beginning of *Les Paysans,* of the second part of *Béatrix,* and of the second part of *Splendeurs et misères des courtisanes.*

1845 Travels in Europe with Madame Hanska and her daughter and future son-in-law.

1846 Stays in Rome and travels in Switzerland and Germany with Madame Hanska. A witness at the marriage of her daughter. Birth to Madame Hanska of a still-born child, who was to have been called Victor-Honoré. Publication of *La Cousine Bette* and of the third part of *Splendeurs et misères des courtisanes.*

1847 Madame Hanska stays in Paris from February till May. Publication of *Le Cousin Pons* and of the last part of *Splendeurs et misères des courtisanes*.

1848 Revolution in France resulting in the abdication of Louis-Philippe and the establishment of the Second Republic. Balzac goes to the Ukraine to stay with Madame Hanska and remains there till the spring of 1850.

1849 His health deteriorates seriously.

1850 Marriage of Balzac and Madame Hanska on 14 March. He returns with her to Paris on 20 May and dies on 18 August.

1869–76 Definitive edition of the *Œuvres complètes* in twenty-four volumes, published by Michel-Lévy and then by Calmann-Lévy.

THE GIRL WITH THE GOLDEN EYES
AND OTHER STORIES

SARRASINE

*To Monsieur Charles de Bernard du Grail**

I WAS immersed in one of those profound daydreams which occasionally seize hold of everyone, even the most frivolous of us, amidst a night of the most riotous revelry. The clock of the Elysée-Bourbon Palace* had just struck midnight. Perched on a window seat and hidden by the voluminous folds of a watered-silk curtain, I was free to contemplate the garden of the mansion where I was spending the evening. The trees, half covered in snow, were sketched in faint relief against the greyish background formed by a cloudy sky, weakly lit by the moon. In this fantastic atmosphere they bore a vague resemblance to ghosts, half hidden by their shrouds, and together formed a gigantic image of the famous 'dance of death'. Turning my gaze in the other direction, I was able to admire the dance of the living taking place in a splendid salon, with walls covered in gold and silver and brightly illuminated by the blaze of a riot of chandeliers. The most rich, beautiful, aristocratic, dazzling, and regal women of Paris were there, swarming and fluttering in a frenzy of movement, decked with diamonds, with flowers crowning their heads, interweaving their tresses and corsages, and decorating their dresses, even garlanding their ankles. The slightest tremor arising from their voluptuous dancing steps sent delicate swaths of pale lace and muslin swirling around their slender forms. Here and there the flash of an eye, eclipsing the candlelight and even the fiery diamonds, would inflame hearts already burning with passion to an even higher degree. I caught those sly movements of the head intended for lovers, those negative expressions and cold postures reserved for husbands. The card-players' shouts which greeted each unexpected trump and the chink of their gold coins mingled with the music and the murmur of conversation, and the scented air and general intoxication had a delirious effect on this crowd, already inebriated by all the seductions of high society. So, to my right lay the sombre and silent image of the dead; to my left, the ordered bacchanalian rites of the living; on the one side Nature, cold and numb, was in mourning; on the other there was nothing but human pleasure. Balancing on the borderline between these two very different tableaux, which, repeated in a thousand variations, make Paris the most entertaining intellectual city in the world, I created in my mind's eye a hotchpotch, part comedy, part tragedy; my left foot tapped to the rhythm of the dance music, while the other felt as if in the grave. And indeed, this leg was frozen by one of those draughts which chill half your body, whilst the other half was bathed in the clammy heat of the social gathering, so familiar at any ball.

'I wonder whether Monsieur de Lanty has owned this house for long?'

'Indeed he has. It is nearly ten years since Marshal de Carigliano sold it to him…'

'Ah!'

'The family must be enormously wealthy, I suppose?'

'Without a doubt.'

'What a celebration! What ostentatious luxury!'

'Do you think they are as rich as Monsieur de Nucingen* or Monsieur de Gondreville?'

'Do you really not know?'

I looked more closely and recognized the two speakers as belonging to that strange class of people in Paris whose conversation consists entirely of whys, hows, what's-the-reason, who-are-they, what's-going-on, and what-did-she-do. They lowered their voices and moved away to a sofa in a more secluded spot in order to be freer in their conversation. Never was there a richer seam of secrets for those seeking mysteries. No one knew what country the Lanty family came from, nor from what line of business, from what expropriation, piracy, or inheritance, they derived their fortune, estimated at several million francs. All the members of this family spoke Italian, French, Spanish, English, and German fluently enough for it to be supposed that they had lived for long periods among these peoples. Were they gypsies, or were they swindlers?

'Even if they got it from the devil,' said some of the young politicians, 'they make wonderful hosts.'

'Even if the Comte de Lanty had plundered some casbah or other, I'd happily marry his daughter,' exclaimed a philosopher.

Who would not have married Marianina, a sixteen-year-old girl whose beauty matched the fabulous imaginings of oriental poetry. Like the sultan's daughter in the tale of the magic lamp,* her veil should never have been removed. The imperfect talents of Malibran, Sontag, or Fodor,* whose achievement of overall perfection has always been prevented by the dominance of one particular quality, would pale by comparison with her singing, for Marianina was able to combine to the same degree purity of sound, sensitivity, felicity of gesture and tone, intuition and technique, accuracy and feeling. This girl was the model of that hidden poetry which is common to all the arts but which forever eludes those who seek it. Sweet and modest, educated and witty, nobody could put Marianina in the shade, except perhaps her mother.

Have you ever met one of those women whose dazzling beauty resists encroaching age, and who at thirty-six seems more desirable than she would have been fifteen years earlier? The passions of such a woman's soul illuminate her radiant face: her every feature radiates intelligence and each pore has a special glow, particularly in the light. Her seductive eyes attract, reject, speak, or are silent; her deportment is artlessly elegant, her voice plays upon the rich melodies of the sweetest and most tender tones of coquetry. She draws on subtle comparisons to flatter the vanity of even the most self-conscious man. A raised eyebrow, a glance of the eye, a curl of the lip can instil a kind of terror in those whose lives and happiness depend upon them. Inexperienced in love and amenable to persuasion, a young girl may allow herself to be seduced; but faced with this kind of woman, a man needs to know how to hide in a wardrobe, like Monsieur de Jaucourt,* and not cry out when the chambermaid crushes a couple of his fingers in the door-jamb. Is he who loves such a powerful siren not risking his life? And perhaps this is why we love them so passionately. The Comtesse de Lanty was such a woman.

Filippo, Marianina's brother, flaunted the same dazzling beauty as the Countess. In a word, this young man was a living image of Antinous,* with frailer forms. But how these slim and delicate proportions suit a youth when an olive skin, strong eyebrows, and the fire of a velvety eye promise virile passions and generous ideas in days to come! If Filippo had his place as an ideal in the hearts of all the young ladies, he was just as firmly fixed in the minds of all their mothers as the most attractive match in France.

The beauty, wealth, wit, and grace of these two children were entirely inherited from their mother. The Comte de Lanty was short, ugly, and skinny; sulky as a Spaniard, boring as a banker. He passed, it should be said, for a profound political thinker because he rarely laughed, and often quoted Monsieur de Metternich or Wellington.*

This mysterious family held all the attractions of a poem by Lord Byron,* and their difficulties were interpreted in different ways by each individual in high society: an ode in which every single verse was both obscure and sublime. The reticence observed by Monsieur and Madame de Lanty as to their origins, their past existence, and their relations with the four corners of the earth would not have been a subject of astonishment for long in Paris, where gold coins, even tainted with blood or mud, betray nothing and count for everything. In no other country perhaps is Vespasian's axiom* better understood. As long as high society knows that you are wealthy, you are ranked with others of equal wealth, and nobody will ask to see the title-deeds of your nobility, since everyone knows how little they cost. In a city where social problems are resolved using mathematical equations, adventurers have excellent chances on their side. Even if they did have gypsy origins, this family was so rich and attractive that high society could easily forgive their petty secrets. Unfortunately, the enigmatic story of the House of Lanty offered a permanent subject of curiosity, not unlike that of an Ann Radcliffe novel.*

Certain observant people, the sort who want to know which shop you buy your candles from, or who ask how much rent you pay when they admire your apartment, had noticed, from time to time, the appearance of a strange character at the parties, concerts, balls, and routs* given by the Countess. It was a man whose first appearance at the family mansion was during a concert, where he seemed to have been drawn to the salon by the enchanting voice of Marianina.

'I'm starting to feel cold,' a lady sitting near the door said to her neighbour.

The stranger, who was standing near to this lady, moved away.

'How strange! Now I'm too hot!' said the lady after he had left. 'And you may accuse me of madness, but I can't help thinking that the gentleman in black standing near me who has just left was the cause of the chill.'

Soon the exaggeration natural to high social circles gave birth to and amplified the most amusing ideas, the strangest remarks, and the most ridiculous tales about this mysterious character. Without being exactly a vampire, a ghoul, an artificial man, or some kind of Faust or Robin Hood,* he shared, according to amateurs of the fantastic, something of their ability to mimic human form. Some Germans even took at face value these ingenious examples of Parisian gossip-mongering. The stranger was quite simply an old man. Several of those young men who every morning are used to deciding the future of Europe in a few elegant phrases claimed to see in the stranger some great criminal, possessed of immense wealth. Novelists told the story of the life of this old man, and gave you really intriguing details of the atrocities committed by him while he served under the Prince of Mysore.* Those more down-to-earth observers, the bankers, made up their own ingenious story. 'Bah!' they would say, shrugging their ample shoulders pityingly, this little old man is a 'Genoese head'.*

'Monsieur, without wishing to be indiscreet, would you be kind enough to explain what you mean by a "Genoese head"?'

'Well, Monsieur, it's a man whose life is mortgaged by an enormous capital outlay, and whose family's income depends on his good health.'

Once at Madame d'Espard's I remember hearing a hypnotist proving, through some very tenuous historical connections, that this old man was the famous Balsamo, known as Cagliostro,* who had been preserved under glass. According to this modern alchemist, the Sicilian adventurer had cheated death and now amused himself by making money for his grandchildren. On another occasion Monsieur de Ferette, the King's Bailiff, claimed to have recognized in this odd character none other than the Comte de Saint-Germain.* All those idiocies, spoken with the sort of witty sarcasm which characterizes our cynical society, fostered a vague atmosphere of suspicion around the House of Lanty. Finally, by a strange set of circumstances, the members of this family justified society's conjectures by acting in a rather mysterious way with this old man, whose life was, as it were, screened from all investigation.

Whenever this character appeared in the doorway of the apartment which he was said to occupy in the Lanty household, his emergence always caused a great commotion among the family. You would have thought it an event of considerable importance. Filippo, Marianina, Madame de Lanty, and an old retainer alone had the privilege of helping the strange man to walk, stand up, or sit down. Each of them watched over his slightest movement. He seemed to be an enchanted character on whom depended the happiness, life, and fortune of all. Was it fear or affection that made them behave in this way? Society could find no clue to resolve the enigma. After remaining hidden for months in some undiscovered sanctuary, this presiding deity would suddenly emerge, surreptitiously and unannounced, and appear in the middle of a salon, like those fairies of days gone by who alighted from their flying dragons in order to spread confusion amid those festivities to which they had not been invited. Only the most experienced observers could detect the anxiety of the heads of the house, as they managed to disguise their feelings with considerable subtlety. But sometimes, while dancing a quadrille, Marianina was naive enough to glance in unguarded terror at the old man as she watched him move among the different groups of people. Or Filippo would rush forward, weaving his way through the crowd to meet him, and would stay by his side, tender and attentive, as if contact with other people or the slightest draught might destroy this strange creature. The Comtesse would manage to get close to him, without appearing to have the intention of seeking him out; then, adopting an attitude and an expression marked with deference as much as tenderness, submission as much as tyranny, she would utter two or three words to which the old man almost always deferred, and he would disappear, led, or rather, in fact, borne away by her. If Madame de Lanty was not there, the Count employed a thousand stratagems to get to his side, but seemed to have trouble in making himself understood, and treated him like a spoilt child whose mother indulged his whims or feared his tantrums. One or two indiscreet acquaintances had spontaneously and rashly questioned the Comte de Lanty, but this cold and reserved man seemed never to understand what it was that his inquisitors wanted to know. Thus, despite a number of attempts, which the prudence of all the members of the family rendered useless, nobody was yet able to decode such a well-hidden secret. In the end, the well-connected spies, gossips, and politicians became war-weary and gave up worrying about this mystery.

But on this occasion there were perhaps amid these splendid salons some philosophical souls who, tasting an ice cream or a sorbet, or placing their empty glass of punch on a side table, said to themselves:

'I would not be surprised to learn that these people are rogues. That old man, who hides away and appears only at the equinox or the solstice, looks very much like an assassin.'

'Or a bankrupt.'

'It's more or less the same thing. Destroying a man's wealth is sometimes worse than destroying the man himself.'

'Monsieur, I bet twenty louis, and I've won forty.'

'Upon my soul, Monsieur, there are only thirty left on the table.'

'Well, that just shows how topsy-turvy this society is. You can't even gamble properly.'

'Too true... but it must be six months since we saw the Phantom. Do you think he's a human being?'

'Well, only just.'

These last phrases were spoken by strangers, standing close by, who were leaving just as I was summing up my last confused thoughts on the contrasts between black and white, life and death. My irrational imagination, as much as my eyes, contemplated in turn the festivities reaching a paroxysm of glamour and the sombre tableau of the gardens. I don't know how long it had taken me to meditate on the two sides of the human coin, but suddenly the stifled laugh of a young woman roused me. By one of nature's rare caprices, the half-mourning thought that rolled through my brain had emerged and I saw it personified, alive; like Minerva who leapt forth tall and strong from Jupiter's head,* it was both a hundred and twenty-two years old, both living and dead. Escaping from his room like a madman from his cell, the little old man must have cleverly slipped in behind a crowd of people attentive to the voice of Marianina, who was finishing the cavatina from *Tancredi*.* He seemed to have risen from the depths of the earth, as if sprung by some theatrical mechanism. He remained motionless and sombre for a moment, watching the festivities, the noise of which had perhaps reached his ears. His almost somnambulistic concern was so concentrated on things that he found himself surrounded by people without seeing any of them. He had emerged unannounced at the side of one of the most ravishing women in Paris, an elegant young dancer, with a delicate physique, a face as fresh as a child's, pink and white, and so frail and transparent that a man's gaze would seem to pass right through her as the sun's rays pass through a clear pane of glass. There they were, the two of them, in front of me, so close together that the stranger was crushing slightly not just her organdie dress and floral wreaths, but even her softly curled hair and her billowing sash.

This was the young lady whom I had invited to Madame de Lanty's ball. As it was the first time that she had entered the house, I excused her stifled giggles; but somehow I managed to convey an urgent signal that made her suddenly subdued and respectful towards the man next to her. She came to sit by my side. The old man was reluctant to leave this delicious creature, to whom he clung capriciously with that silent and apparently unreasonable obstinacy which affects the extremely aged and makes them seem like children. To sit next to the young lady, he had to fetch a folding chair. His slightest movements were imbued with that cold languor and stupid indecision which characterize the movements of the paralytic. He placed himself slowly and cautiously on his chair, mumbling something incoherent. His hoarse voice sounded like the echo of a stone dropped into a well. The young lady squeezed my hand sharply, as if she wanted to be saved from falling off a cliff, and shuddered when the man whom she was watching turned upon her a pair of cold, rheumy eyes which resembled nothing more than tarnished mother of pearl.

'I'm frightened,' she whispered in my ear.

'You can speak normally,' I answered. 'He's very hard of hearing.'

'So you know him?'

'Yes.'

She then plucked up the courage to scrutinize for a moment this creature with no name in human language, a form without substance, a being without life, or rather, a life without action. She was under the spell of that nervous curiosity which drives women to seek dangerous excitement, watching chained tigers or boa constrictors, terrified at being separated from them by only the flimsiest of barriers. Although the little old man had a back bent like that of a farm labourer, it was easy to see that he had once been of normal build. His excessive thinness and the frailty of his limbs proved that his proportions had always been slender. He wore breeches of black velvet, floating in folds around his bony thighs, like a sail becalmed. A student of anatomy would have immediately recognized the symptoms of acute phthisis* on seeing the short legs which served to prop up this strange body. It made one think of crossbones carved on a tombstone. A feeling of profound horror for this man seized the heart as one's eyes were fatally drawn to the marks that decrepitude had etched on this fragile machine. The stranger wore a white waistcoat with gold embroidery, in the old fashion, and his linen was sparkling white. A jabot of slightly tawny English lace, whose richness would have made a queen envious, fell in golden folds over his chest; but on him this lace seemed more of a rag than an ornament. At the centre of the jabot a diamond of incalculable value sparkled like the sun. Such old-fashioned luxury, such obviously valuable yet tasteless treasure, set off even more clearly the face of this strange person.

The frame was worthy of the portrait. The dark face looked

bony and angular from all sides. The chin was hollow; the temples were sunken; the eyes disappeared into yellow sockets. The jaw-bones, accentuated by his incredible thinness, carved out a cavity in the middle of each cheek. These protuberances produced curious shadows and reflections, depending on the lighting, and removed all remaining characteristics of a human face. In addition, the years had stretched the fine yellow skin so tightly over the bones of this face as to inscribe it with a multitude of wrinkles, either circular like the ripples of waters disturbed by a stone thrown by a child, or crazed like a cracked glass, but still as deep and compressed as the edges of the pages of a book. It would not be difficult to find old men with even more repulsive features; but what contributed most to the artificial appearance of the ghostly apparition in our midst were the red and white tints with which his face gleamed. The eyebrows on his mask reflected the light as if on some carefully crafted painting. Fortunately for any onlooker concerned by such decrepitude, the cadaverous skull was concealed beneath a blonde wig whose profusion of curls betrayed an overweening pretence. Besides, the feminine coquetry of this fantastical character was pronounced just as energetically by the gold rings dangling from his ears, the magnificent gemstones shining on his skeletal fingers, and a watch-chain which sparkled like the stones on a lady's diamond necklace. Finally, this kind of Japanese idol kept a stiff, congealed smile on his bluish lips, an implacable and mocking grimace like that of a skull. Silent and motionless as a statue, he exuded the musty smell of the dresses of a duchess exhumed by her heirs when they open her wardrobe, looking for the inheritance. If the old man turned his eyes towards the assembly, it seemed that the movements of those orbs, unable to reflect any light, were operated by some imperceptible device; and when the eyes stayed still, the person observing them ended up doubting whether they had ever moved at all.

Alongside this human wreckage was a young woman whose neck, arms, and bust were naked and white, and whose beautifully shaped and ample form and rich profusion of hair shading an alabaster brow inspired love, and whose eyes, rather than drinking in light, poured it forth. She was subtle, youthful, and yet even her diaphanous curls and her fragrant breath seemed too heavy, harsh, and strong for this shadow, this man of dust. Ah! This was truly to see life and death together; and it seemed to me in the imaginary arabesque of my thoughts that they became a chimera,* hideous below the waist but divinely female above.

'And yet that sort of marriage happens quite often in society,' I mused.

'He reeks of the graveyard!' cried the young lady in terror, pressing against me as if to assure herself of my protection, and whose nervous movements told me that she was truly afraid. 'What a horrible vision!' she continued. 'I can't stay here much longer. If I keep looking at him I shall think that death itself has come to collect me. Is he even alive?'

She reached out and touched the creature with that boldness which arises in women from the depths of their desires, but a cold sweat exuded from her pores, for just as she touched the old man she heard a cry resembling a death-rattle. This harsh voice, if indeed it was a voice, arose from an almost entirely desiccated throat. Then this cry was followed immediately by the strange tones of a small child's whooping-cough. Hearing this, Marianina, Filippo and Madame de Lanty looked towards us, and their eyes struck us with the power of lightning. The young lady must have wished herself at the bottom of the Seine. She took my arm and quickly escorted me towards a boudoir. Men and women alike made way for us. We entered a small, semicircular room, lying behind the reception suite. My companion threw herself down on a divan, trembling with fright, not knowing where she was.

'Madame, you must be out of your mind,' I said.

'But', she said, after a moment of silence during which I looked on her in wonder, 'is it my fault? Why does Madame de Lanty allow these ghosts into her mansion?'

'Come now,' I said, 'you sound like a fool, taking a little old man for a ghost.'

'Be quiet!' she replied, with that imposing and mocking air which women adopt so cleverly when they want to win an argument. 'What a pretty boudoir!' she exclaimed, looking around her. 'Blue satin always makes such a good drape. It looks so fresh. Oh, what a lovely painting!' she added, getting up to go and stand in front of a sumptuously framed canvas.

We remained for a moment contemplating this marvel, which seemed to have been painted by some supernatural brush. The painting represented Adonis* reclining on a lion-skin. The lamp in an alabaster vase suspended in the middle of the boudoir illuminated the painting with a soft light that highlighted all its beautiful features.

'Can such a beautiful creature exist?' she asked, after examining, not without a smile of pleasure, the exquisite grace of the contours, the pose, the colour, the hair, and everything else. 'He is too beautiful to be a man,' she added, after a scrutiny equal to that to which she would have subjected a rival.

Oh, how I then felt the effects of that jealousy in which poets had previously failed to make me believe. Jealousy of prints, paintings, and statues, where artists exaggerate human beauty, following the doctrine which leads artists to idealize everything!

'It is a portrait', I replied, 'from the talented brushwork of Vien.* But the great painter never saw the model, and perhaps your admiration will be mitigated when you learn that this study was based on the statue of a woman.'

'But of whom?'

I hesitated.

'I want to know,' she added urgently.

'I believe', I replied, 'that this Adonis represents a... eh... relation of Madame de Lanty's.'

I suffered to see her plunged in such sad contemplation of this figure. She sat down in silence, I sat beside her and held her hand without her taking any notice. Jilted for a portrait! At that moment the slight noise of the footsteps of a woman and her rustling dress broke the silence. We saw young Marianina enter, with an expression of innocence even more dazzling than her grace and her youthful dress; she walked in slowly, supporting with motherly care and filial concern the living ghost who had caused us to flee the music room and guided him with a certain anxiety as he slowly placed his feeble steps. They made their way laboriously together towards a door hidden behind a curtain. Marianina tapped gently on it. Thereupon appeared, as if by magic, a tall, slim man, like a sort of household deity. Before entrusting the old man to this mysterious guardian, the girl kissed the walking corpse respectfully, and her chaste embrace was not devoid of the sort of subtle tenderness whose privileged secret is known only to certain women.

'*Addio, addio!*'* she said, with the prettiest inflection of her young voice.

She even added to the last syllable an admirably executed trill, but *sotto voce*, as if this poetic expression depicted the effusion of her heart. The old man, suddenly struck by some memory, hesitated on the threshold of the secret closet. Then, in the depths of the silence we heard a heavy sigh arise from his breast, as he took off the finest of the rings which decorated his fingers and placed it in Marianina's bosom. The young lady started to laugh wildly, took out the ring and slipped it onto one of her fingers over her glove, and began to rush back to the salon, where the first bars of a quadrille were sounding. Then she noticed us.

'Oh, you were there all the time!' she said, blushing.

After looking at us as if she were about to question us, she ran off to meet her dance partner with all the careless impetuousness of youth.

'What does this mean?' my young partner asked. 'Is he her husband? This must be a dream. Where am I?'

'You, my dear Madame,' I replied, 'exalted as you are and able to comprehend the most subtle feelings; knowing, as you do, how to cultivate in a man's heart the most delicate of emotions without withering or crushing them as they start to flourish; you, who sympathize with the heart's pains, and who add to the wit of a Parisian lady a passionate soul worthy of Italy or Spain...'

She saw that my language was imbued with bitter irony and, paying no attention, interrupted me to say:

'Oh! That is how you wish to see me. What a curious tyranny! You want me to be something other than myself.'

'Oh! I want nothing of the sort!' I cried, shocked by her severity towards me. 'Is it true, at least, that you like to be told about the violent passions that these beautiful Mediterranean women arouse in our hearts?'

'Yes. And so?'

'Well then, tomorrow evening I shall come to meet you at nine o'clock and I shall reveal the mystery.'

'No,' she replied with a mutinous air, 'I want to know it right now.'

'You say "I want", but you have not yet done me the honour of permitting me to obey you by accepting my suit.'

'At this moment', she replied with exasperating charm, 'I have the most urgent desire to discover the secret. Tomorrow, I may not even listen to you...'

She smiled, and we separated; she, proud and brusque as ever, and I as ridiculous as always. She was brazen enough to waltz off with some aide-de-camp, and I remained by turns angry, sulky, worshipful, smitten, and jealous.

'I will see you tomorrow,' she said, as we left the ball at about two o'clock in the morning.

'I shan't come,' I thought. 'You are more capricious and a thousand times more whimsical than even I could imagine you.'

The next day the two of us were seated in front of a warm fire in a small, elegant salon, she on a little sofa, I on a pile of cushions by her feet, gazing into her eyes. The street was quiet. The lamp shed a soft light. It was one of those evenings which delight the soul, one of those unforgettable moments that are bathed in peace and desire, and whose charms, much later, always give a sense of regret, even in happier days. Who can forget the vivid impression made by love's first promise?

'Tell me,' she said. 'I am listening.'

'But I hardly dare begin. This tale contains passages which are dangerous for the teller. If I get carried away, you will want to silence me.'

'Tell me.'

'As you wish.'

'Ernest-Jean Sarrasine was the only son of a public prosecutor in Franche-Comté,' I continued, after a pause. 'His father had quite decently amassed an income of between six and eight thousand livres from his legal practice, which in those days in the provinces seemed an enormous sum. The old master Sarrasine, having only one child, left no stone unturned for his son's education: he hoped to make him a magistrate and to live long enough to see in his dotage the grandson of Matthieu Sarrasine, farm labourer in the village of Saint-Dié, sit on a lily-gilded throne* and snooze through legal proceedings for the greater glory of the law-courts; but the heavens had not such joy in mind for the prosecutor.

'The young Sarrasine, entrusted from an early age to the Jesuits, showed signs of uncommon indiscipline. He would study only when it suited him, frequently rebelled, and would sometimes spend hours on end plunged in some confused meditation, at times busying himself with studying his comrades at play, at other times with imagining the heroes of Homer. Then, when he did turn to amusement, he invested an extraordinary passion in his game. If a fight erupted between himself and a comrade it rarely ended without bloodshed. If he was the weaker he would bite. By turns active or passive, witless or too clever; his odd character made him feared as much by his masters as by his comrades. Instead of learning the elements of the Greek language, he used to draw the reverend father expounding a passage from Thucydides, sketched the mathematics master, the prefect,* the servants, the monitor,* and daubed every wall with shapeless sketches. In church, instead of singing the praises of the Lord he amused himself during the service by hacking away at a bench; or, if he had stolen a piece of wood, he would carve some figure of a saint. If he could not lay hands on wood, stone, or pencil, he would express his ideas in soft white bread. He would either copy figures from the paintings which decorated the choir-stall or simply improvise, always leaving behind him crude sketches whose licentious character was the despair of the younger fathers, while rumour had it that the older Jesuits found them amusing. In the end, if the college records are to be believed, he was expelled for carving a log into the form of Christ one Good Friday, while waiting his turn to confess. The impiety engraved into this statue was too strong not to attract punishment for the artist. If only he had not had the audacity to place such a cynical figure on top of the tabernacle!*

'Sarrasine then came to Paris to seek sanctuary from the threat of his father's curse. As he had the sort of will that knew no obstacle, he obeyed only the orders of his genius and enrolled in the studio of Bouchardon.* He worked all day, and at night went begging for subsistence. Bouchardon, admiring the progress and intelligence of the young artist, soon guessed the poverty of his pupil; he came to his aid, felt affection for him, and treated him as his son. Then, when Sarrasine's genius was revealed in one of those works where a nascent talent struggles to emerge from the whirlwind of youth, Bouchardon generously attempted to reinstate him in the good books of the old prosecutor. Bowing to the authority of the famous sculptor, the paternal anger abated. The whole city of Besançon was proud of having given birth to a great man of the future. In the first moments of joy brought on by his flattered vanity, the avaricious lawyer arranged for his son to go into the world in the best possible way. For some considerable time the long and laborious studies required by sculpture held the impetuous character and untamed genius of Sarrasine in check. Bouchardon, intuiting the violence of the passions which raged in this young soul, which was perhaps as vigorously forged as that of Michelangelo, channelled the young man's energies into endless work. He managed to contain the extraordinary *élan* of Sarrasine within reasonable limits by forbidding him to work and offering him distractions when he saw him carried away by some furious idea, or by entrusting him with an important piece of work just when he was about to give way to dissipation. But, with such a passionate soul, tenderness was always the most powerful weapon, and the master was able to gain such a hold over his pupil only by provoking gratitude for his fatherly kindness.

'When he was twenty-two years of age Sarrasine was by necessity removed from the salutary influence that Bouchardon wielded over his habits and morals. He paid the price for his genius when he won the prize for sculpture* endowed by the Marquis de Marigny, the brother of Madame de Pompadour,* who did so much to aid the arts. Diderot* praised the statue of Bouchardon's pupil as a masterpiece. It was not without profound sadness that the sculptor appointed to the king watched this young man, in whom he had carefully inculcated a profound ignorance of life's realities, prepare to depart for Italy.

'For six years Sarrasine had been Bouchardon's companion. As passionate a devotee of his art as Canova* was to be later, he was used to rising at dawn, going to the studio, and leaving it only at nightfall, with no companion but his muse. If he went to the Comédie-Française,* he went there only when his master invited him. He felt so uncomfortable at Madame Geoffrin's salon* and in the high society to which Bouchardon tried to introduce him, that he preferred to remain alone, and he repudiated the pleasures of his licentious age. His only mistresses were sculpture, and Clotilde, one of the stars of the Opéra. And even this affair was of short duration. Sarrasine was rather ugly, always badly dressed, of so free a nature and so haphazard in his private life that the illustrious nymph, fearing some disaster, very soon sent the sculptor back into the arms of the arts. Sophie Arnould* has written a witty comment somewhere on the subject. I believe that she was surprised that her friend had been able to get the better of this man's statues.

'Sarrasine left for Italy in 1758. During the journey his ardent imagination was aroused by the sight of the copper skies and the marvellous monuments that mark the homeland of the arts. He admired the statues, the frescos, and the paintings and, inspired to emulate them, he arrived in Rome seized with a desire to inscribe his name between those of Michelangelo and Monsieur Bouchardon. Thus, during his first few days there he divided his time between working in the studio and studying the works of art which are so abundant in Rome. He had already spent two weeks in that state of ecstasy which grips any imaginative young man when faced with this empire of ruins, when one evening he entered the Teatro d'Argentina,* only to find it besieged by crowds. He enquired after the reason for this throng, and everyone replied with two names: "Zambinella!" "Jommelli!"* He entered and sat in the stalls, squeezing in between two remarkably plump monks, but was fortunate enough to find himself close to the stage. The curtain was raised. For the first time in his life he heard the music whose delights Jean-Jacques Rousseau* had so eloquently praised on hearing it one evening at the Baron d'Holbach's salon.* The senses of the young sculptor were, so to speak, finely tuned by the accents of the sublime harmonies of Jommelli. The languorous originality of the skilfully interwoven Italian voices plunged him into an ecstasy of bliss. He was speechless, motionless, and did not even feel the weight of the two priests on either side of him. His soul seemed to flow into his sense of sight and hearing; he drank in the sound through the very pores of his skin. Suddenly, a burst of applause strong enough to bring the house down welcomed the arrival on stage of the prima donna. She advanced coquettishly towards the front of the stage and welcomed the public with infinite grace. The lights, the enthusiasm of the crowd, the illusion of the stage, and the glamorous costume, which was rather striking for the time, conspired in favour of this woman. Sarrasine sighed with pleasure.

'At this moment he admired an ideal beauty whose perfections he had thus far sought here and there in nature, seeking in one model, however humble, the perfect curves of a leg, in another the shape of a breast, and in a third white shoulders; here the neck of some young girl, there the hand of another woman and the rounded knees of a child, without ever finding the rich and smooth creations of ancient Greece beneath the cold skies of Paris. La Zambinella presented him with all the living, subtle, and exquisite proportions of feminine nature, so ardently desired, of which the sculptor is at once both the most severe and the most passionate judge. Her mouth was expressive, her eyes brimmed with love, her complexion was of a dazzling whiteness. Add to these details, which would have ravished any painter, all the marvels of Venus revered and rendered by the chisel of the Greeks. No artist could tire of admiring the inimitable grace with which the arms merged with the bust, the elegant curves of the neck, the lines harmoniously described by the eyebrows and the nose; and then there was the perfect oval of the face, the purity of its lively contours and the effect of the thick, curving eyelashes at the end of voluptuous eyelids. This was more than a woman, this was a masterpiece. There was in this unprecedented creation a love to ravish all men, and beauty enough to satisfy any art critic.

'Sarrasine devoured with his eyes this statue by Pygmalion* who had come down for him alone from her pedestal. When la Zambinella sang, pandemonium broke out. The artist felt a chill, then a sudden burning in the depths of his inner being—in what we call our heart, for want of a better word. He did not applaud, and said nothing, but he felt a surge of madness, the kind of frenzy that moves us only at that age when our desires are tinged with something terrible and infernal. Sarrasine wanted to leap onto the stage and seize hold of this woman: this impulse, multiplied a hundredfold by a moral abandon which is impossible to explain, since these phenomena occur in a sphere inaccessible to human observation, tore through him with irresistible force. To look at him, you would have thought him a cold and stupid man. All thought of fame or knowledge, of career or rewards, of life itself, collapsed.

' "To gain her love, or die!"—such was the order that Sarrasine imposed upon himself. He was so completely intoxicated that he saw neither the room nor the spectators and actors, and did not hear the music. What was more, all distance between him and la Zambinella seemed to have been swept away: he possessed her; his eyes, fixed on her, held her in their grasp. An almost diabolical power enabled him to feel the breath of her voice, to breathe in the fragrant powder which impregnated her hair, to see the contours of her face, to count the blue veins which subtly emphasized her satin skin. Finally the agile, fresh, and silvery tones of that voice, as supple as a thread that the slightest breath of air shapes, coils and unravels, modulates and disperses, that voice attacked his soul, so that more than once he let out the sort of involuntary cry born of convulsive delight which is all too rarely torn from us by human passions.

'Soon he had to leave the theatre. His trembling legs supported him no more. He was drained, with the weakness of a nervous man who has given way to some terrible fit of rage. He had had so much pleasure, or perhaps he had suffered so much pain, that his life had ebbed away like the water from a vase knocked over and spilt. He felt within him a void, a collapse similar to those depressions which are the despair of convalescents as they emerge from a serious illness. Filled with an inexplicable sadness, he went to sit down on the steps of a church. There, leaning against a column, he became lost in a confused, dream-like meditation. Passion had struck him like lightning. Back once more in his lodgings, he fell into one of those paroxysms of activity which reveal to us the presence of some new principles in our existence. A prey to that first fever of love which brings as much pain as it does pleasure, he wanted to temper his impatience and his desire by drawing la Zambinella from memory. It was a kind of material meditation. On one sheet of paper la Zambinella adopted the apparently calm and cold posture preferred by Raphael, Giorgione, and all great painters. On another she turned her head gracefully at the end of a trill, as if to listen to herself. Sarrasine drew his mistress in every possible pose; he caught her naked, seated, standing, lying, chaste, or amorous, and he was able to realize through the delirium of his pencil all the capricious ideas that tempt our imagination when we think intensely of our beloved. But his frenzied thoughts went further than his drawing. He saw la Zambinella, spoke to her, beseeched her, exhausted a thousand years of life and happiness with her, placing her in every imaginable situation and testing out, so to speak, his future with her.

'The next day he sent his valet to rent a box at the opera close to the stage for the whole season. Then, like all impassioned young men, he exaggerated the difficulty of his enterprise, and his passion doted on the new delight of being able to admire his beloved unencumbered. This golden age of love, during which we enjoy our feelings and are able to create our own happiness almost unaided, was not to last long for Sarrasine.

'However, events took him by surprise while he was still bewitched by this springtime hallucination, as naive as it was voluptuous. For a week or so he lived the experience of a lifetime, busy in the morning kneading the clay with whose help he managed to copy la Zambinella despite the veils, skirts, corsets, and ribbons which hid her from him. In the evening, settling early in his box, reclining on a sofa, he created his own private happiness, like a Turk intoxicated with opium, a happiness as rich and bountiful as he could wish. First he gradually got used to the excessive emotions that his mistress's singing aroused in him, then he taught his eyes to watch her, and finally he was able to contemplate her without fearing the explosion of mute rage that had shaken him the first time. As his passion became less turbulent, so it grew in strength. Moreover, the shy sculptor found it hard to have his solitude, peopled as it was with images, embellished with fantasies, hope, and boundless happiness, disturbed by his comrades. He loved so strongly and so naively that he was bound to suffer those innocent scruples which assail us when we fall in love for the first time. As he began to realize that he would soon have to act, to make plans, to ask where la Zambinella lived, find out if she had a mother, an uncle, a guardian, a family, and as he wondered about how to find a way of seeing her and speaking to her, he felt his heart swelling so strongly with such ambitious ideas that he postponed these cares to the morrow, enjoying his physical suffering as much as his mental pleasure.'

'But', Madame de Rochefide interposed, 'I still don't see how Marianina or her little old man fit into this.'

'You see only him!' I exclaimed, as impatient as a playwright whose dramatic effect has been spoiled.

I paused. 'After a few days Sarrasine settled so regularly in his box, and his eyes expressed so much love, that his passion for la Zambinella's voice would have been the talk of Paris if this adventure had taken place there; but in Italy, Madame, at the theatre, each person is interested only in the dictates of his own heart, leaving no time for spying through opera-glasses. And yet the frenzy of the sculptor did not long escape the eyes of the singers themselves, both male and female. One evening the sculptor noticed them in the wings, laughing at him. It is difficult to tell to what extremes this might have led him, if la Zambinella had not entered the stage at that point. She cast one of those eloquent gazes at Sarrasine which often say more than women intend them to. This gaze was a revelation. Sarrasine felt that he was loved!

'"If this is only a whim," he thought, already accusing his mistress of too much ardour, "she does not know the force of will that shall dominate her. Her whim shall last, I hope, as long as my life."

'At that moment three quiet knocks at the door of his box caught the attention of the artist. He opened the door. An old woman slipped in mysteriously.

'"Young man," she said, "if you seek happiness, be cautious. Wrap yourself in a cape, cover your eyes with a broad-brimmed hat; then at about ten o'clock this evening come to the Rue du Corso, in front of the Hôtel d'Espagne."

'"I shall be there," he replied, placing two louis in the wrinkled hand of the duenna.

'He slipped away from his box, having exchanged a complicit glance with la Zambinella, who shyly lowered her voluptuous eyelids, like a woman happy at last to be understood. Then he rose in order to rush home, hoping to borrow all the elegance the dressing-table would afford him, to appear as seductive as possible. But, as he was leaving the theatre, a stranger seized his arm.

'"Take care, my French lord," the man whispered in his ear. "This is a matter of life or death. Cardinal Cicognara is her protector, and he takes no hostages."

'If some demon had placed the depths of hell between Sarrasine and la Zambinella, at that moment he would have crossed them in a single bound. Like the horses of the immortals depicted by Homer,* the sculptor's love crossed immense spaces in the blink of an eye.

'"Even if death were to await me as I left my house, I would go all the quicker," he replied.

'"*Poverino!*"* cried the stranger, as he disappeared.

'To speak of danger to a man in love, is that not to tempt him with greater pleasures? Never had Sarrasine's valet seen him prepare his dress so carefully. His finest sword, a present from Bouchardon, the cravat which Clotilde had given him, his suit sewn with spangles, his waistcoat of silver cloth, his gold snuff-box, his precious watches, everything was taken from his trunks, and he adorned himself like a girl preparing to parade in front of her first lover. At the stated time, drunk with love and bursting with hope, Sarrasine ran to the appointment set by the old woman, hiding his face in his cloak. The duenna was waiting for him.

'"You took your time," she said. "Come."

'She drew the Frenchman through several side-streets and stopped in front of a rather elegant mansion. She knocked. The door opened. She led Sarrasine through a labyrinth of stairs, galleries, and apartments lit only by the uncertain glow of the moon, and soon arrived at a door between whose slats escaped flashes of light and the sound of various joyful voices. Suddenly Sarrasine was dazzled when, at a word from the old lady, he was admitted into this mysterious apartment and found himself in a room as brightly lit as it was sumptuously furnished, in the midst of which was a table richly laden with decanters of venerable vintage, their crystal sparkling with wine-dark reflections. He recognized the male and female singers from the theatre, mingling with other charming women. The artists were waiting for him to arrive before starting their festivities. Sarrasine suppressed a reaction of disappointment and put a brave face on it. He had hoped for a dimly lit room, his beloved by the fireside, a jealous lover nearby, death and danger, confidences exchanged under their breath, heart to heart, perilous kisses, their faces close enough for la Zambinella's hair to brush his brow heavy with desire and burning with happiness.

'"Long live madness!" he cried. "*Signori e belle donne*, you must allow me to repay you one day, to thank you for the welcome you have given a poor sculptor."

'Having received the rather effusive greetings of most of the company, whom he recognized by sight, he attempted to draw closer to the wing-chair where la Zambinella was nonchalantly lounging. Oh! How his heart beat when he saw a dainty foot, wearing one of those slippers which in those days, if you will permit me to say so, Madame, gave a woman's foot such a coquettish and delectable expression that I don't know how a man could resist it. The tight white stockings picked out with green embroidery, the short skirts, and pointed high-heeled slippers of the reign of Louis XV may even have played their part in demoralizing Europe and the clergy.'

'May have?' said the Marquise. 'Have you read nothing?'

'La Zambinella', I replied, smiling, 'had boldly crossed her legs, and was dangling the upper one, quite like a duchess, an attitude which suited her type of wayward beauty, full of a kind of engaging indolence. She had removed her theatrical costume and donned a bodice which silhouetted her slim waist and set off the panniers of her skirt and her satin dress embroidered with blue flowers. Her bosom, whose treasures were concealed by a coquettish profusion of lace, was dazzlingly white. Her hair was styled rather like that of Madame du Barry,* and her face, although overshadowed by a wide bonnet, appeared all the sweeter and her powder became her perfectly. To see her thus was to adore her. She smiled gracefully at the sculptor. Sarrasine, upset at being unable to speak to her without being overheard, sat down politely beside her and talked to her of music, praising her prodigious talent, but his voice trembled with love, fear, and hope.

'"What are you afraid of?" asked Vitagliani, the most renowned singer in the company. "Come, you need fear no rival here."

'The tenor smiled and said no more. His smile was reflected in the faces of the other guests, whose attentiveness disguised a mischievous complicity that a lover was not supposed to notice. This public acknowledgement struck Sarrasine like a sudden dagger-blow to the heart. Although he had a certain strength of character, and no adverse circumstances could have lessened his love, he had perhaps never dreamed that la Zambinella was something akin to a courtesan; he had never imagined that he would not be able to enjoy all at once the pure joys that make the love of a young woman so delightful and the fiery passion offered by a woman of the theatre seeking to sell the treasures of her love. He pondered the problem, then resigned himself. Supper was served. Sarrasine and la Zambinella sat down quite casually side by side. During the first half of the soirée the artists were fairly restrained, and the sculptor was able to converse with the singer. He discovered that she had wit and discrimination, and yet was surprisingly lacking in knowledge, and showed herself to be weak and superstitious. The delicacy of her senses was apparent in her sensitivity to sound. When Vitagliani uncorked the first bottle of champagne, Sarrasine read in his neighbour's eyes a moment of panic at the small explosion caused by the escaping gas. The involuntary shudder of this feminine creature was interpreted by the amorous artist as a sign of extreme sensibility. Her vulnerability charmed the Frenchman. A man's love depends so much on his need to protect!

'"My power shall serve as your shield!" Is not this phrase inscribed in the heart of every declaration of love? Sarrasine was too impassioned to play the game of gallantry with the beautiful Italian woman. Like all lovers, he was in turn serious, merry, and thoughtful. Although he seemed to be listening to the other guests, so absorbed was he in the pleasure of being beside her, of lightly touching her hand, of being at her service, that he heard not a word they said. He was afloat in a sea of secret joy. Despite the meaningful looks they exchanged from time to time, he was surprised by the reserve that she maintained towards him. Even though it was she who had first pressed her foot against his, and teased him with all the wiles of a free and amorous woman, yet she suddenly veiled herself in maidenly modesty on hearing a remark by Sarrasine which revealed the excessive violence of his nature. When the supper turned into riotous revelry, the guests broke into song, inspired by the Peralta wine and the Pedro Ximenez sherry.* They sang ravishing duets, Calabrian airs, Spanish *seguedillas*, Neapolitan *canzonets*. Intoxication was in their eyes, in the music, in their hearts and voices. Now the company overflowed with sparkling enchantment, convivial abandon, and that Italian bonhomie which those who are familiar only with Parisian assemblies, London dances, or the circles of Vienna cannot imagine. Words of wit and love were exchanged like bullets on a battlefield, mingling with laughter, oaths, and appeals to the Virgin Mary or her *bambino*. One man stretched out on a sofa and fell asleep. A young woman listened to a declaration of love without realizing that she was spilling her sherry all over the tablecloth. In the midst of this chaos la Zambinella looked at times terrified, at others lost in thought. She refused to drink, ate perhaps a little too much; but appetite, so they say, is charming in a woman. As he admired the modesty of his beloved, Sarrasine started to think seriously about the future.

'"I'm sure she wants to be married," he said to himself.

'Then he gave himself up to imagining the delights of this marriage. His whole life seemed to him too short to drink dry the well of happiness which he found in the depths of his soul. Vitagliani, his neighbour, filled his glass so often that at around three o'clock in the morning Sarrasine, although not completely drunk, was powerless to control his delirious passion. An impetuous urge made him seize the woman and carry her out of the salon into a kind of boudoir whose door had caught his eye more than once. The Italian woman was armed with a dagger.

'"If you come closer," she said, "I shall be forced to thrust this knife in your heart. Admit it, you would despise me! I have come to respect your character too much to yield in this way. I do not want to betray the feelings with which you honour me."

'"No, no!" said Sarrasine, "you cannot extinguish passion by exciting it. Are you already so corrupt that your hardened heart would make you act like a young courtesan, who fans the emotions of all those who fill her purse?"

'"But today is Friday,"* she answered, terrified by the Frenchman's violence.

'Sarrasine, who was not religious, began to laugh. La Zambinella, starting like a young deer, fled towards the ballroom. When Sarrasine appeared in hot pursuit, he was greeted with peals of devilish laughter. He saw Zambinella in a faint on a sofa. She was pale and seemed exhausted by the extreme effort she had just made. Although Sarrasine knew very little Italian, he understood his mistress as she whispered to Vitagliani: "Oh, he will be the death of me!"

'This strange scene utterly confused the sculptor. Then he regained his wits. At first he did not move, but then recovered the power of speech, sat down beside his mistress, and declared his respect for her. He found the strength to mute his passion by talking in the most exalted phrases; and in describing his love for her he deployed those gems of rhetorical magic which act as an obliging go-between that women rarely refuse to believe.

'As the first rays of morning light surprised the revellers, one of the women suggested going to Frascati.* Everyone enthusiastically cheered the idea of spending the day at the Villa Ludovisi.* Vitagliani went down to hire the carriages. Sarrasine was delighted to accompany la Zambinella in a phaeton.* Once they had left

Rome, the cheerful mood, briefly subdued by everyone's attempt to fight off sleep, was suddenly reawakened. The men and women alike seemed accustomed to this strange way of living, with its succession of pleasures and artistic impulses which makes of life an endless celebration, and where laughter has no thought for the morrow. The sculptor's companion was the only one who seemed downcast.

'"Are you unwell?" asked Sarrasine. "Would you prefer to return home?"

'"I don't have the strength to endure such excess," she replied. "I need to be treated very gently, but with you by my side I feel so well. Without you I would never had stayed at that supper. A night without sleep leaves me drained."

'"How delicate you are!" Sarrasine replied, studying the dainty features of his charming companion.

'"These drunken revels ruin my voice."

'The artist exclaimed, "Now that we are alone, and you no longer need fear my outbursts of passion, tell me that you love me."

'"Why?" she answered. "What good would that do? You thought me pretty. But you are a Frenchman. Your feelings will pass. Oh, you would never love me as I would wish to be loved."

'"What do you mean?"

'"Not with base passion, but purely. I abhor men perhaps even more than I hate women. I need to find refuge in friendship. To me the world is a wilderness. I am a damned creature, condemned to understand happiness, to feel it, to desire it, and, like so many others, forced to see it escape me again and again. Remember, my lord, that I would never have deceived you. But I forbid you to love me. I can be your devoted friend, for I admire your strength and character. I need a brother, a protector. Be all that for me, but nothing more."

'"Not love you!" exclaimed Sarrasine, "but you, my dear angel, are my life, my happiness!"

'"I could say one word which would make you reject me in horror."

'"You are toying with me! Nothing can frighten me off. Tell me that you will rob me of my future, that in two months I shall die, that I shall be damned simply for having kissed you." Despite la Zambinella's efforts to escape his impassioned embrace, he kissed her and said: "Tell me that you are a devil, that you demand my fortune, my reputation, all hope of fame! Do you want me never to be a sculptor? Just say the word!"

'"What if I were not a woman?" asked la Zambinella shyly, in soft and silvery tones.

'"What a joke!" exclaimed Sarrasine. "Do you think you could deceive the eye of an artist? Have I not spent ten days devouring, studying and admiring your perfections? Only a woman could possess such softly rounded arms, such elegant curves. Oh, you are fishing for compliments!"

'She smiled sadly and murmured, "Fatal beauty." She looked up towards the heavens. At that moment her countenance took on such a powerful and vivid expression of horror that it made Sarrasine shudder.

'"My French lord," she continued, "forget for ever this one moment of madness. I hold you in esteem, but, as for love, do not ask it of me, for that feeling has been stifled in my heart. I have no heart!" she cried, breaking down in tears. "The stage on which you saw me, the applause, the music, the fame to which I have been sentenced, that is my life, I have no other. In a few hours you will no longer see me with the same eyes. The woman that you love will be dead!"

'The sculptor did not reply. He was gripped by a mute rage which choked his heart. He could only look at this extraordinary woman with eyes that blazed and scorched. That voice imbued with weakness, the demeanour, manners, and movements of la Zambinella, so suffused with sadness, melancholy, and despondency, awakened in his soul all his reserves of passion. Her every word was a spur. At that moment they arrived at Frascati. When the artist gave his beloved his arm to help her alight from the carriage, he felt how much she was shivering. "What is the matter?" he exclaimed as he saw her grow pale. "I should die if I ever caused you the slightest pain, even without meaning to."

'"It's a snake!" she said, pointing at a grass-snake slithering along a ditch. "I'm afraid of those hateful creatures." Sarrasine crushed the grass-snake's head with a stamp of his heel.

'"How can you be so brave?" asked la Zambinella, visibly terrified as she stared at the lifeless reptile.

'"So now," said the artist with a smile, "do you still dare to claim that you aren't a woman?"

'They caught up with the group and walked through the woods of the Villa Ludovisi, which in those days belonged to Cardinal Cicognara. The morning passed too quickly for the lovesick sculptor, but it was crowded with incidents which revealed to him the coquetry, frailty, and fastidiousness of this passive and pliant soul. She had a woman's sudden fears, irrational whims, instinctive nervous reactions, impetuous audacity, daring outbursts, and deliciously refined sentiments. There came a moment when, as they roamed through the countryside, the merry little band of singers saw in the distance a group of men armed to the teeth, with a threatening appearance. Someone shouted, "Look out, bandits!" They all quickened their pace to reach the safety of the grounds of the Cardinal's villa. At this critical moment Sarrasine noticed from la Zambinella's pallor that she no longer had the strength to keep walking. He caught her up and ran for a while with her in his arms. When he reached a nearby vineyard he set his beloved back on her feet.

'"Why is it", he said, "that in any other woman I would find such excessive weakness unpleasant, repulsive even, and the slightest sign of it would be almost enough to extinguish all my feelings for her? Yet in you it seems to me so appealing and charming! Oh how I love you!" he went on. "All your faults and fears and failings lend a certain grace to your soul. I feel that I would hate a strong woman, a Sappho* who was brave and full of energy and passion. Oh, you frail and gentle creature! How could you be otherwise? That delicate, angelic voice would have seemed quite unnatural if it had come from any other body but yours."

'"I cannot offer you any hope," she said. "Stop speaking to me in this way, or you will become a laughing stock. I cannot bar you from entering the theatre, but if you love me or if you have any sense, you will not go there again." She continued gravely: "Listen, Monsieur..."

'"Oh, no more," interjected the artist, beside himself. "Your resistance inflames the love in my heart."

'La Zambinella maintained a graceful and modest demeanour, but fell silent, as if her thoughts were consumed by some dreadful misfortune. When the time came to return to Rome she chose a four-seater berlin,* ordering the sculptor with a cruel, imperious air to go back alone in the phaeton. During the journey Sarrasine resolved to abduct la Zambinella. He spent the whole day devising increasingly extravagant plans. Night was falling as he left his house to enquire of certain people where to find the mansion in which his mistress was living, and at that moment he met one of his friends on his doorstep.

'"Dear friend," said the latter, "I have been asked by our ambassador to extend an invitation to you to attend his residence this evening. He is giving a magnificent concert, and when I tell you that Zambinella will be there..."

'"Zambinella!" exclaimed Sarrasine, in a turmoil at hearing the name. "I am mad about her!"

'"As is everybody," his friend replied.

'"Now, if you are my friends, you and Vien, Lauterbourg, and Allegrain,* will you lend me a hand in a matter I have to settle after the party?" asked Sarrasine.

'"As long as there's no cardinal to kill, or..."

'"No, no," said Sarrasine, "I do not ask for anything that a gentleman would not do."

'A little later the sculptor had made all the arrangements necessary for the success of his enterprise. He was one of the last to arrive at the ambassador's, but he came in a closed carriage drawn by sturdy horses driven by one of the most resourceful coachmen in Rome. The ambassador's palace was crowded, and the sculptor, who was unknown to any of the other guests, struggled to make his way to the salon where Zambinella was singing at that moment.

'"I suppose it is out of respect for the cardinals, bishops, and priests who are here", asked Sarrasine, "that *she* is dressed as a man, her hair bound up in a net at the back of her head, and a sword by her side?"

'"She! Who do you mean?" asked the elderly nobleman addressed by Sarrasine.

'"La Zambinella."

'"La Zambinella!" echoed the Roman prince. "Do you speak in jest? Where have you spent all your life? Was ever a woman allowed on stage in Rome? And do you not know the nature of the creatures who play the parts of women in the theatres of the Papal States? It was I, my dear Sir, who endowed Zambinella with his voice. I paid for everything that this rascal has ever wanted, even his singing lessons. Well, he has shown so little gratitude for what I did for him that he has never yet deigned to cross my threshold. But if he does get rich he'll owe every cent to me."

'Prince Chigi* could easily have continued at greater length, but Sarrasine was not listening to him. A terrible truth had penetrated his soul. It was as if he had been struck by lightning. He was paralysed; he could not take his eyes from the figure of the now allegedly male soprano. His intense gaze worked a sort of magnetic attraction on Zambinella, until finally the singer could not prevent himself from turning to look at Sarrasine, and at that moment the divine voice broke. He trembled. An involuntary murmur that escaped the lips of the audience, who seemed to hang on his every note, disconcerted him entirely; he sat down and stopped singing. Cardinal Cicognara, who had been discreetly following the angle of his protégé's gaze, then noticed the Frenchman; he leant towards one of his ecclesiastical aides and apparently asked the name of the sculptor. Once he had obtained the response he required he scrutinized the artist intently, and gave instructions to a priest, who promptly disappeared. Meanwhile Zambinella, who had recovered, took up the phrase which he had so abruptly interrupted, but performed it poorly and, despite the audience's solicitations, he refused to sing anything else. This was the first time that he threw one of those capricious tantrums for which he would become just as famous as for his talent and immense wealth, and which people attributed at least as much to his beauty as to his voice.

'"She is a woman," said Sarrasine, as if there were no one to hear him. "There is some secret intrigue behind the scenes. Cardinal Cicognara is deceiving the Pope and the whole city of Rome!"

'The sculptor immediately left the salon, rallied his friends, and had them lie in wait in the palace courtyard. When Zambinella was sure that Sarrasine had left, he seemed to recover some composure. At around midnight, after wandering from salon to salon like someone on the lookout for an enemy, the singer left the party. Just as he crossed the threshold of the palace he was seized deftly by men who gagged him with a handkerchief and placed him in the carriage that Sarrasine had hired. Frozen with terror, Zambinella huddled into a corner of the carriage, not daring to move. He was faced with the terrifying countenance of the artist, who preserved a death-like silence. It was a short journey. Captured by Sarrasine, Zambinella suddenly found himself in a dark, sparsely furnished studio. The singer, only half alive, did not move from his chair and did not dare look at the sculpture of a woman whose features were all too familiar. He was unable to utter a word, but his teeth chattered and he was transfixed with fear. Sarrasine paced nervously around the room. He stopped abruptly, facing Zambinella.

'"Tell me the truth," he demanded, in a hoarse, strained voice. "Are you a woman? Cardinal Cicognara..."

'Zambinella fell to his knees, and his only answer was to lower his head.

'"Oh, you are a woman," cried the distraught artist, "for even a..." He stopped short. "No," he began again, "no man would stoop so low."

'"Oh, do not kill me!" cried Zambinella, bursting into tears. "I agreed to deceive you only to please my friends, just for a joke."

'"A joke!" the sculptor responded, with a diabolical edge to his voice. "A joke, a joke! Who are you to dare play with a man's passion?"

'"Oh, have mercy!" replied Zambinella.

'"I should put you to death!" cried Sarrasine, violently drawing his sword. "But", he continued with icy disdain, "if I plunged this blade into the heart of your being, would I find any feelings to destroy, would it satisfy my vengeance? You are nothing. I would kill you, whether you be man or woman, and yet..."

'Sarrasine, recoiling in disgust, turned his head away, and then saw the statue.

'"So it is all an illusion!" he cried, then turning to Zambinella, said: "For me a woman's heart was a haven and a homeland. Do you have any sisters to compare with you? No. Well then, die! Or rather, no, you shall live. Is not letting you live sentencing you to something worse than death? I fear neither dying nor ceasing to exist, but I grieve for my lost future and my fortune in love. Your feeble hand has swept my happiness aside. What hope of yours might I crush in exchange for all those of mine that you have blighted? You have brought me down to your level. 'To love, to be loved' are henceforth words empty of meaning for me, as they are for you. Every time I see a real woman I shall think of that imaginary one," he said, pointing to the sculpture with a gesture of despair. "I shall forever have in my mind a divine harpy* who will dig her claws into all my natural feelings as a man and stamp every woman I meet with the seal of imperfection. You monster! You who can give birth to no form of life, you have killed all the women in the world for me!"

'Sarrasine sat down opposite the terrified singer. Two large tears welled up in the sculptor's dry eyes and rolled down his manly cheeks and fell upon the ground. Two tears of rage, two bitter and burning tears.

'"Away with love! I am dead to all pleasure, to all human emotion."

'Saying this, he seized hold of a hammer and threw it at the statue with such excessive force that he missed it. But thinking he had destroyed this monument to his folly, he grasped his sword and swung it in order to kill the singer. Zambinella gave a piercing shriek. At that moment three men entered, and suddenly the sculptor fell, stabbed by the blows of three daggers.

'"With the compliments of Cardinal Cicognara," said one of the men.

"A good deed worthy of a Christian," the Frenchman replied

with his dying breath. The sinister emissaries informed Zambinella that his protector was concerned for his safety, and that he awaited him at the door in a closed carriage to take him away as soon as he was freed.'

'But', asked Madame de Rochefide, 'what is the connection between this story and the little old man whom we saw at the Lantys'?'

'Madame, Cardinal Cicognara took possession of the sculpture of Zambinella and had it carved in marble; it is now in the Albani museum. It was there, in 1791, that the Lanty family found it and asked Vien to copy it. The portrait which you saw showing Zambinella at twenty, a moment after you saw him aged a hundred, was used later as a model by Girodet for his *Endymion*,* and you might have recognized the ideal figure you saw in Vien's Adonis.'

'So Zambinella himself, or herself...?'

'Can be no other, Madame, than Marianina's great-uncle. You might now be able to understand Madame de Lanty's interest in concealing the source of a fortune which comes from...'

'Enough!' she said with an imperious gesture.

We remained for a moment plunged in the deepest silence.

'Well, then?' I asked.

'Ah,' she exclaimed, standing up and starting to pace around the room. She came to look me in the face, and said with a broken voice:

'You have filled me with a lasting disgust for life and its passions. Unless one is a monster, do not all human emotions share the same fate, ending in such terrible disappointment? If we are mothers, our children destroy us with their wicked behaviour or their indifference. If we are wives, we are deceived. If we are lovers, we are discarded, abandoned. As for friendship, is there such a thing? I would enter a convent tomorrow if I thought I could not remain an unassailable rock in the midst of life's tempests. If the Christian afterlife is another illusion, at least it is only dispelled after death. Let me be alone.'

'Ah!' I replied. 'You know how to punish a man.'

'And would I be wrong to do so?'

'Yes, you would,' I replied, summoning up my courage. 'By telling you the whole story, which is quite well known in Italy, I have shown you a decent idea of the progress made by our modern civilization. We no longer create such unfortunate wretches.'

'Paris', she replied, 'is indeed a hospitable place; it welcomes all, including those whose paths to glory are besmirched with shame and blood. Crime and infamy have a right of asylum here; only virtue lacks an altar. Yes, the pure in heart have a home in heaven! No one will have ever truly known me! I am proud of it.'

The Marquise remained plunged in thought.

Paris, November 1830

THE UNKNOWN MASTERPIECE

To a Lord

. . . .
. . . .
. . . .
. . . .
. . . .

1845

I
GILLETTE

TOWARDS the end of 1612,* one cold December morning, a young man whose clothes appeared decidedly threadbare was walking past the door of a house located in the Rue des Grands-Augustins in Paris. Having spent quite some time walking the length of the street, with all the uncertainty of a lover afraid of presenting himself to his first mistress, no matter how compliant she might be, he finally crossed the threshold and asked if Maître François Porbus* was at home. On receiving an affirmative reply from an old woman who was busy sweeping a low-ceilinged room, the young man slowly climbed the stairs, hesitating on every step like some newly appointed courtier fretting over the way the king would receive him. When he reached the top of the spiral staircase he stood still for a moment on the landing, uncertain whether to grasp the grotesque knocker embellishing the door of the studio where Henri IV's former portrait painter, once spurned by Marie de Medici in favour of Rubens,* was no doubt working. The young man was deeply moved by those feelings that make all great artists tremble, when, in the full flush of their youth and their love for art, they come face to face with a man of genius or a masterpiece. Common to all human emotions is a first flowering born of noble enthusiasm, which gradually fades, until happiness is no more than a memory and fame merely a lie. Of all our fragile emotions, the one most akin to love is the nascent passion of an artist discovering the exquisite torment of the fame and misery which are to be his lot; a passion brimming with audacity and inhibition, with vague beliefs and inevitable moments of discouragement. If any budding genius of slender means does not tremble in body and soul when he comes face to face with a master, then he will always be lacking some chord in his heart, what you might call a touch of the brush, some feeling within his work, a certain lyric expression. There may well be braggarts, bloated with pride, who believe their future fame inevitable, but they are men of wit only in the eyes of fools. Following this reckoning, our unknown young man would seem to have true merit, if talent can be measured by initial inhibition or by that indefinable modesty which those destined for fame are able to shed when they exercise their art, as beautiful women do when they learn the skills of coquetry. A succession of triumphs lessens self-doubt, and modesty may well be a form of self-doubt.

Overcome by feelings of inadequacy and shocked at that instant by his own bravado, this poor novice would never have crossed the threshold of the painter to whom we owe that admirable portrait of Henri IV, if chance had not paid him an extraordinary favour. An old man had come up the stairs. From the strangeness of his costume, the splendour of his lace collar, and the imposing confidence of his gait, the young man guessed this character to be the painter's patron or friend; he stepped back to let him pass on the landing, scrutinized him with curiosity, hoping to discover in him the good will of a fellow artist or the amiable disposition of an art lover; but he detected something diabolical in this figure, and above all that 'certain something' which excites every artist. Picture a prominent, balding brow, jutting over a short, flattened snub nose, similar to that of Rabelais or Socrates, a wrinkled, laughing mouth, a short but proudly lifted chin, sporting a neatly trimmed grey, pointed beard, sea-green irises, seemingly dulled by age, but which, in contrast to the mother-of-pearl surrounding them, could at times flash magnetic looks charged with anger or enthusiasm. His face, moreover, was singularly worn by the ravages of age, and even more by thought, which eats away at both body and soul. His eyes had lost their lashes, and traces of eyebrows were barely discernible on the arches above them. Place this head upon a weak and insubstantial body, surround it with sparkling white lace as intricately worked as a fish-slice, throw a heavy golden chain over the old man's black doublet and you will have but an imperfect image of this figure, to which even the dim light of the staircase lent a fantastical colour. You might have taken him for a Rembrandt* painting, walking silently and frameless through the atmospheric darkness which that painter made his own. The old man glanced at the younger man with eyes full of wisdom, knocked three times at the door, and said to the frail-looking man in his forties who had come to open it, 'Good day, Maître.'

Porbus bowed respectfully and invited the young man in, believing him to be accompanying the elder, and took all the less notice of him as the novice remained spellbound by the emotion common to all natural artists when they see for the very first time a studio where some of the material processes of their art are revealed to them. Daylight entered the studio of Maître Porbus through a skylight in the vaulted roof. The sun's rays fell upon a canvas resting on an easel, on which there were only three or four white brushstrokes, but failed to reach into the furthest black corners of the vast room. However, in the reddish half-light a few stray beams glinted on the silver facets of a medieval soldier's breastplate hanging on the wall, and fell in a sudden shaft of light across the carved and polished cornice of an antique dresser laden with curious chinaware, and embroidered bright stitches on the rough material and broken folds of the old gold brocade curtains that were draped there for occasional copying. Male anatomical models and torsos and other fragments of classical goddesses, lovingly smoothed by the kiss of centuries, were strewn over the benches and side tables. Countless studies and sketches in three colours of crayon,* in red wash or black ink, covered the walls from floor to ceiling. Pots of paint, flasks of oil and spirits, and upturned stools left only a narrow passage leading towards the halo cast by the pool of light from the high window, its rays falling directly on Porbus's pallid face and the ivory pate of the strange man. The young man's attention was soon captured by a painting which, in those troubled revolutionary times, had become famous. This striking image was still venerated by some of those diehards who keep the sacred flame burning in difficult times. It represented Saint Mary of Egypt* preparing to pay the boatman. This masterpiece had been intended for Marie de Medici, who later, finding herself in financial straits, had been forced to sell it.*

'I like your saint,' the old man said to Porbus, 'and I would give you ten gold crowns more than what the Queen is offering, but I wouldn't want to enter into the lists with her, devil take it!'

'Do you really like her?'

'Well,' said the old man, ' "like her"? Yes and no. You've fitted her out nicely enough, but there's no life in her. You lot think you've done your job when you've drawn accurately and got the parts of the body in the right place according to the laws of anatomy! You colour in their contours using flesh tones mixed in advance on your palette, taking care to keep one side darker than the other, and because from time to time you look at a naked woman standing on a table, you think that you have copied nature, you believe yourselves to be painters and have discovered God's secrets... Pah! In order to be a great poet it's not enough to know your grammar by heart and avoid misuse of our language. Take a look at your saint, Porbus! At first glance she seems much to be admired, but when you look more closely you'll see that she is pasted onto the flat of the canvas and you couldn't walk round behind her. She's an outline with only one plane, she's a cardboard cut-out, an image unable to turn around or change position. I don't sense any air between her arm and the background of the painting; there's no space, no depth, although you have strictly obeyed the laws of linear and aerial perspective;* but despite such laudable efforts, I can't bring myself to believe that the warm breath of life animates this beautiful body. It seems to me that if I were to place my hand on that beautifully firm and shapely breast it would feel as cold as marble! No, my friend, there's no blood flowing beneath that ivory skin, there's no crimson life-force swelling through the tangled tracery of veins and capillaries running beneath the amber transparency of her temples and her breast. This part throbs with life, but that one is completely inanimate; life and death are in conflict in every corner. Here she's a woman, there she's a statue, and over here she's a corpse. Your creation is unfinished. You haven't managed to breathe more than part of your soul into your cherished work. More than once you have allowed the Promethean torch that you were holding to be extinguished, and many parts of your painting have not even been touched by the divine fire.'*

'But why is this so, dear master?' Porbus asked the old man respectfully, while the young man could barely resist a strong temptation to strike that venerable gentleman.

'Ah, you see,' said the little old man, 'you have been dithering between two systems, between line and colour, between the rigid attention to detail and rigorous design of the old German masters and the dazzling passion and joyful abundance of the Italian painters. You wanted to imitate Hans Holbein and Titian, Albrecht Dürer and Paolo Veronese* at the same time. An admirable ambition in its way, no doubt—but what has happened? You have captured neither the austere charm of draughtsmanship nor the enchanting illusions of chiaroscuro. In this patch here, just as the molten bronze of a sculpture breaks a too-fragile mould as it sets, so Titian's rich, golden hues burst through Albrecht Dürer's frail framework into which you have poured them. In other places the mould has withstood the pressure and restrained the wonderful exuberance of the Venetian palette. The face is neither perfectly drawn nor perfectly painted, and reveals so many traces of your wretched indecision. If you did not feel strong enough to use the fire of your genius to fuse these two rival approaches, then you should have made a clear choice for one or the other in order to achieve that coherence which imitates one of the principles of life. You are convincing only in the middle parts, your outlines are wrong, they don't match up, and have no depth. There is some truth here', the old man pointed to the breast of the saint, 'and here,' he went on, indicating the spot where the shoulder ended, 'but there', he said, pointing to the centre of the breast again, 'it's all wrong. Let us not analyse it, that would only lead you to despair.'

The old man sat on a pair of steps, holding his head in his hands, and fell silent.

Porbus replied, 'Yet, Master, I did carefully study that breast on a model, but unfortunately for us, some of nature's real manifestations look implausible on the canvas.'

'The purpose of art is not to copy nature, but to express it. It's not about making good or bad copies, it's about poetry!' said the old man, interrupting Porbus with a tyrannical wave of his hand. 'Otherwise a sculptor could save himself the trouble and take a cast of a woman! And yet, try making a cast of your mistress's hand and putting it in front of you, and you will see something horribly corpse-like and totally unconvincing, and then you will have to go in search of the man's chisel which won't make an exact copy, but will capture its life and movement. It is our task to capture the spirit, the soul, and the physiognomy of objects and living things. Appearances are only the accidents of life, not life itself. This hand, since I chose that example, isn't just a part of the body, it is also the expression and extension of a thought waiting to be captured and rendered. Neither painter, nor poet, nor sculptor should separate cause and effect, which are inextricably linked together. That's where the real struggle takes place. Many painters succeed instinctively without being aware of this artistic debate. You draw a woman, but you do not see her. This is not the way to force open Nature's store of mysteries. Though you are not aware of it, your hand is reproducing another copied from your teacher's studio. You do not delve far enough into the deepest recesses of form, you do not pursue it with enough love and perseverance in its flights and fancies. Beauty is something austere and difficult which will not be captured in that way, you have to wait for the right moment, lie in wait, watch carefully, corner it, and fiercely embrace it to force it to surrender. Form is a Proteus far more elusive and devious than the Proteus of myth,* it is only after prolonged struggles that we may constrain it to show its true face; you and your kind are content with the first appearance that form assumes, or at most the second or the third; that is not the way that the best wrestlers go about it. The painters who win through do not let themselves be deceived by such lures, they persevere until Nature has no choice but to reveal itself in all its naked and essential truth. That was Raphael's* method,' said the old man, doffing his black velvet cap to indicate the respect inspired in him by the king among painters; 'his great superiority comes from a sense deep within himself which seems to want to shatter form. In his images, form is what it is for us, a medium for communicating our ideas and sensations, an immense work of poetry. Every poetic image is a world in itself, a portrait whose original appeared in a sublime vision, bathed in light, invoked by an inner voice, and laid bare by a divine hand, pointing to the sources of expression of a whole lifetime. You dress your women in robes of fine flesh and draperies of beautiful hair, but where is the blood that engenders peace or passion, which creates individual effects? Your saint had a dark complexion but here, my poor Porbus, you have made her fair! So your figures are pale, tinted phantoms that you would parade before our eyes, and you call that painting and art. Just because you have created something that looks more like a woman than a house, you think you have reached your goal, and proud of not needing to write beside your figures *currus venustus* or *pulcher homo*,* as early painters did, you think that you are wonderful artists. Ha, ha! My fine fellow, you are still in the dark, you will need to wear out many more crayons and cover many more canvases before you see the light. Of course a woman carries her head in this way, she holds her skirt like that, her eyes languish and melt with that air of gentle resignation, the shadow of her fluttering eyelashes hovers over her cheeks in just that way. That's it, yet that's not it at all. What is missing? Next to nothing, but that nothing is everything. You have created a semblance of life, but you do not express its overflowing energy, that certain something which perhaps may be the soul, floating cloudlike around her outer form; that is, that bloom of life caught by Titian and Raphael. Starting from the best you have achieved, one might perhaps create excellent paintings; but you tire too easily. The crowd admires, and the real connoisseur smiles. Oh Mabuse,* oh my master,' continued this strange character, 'you are a thief, you took life away with you. But', he went on, 'apart from that, this one canvas is worth all the paintings by that charlatan Rubens, with his mountains of Flemish flesh sprinkled with vermilion, his waves of red hair, and his garish array of colours. At least here you have got colour, feeling, and line, the three essential elements of Art.'

'But that saint is sublime, my good man!' shouted the young man as he emerged from a state of deep contemplation. 'Those two figures, the saint and the boatman, have a sense of subtlety unknown to the Italian painters. I can't think of a single one who could have imagined the boatman's hesitation.'

'Is this rascal one of yours?' Porbus asked the old man.

The novice blushed. 'Alas, Master, pardon my boldness. I am a nobody, I only paint by instinct, and I have just arrived in this city, the source of all learning.'

'To work!' replied Porbus, offering him a red crayon and a sheet of paper. The stranger sketched a fluent copy of the saint.

'Oh, oh!' exclaimed the old man. 'Your name?'

The young man signed his sketch *Nicolas Poussin*.*

'It's not bad for a beginner,' said the strange character, who had spoken so wildly before. 'I see that we can talk of painting in your company. I don't blame you for admiring Porbus's saint. Everyone agrees that it is a masterpiece, and only those initiated in the most profound secrets of art can discover where it falls short. But since you are worthy of the lesson and capable of understanding, I shall show you how little is needed to complete this work. Open your eyes, give me all of your attention, you may never again have such an opportunity to learn. Your palette, Porbus?'

Porbus went to fetch palette and brushes. The little old man rolled up his sleeves with a brisk, impetuous movement, hooked his thumb into the palette, overflowing with all the colours of the rainbow, that Porbus held out. He snatched rather than took from his hands a fistful of brushes of all sizes, and his pointed beard twitched suddenly with an alarming surge of energy, as if the man were in the throes of some erotic fantasy. As he loaded his brush with paint he muttered under his breath: 'These colours should be thrown out of the window along with the man who mixed them; they are revoltingly crude and unnatural, how could anyone paint with them?' Then, with feverish animation, he dipped the tip of the brush into the various pools of colour, his fingers sometimes skipping through the entire spectrum more rapidly than those of a cathedral organist raiding the whole keyboard in a rendering of 'O Filii' at Easter.*

Porbus and Poussin stood motionless at either side of the canvas, plunged in the most intense contemplation.

'Look, young man,' said the old man, without turning round, 'look how with two or three brushstrokes and some blue-tinted glaze we can get the air to flow around the head of this poor saint, who must have been stifling and paralysed in that unbreathable atmosphere! See how the cloak floats freely now, and how we can tell that the breeze wafts it! A moment ago it looked like starched linen held in place by pins. Don't you see how the satin sheen that I have just brushed over her breast enhances the supple, fleshy texture of a maiden's skin, and how the mingled tones of reddish brown and burnt ochre warm the grey chill of that patch of shade where the blood was freezing instead of flowing? Young man, young man, what I am showing you now, no master could teach you. Mabuse alone knew the secret of giving life to faces and figures. I was the only pupil that Mabuse ever had. I had none myself, and I am old! From the few hints I'm giving you, you will have intelligence enough to work out the rest.'

All the while he was speaking the strange old man was touching up every part of the painting; a couple of brushstrokes here, a single one there, but always applied so skilfully that it looked like an entirely new painting; a painting bathed in light. He worked so ardently and passionately that beads of sweat broke out on his bald forehead; he proceeded so rapidly and with such jerky, impatient little movements that the young Poussin had the feeling that there was a demon inside this odd character who was capriciously manipulating his hands against their owner's will. The supernatural glint in his eyes, the nervous tics that seemed to stem from some resistance, gave this idea a semblance of truth that deeply stirred his youthful imagination. As he walked to and fro the old man said: 'Whack! Whack! Whack! That's how to butter your bread, young man. Come, my little brushstrokes, help me light a fire under those icy tones. Bang, bang, bang!' he cried, firing up those parts of the canvas where he had detected a lack of life, using just a few daubs of colour to redress the emotional discord and re-establish the unity of tone required for a passionate Egyptian woman.

'Look, young lad, it's only the last brushstroke that counts. Porbus has used a hundred, I have used only one. Nobody thanks us for what lies underneath. Remember that!'

At last the demon desisted and turned towards Porbus and Poussin, who were struck dumb with admiration: 'It is still not as good as my *Belle Noiseuse*,* yet you could put your signature to a work like that. Yes, I would sign it,' he added, getting up and fetching a mirror in which to look at the portrait.

'Now let's have luncheon,' he said, 'come both of you to my lodgings. I have smoked ham and some good wine! Aha, despite these troubled times we shall talk painting! We have the strength.' He clapped Nicolas Poussin on the shoulder, and added, 'Here is a young lad who has real talent.'

Then, taking note of the Norman's wretched jacket,* he drew from his belt a leather purse, delved into it, took out two gold coins, held them out, and said: 'I'll buy your sketch.'

'Take it,' said Porbus to Poussin, seeing him start and redden with shame, for the young disciple had the pride of the poor, 'he has in his knapsack a king's ransom twice over!'

Leaving the studio, the three of them went downstairs and walked down the street, discussing the arts all the time, until they reached a fine, timbered house situated near the Pont Saint-Michel, whose decoration, door-knocker, window-frames, and arabesques filled Poussin with wonder. The aspiring painter found himself at once in a low room, before a good fire, beside a table laden with appetizing dishes, and by an extraordinary stroke of fortune, in the company of two great artists brimming with good humour.

'Young man,' said Porbus, seeing him awestruck before a painting, 'don't spend too much time looking at that painting, or you will fall into despair.'

It was the *Adam** that Mabuse had painted to secure his release from prison where his creditors had kept him for so long. This figure did indeed offer such a powerful sense of reality that Nicolas Poussin started at that moment to understand the true sense of the old man's confused words. The latter was looking at his painting with satisfaction but without enthusiasm, as if to say: 'I have done better!'

'There is life in it, my poor master was at his best there; but there is still some lack of truth in the background of the canvas. The man is certainly alive, he is standing up and about to come towards us. But the air and sky and wind that we breathe are not there. And it's a mere man that we see here! Yet the only man who issued directly from the hands of God should have some divine quality, and that is missing. Mabuse said so himself, with disdain, when he wasn't drunk.'

Poussin looked from the old man to Porbus, disturbed and curious. He approached the latter as if to ask him the name of their host; but Porbus held his finger to his lips with a mysterious air and the young man, despite his lively curiosity, held his tongue, in the hope that sooner or later a word might enable him to guess the name of the man whose wealth and talent were sufficiently attested by the respect Porbus showed him, and by the wonderful works crammed into his salon.

Poussin, seeing a magnificent portrait of a woman on the sombre oak panelling, exclaimed: 'What a beautiful Giorgione!'*

'No,' replied the old man, 'you are looking at one of my first daubs!'

'Heavens above, so I must be in the presence of the god of painting,' said Poussin naively.

The old man smiled with the air of one long accustomed to such praise. 'Maître Frenhofer!' said Porbus, 'might you summon up a little of your good Rhenish wine for me?'

'Two casks,' the old man replied, 'one to repay the pleasure I had this morning on seeing your beautiful sinner, and the other as a pledge of friendship.'

'Ah, if I were not always ill,' Porbus continued, 'and if you would allow me to see your *Belle Noiseuse*, I could paint something with depth and generous dimensions, where the figures would be life-size.'

'Show you my work?' exclaimed the old man, in consternation. 'No, no, I must still perfect it. Yesterday, towards evening, I thought that I had finished. Her eyes seemed moist, her flesh stirred. The locks of her hair waved freely. She was breathing! Although I managed to use a flat canvas to depict the relief of nature in the round, this morning by the light of day I discovered my error. Ah, to arrive at that glorious result I have studied in depth the great masters of colour, I have analysed the paintings of Titian, the king of light, stripping them layer by layer. Like that sovereign painter, I have sketched my figure in pale tones with a soft, rich texture, for shadow is merely an accident of light, remember, my lad. Then I went back over my work, and using half-tones and glazes I kept reducing its transparency, I made the shadows more vigorous and the blacks a deeper shade, for the shadows of ordinary painters are of a different nature to their light tones, they are wood, they are bronze, they are anything you like, except flesh in shadow. You feel that if their figure changed position the patches of shade would not be wiped clean and would not grow luminous. I have avoided this trap, into which many of the most illustrious have fallen, and in my work you can detect whiteness beneath the opacity of the deepest shadow! Unlike those hordes of ignorant men who believe that they draw correctly because their lines are cleanly defined, I have not outlined my figure dryly nor have I drawn attention to the slightest anatomical detail, for the human body is not enclosed by lines. In this respect sculptors can approach reality more closely than we painters. Nature proceeds in a series of curves, each enveloping the other. Strictly speaking, drawing does not exist! Don't laugh, young man! However peculiar that phrase might seem, you will one day understand the truth of it.* Line is the means whereby man notes the effect of light on objects; but there are no lines in nature, where all is plenitude; it is by modelling that we draw, that is to say that we detach objects from their environment, it is only the distribution of light which gives the body its appearance! So I have not defined the outlines, I have spread a cloud of warm, golden half-tones over the contours so that you can't quite put your finger on the exact place where the outlines meet the background. Seen close up, the whole process seems woolly and lacking in clarity, but if you step back a pace or two everything becomes clear, fixed, and precise; the body moves round, its forms take on relief, you feel the air circulate all round it. And yet I am still not satisfied, I still have my doubts. Perhaps I should not draw with a single line, perhaps I should start in the middle of a figure by first grasping its most prominent highlights, and then move on into the parts which lie in darkness. Is this not how the sun, the divine painter of the universe, proceeds? Oh, nature, nature! Who ever managed to unveil your disguises? Just think, too much knowledge, like too much ignorance, leads to a dead end. I have such doubts about my work!'

Frenhofer paused and then continued: 'I've been working on this for ten years now, young man, but what are ten short years when the problem is a struggle with nature? We don't know how long it took for the great Pygmalion* to create the only statue which ever walked!'

The old man fell into a profound reverie, and stared into space while playing mechanically with his palette-knife.

'Now he is communing with his muse,' said Porbus under his breath.

On hearing this, Nicolas Poussin felt himself caught up in the unfathomable curiosity of an artist. This intent and obtuse old man, with his white eyes, had come to be for him more than a man, and appeared to him as a fairy-tale spirit from some other world. He awakened a thousand confused ideas in his soul. The moral characteristics of this kind of fascination can no more be defined than one may translate the emotion aroused in the heart of an exile by a song which recalls his homeland. Everything about this old man went beyond the bounds of human nature: the contempt which he professed to feel for the most beautiful examples of art, his wealth, his manners, Porbus's deference, his painting—kept hidden for so long—a work no doubt of patience and genius, judging by the head of the Virgin which young Poussin so frankly admired. Its beauty could be compared to that of Mabuse's *Adam* and proved that this old man was one of the princes of Art. What Nicolas Poussin could most perceptibly grasp with his rich imagination, as he looked at this supernatural being, was a complete image of the nature of the artist, this mad nature on which so much power is conferred, and which so often takes advantage of it, leading cool reason, the bourgeois public, and even some lovers of art across a thousand rocky roads, where they find nothing; while, footloose and fancy-free, that girl with white wings discovers epics, palaces, and works of art there. Nature, mocking and kind, fertile and poor! Thus, for the enthusiastic Poussin, this old man in a sudden transfiguration had become art itself, art with all its secrets, passions, and daydreams.

'Yes, my dear Porbus,' Frenhofer went on, 'what I have missed so far is the acquaintance of an irreproachable woman, a body with contours of perfect beauty, and the bloom of whose flesh... but where would I find that living woman,' he said, interrupting himself, 'that lost Venus of the ancient world, so often sought, but whose beauty we find only in fragmented form? Oh, to see if only for a moment, just once, divine nature complete, the ideal at last, I would give my whole fortune, I would descend into limbo to seek you, divine beauty! Like Orpheus,* I would descend into hell to bring her back alive!'

'We might as well leave,' said Porbus to Poussin, 'he is not listening to us, he cannot see us!'

'Let's go to his studio,' replied the young man, in a state of wonder.

'Oh, the old ruffian* has hidden it away carefully. His treasures are too well guarded for us to get near them. I was not waiting for your advice and wishful thinking to try to unlock the mystery.'

'So there is a mystery?'

'Yes,' replied Porbus. 'This old Frenhofer is the only pupil that Mabuse agreed to take on. Frenhofer became his friend, his saviour, his father figure, and gave away most of his wealth to satisfy the passions of Mabuse; in exchange, Mabuse transmitted the secret of painting in relief, the ability to give his figures that extraordinary life, that bloom of nature that we despair of ever finding, but whose *savoir faire* he possessed so well that one day, having sold and drunk away the damask cloak, gilded with lilies, which he was to wear in the presence of Charles Quint,* he appeared accompanied by his pupil dressed in a paper cloak painted to look like damask. The unusual splendour of the material worn by Mabuse surprised the Emperor, who, wishing to compliment the old drunkard's protector, discovered the fraud. Frenhofer is a man with a great passion for our art, who sees higher and further than other painters. He has meditated profoundly on colours, on the absolute truth of line; but after so much research he has come to doubt the very object of his research. In his moments of despair he claims that drawing does not exist and that with line one can render only geometrical figures; which is stretching the truth, for with line and with black, which is not a colour, one can create a figure; which proves that our art, like nature, is composed of an infinite number of elements: drawing provides a skeleton, colour gives life, but life without its skeleton is even more incomplete than a skeleton without life. Finally, there is something truer than all that, which is that practice and observation are everything for a painter, and if argument and poetry ever quarrel with brushes, we end up as confused as this fellow, who paints to perfection but is perfectly mad. This sublime painter was unfortunate enough to be born rich, allowing him to go astray—don't imitate him! Work! Painters should never have deep thoughts without a brush in their hand.'

'We'll solve the mystery,' cried Poussin, paying no more attention to Porbus, casting care to the winds.

Porbus smiled at the enthusiasm of the young stranger, and left him with an invitation to return to see him.

Nicolas Poussin walked slowly back to the Rue de la Harpe and went past, without noticing, the modest hostelry where he was lodging. Turning back with anxious haste to climb his dingy staircase, he reached his attic room, situated under a half-timbered roof, the simple, light structure common to the houses of old Paris. By the single gloomy window of the room he saw a young woman who, when she heard the door open, jumped up with the sudden movement of one in love; she had recognized her painter by the way he turned the latch.

'What is the matter?' she asked.

'It's just that', he exclaimed, choking with pleasure, 'I feel I am a painter! I had my doubts until now, but this morning I believed in myself? I can be a great man! Look, Gillette, we shall be rich and happy! There is gold in these brushes.'

But suddenly he fell silent. His grave and vigorous face lost its expression of joy when he compared the immensity of his hope to the mediocrity of his resources. The walls were covered with simple crayon sketches on sheets of paper. He did not even have four bare canvases. Paint was expensive in those days, and the poor gentleman found his palette almost empty. In the depths of this poverty, he possessed incredible richness of heart and a superabundance of hungry genius. Brought to Paris by a gentleman of his acquaintance, or perhaps by his own talent, he had suddenly found a mistress, one of those noble souls drawn to suffer at the side of a great man, espousing his miseries and tolerating his moods; as strong in adversity and in love as others are intrepid in showing their finery and flaunting their insensitivity. The smile that played on Gillette's lips lit up the attic and challenged the brilliance of the sky. The sun did not always shine, whereas she was always there, caught up in her passion, following her happiness and her suffering, consoling the genius who was brimming with love before he came to grips with his art.

'Listen, Gillette, come here.'

She sprang obediently and joyfully into the painter's lap. She was elegance and beauty personified, as pretty as springtime, endowed with every feminine charm and animated by spiritual passion.

'Oh, heavens,' he exclaimed, 'I shall never dare tell her…'

'A secret?' she said. 'I have to know.'

Poussin remained thoughtful.

'Tell me.'

'Gillette, my poor beloved sweetheart!'

'Oh! Do you want me to do something for you?'

'Yes.'

'If you want me to pose for you again like the other day,' she continued with a slightly sulky air, I shall never agree, for when that happens your eyes don't meet mine. You are not thinking of me, although you are looking at me.'

'Would you prefer to see me use another model?'

'Perhaps, if she were ugly enough.'

'Well then,' continued Poussin on a serious note, 'to make me a great painter, for my future glory, what if you were to pose for someone else?'

'You are testing me. You know that I wouldn't do it.'

Poussin let his head sink onto his chest, like a man giving way to a joy or pain too strong to bear.

'Listen, Nick,' she said, pulling at the sleeve of Poussin's worn doublet, 'I've told you that I would give my life for you; but I've never promised that I would give up my love, not as long as I live.'

'Give up?' exclaimed Poussin.

'If I revealed myself like that to someone else, you wouldn't love me any more. And I too would find myself unworthy of you. Acting out your fantasy, isn't that natural and simple? In spite of myself, I can't help feeling happy, and proud to obey your dearest wish. But to do that for someone else? No, what are you thinking of!'

'Forgive me, my dear Gillette,' said the painter, throwing himself at her feet. 'I'd rather be loved than famous. For me you are more beautiful than wealth and honours. Go on, throw away my brushes, burn those sketches. I was wrong. My vocation is to love you. I am not a painter, I am a lover. May art and all its secrets perish!'

Delighted, entranced, she wondered at him. She reigned supreme, and felt instinctively that the arts were forgotten in her favour and thrown at her feet like an offering of incense.

'Yet he's just an old man', continued Poussin. 'He would see nothing in you but the woman. You are so perfect!'

'We have to love one another!' she cried, ready to sacrifice her amorous scruples in favour of a lover who had sacrificed so much for her. 'But', she continued, 'I should be lost. Ah, to be lost for your sake. What a beautiful fate! But you will forget me. Oh, what dreadful thoughts you have had!'

'I have had them, and I do love you,' he said, almost contrite, 'but I'm still loathsome, all the same.'

'Shall we consult Father Hardouin?' she asked.

'Oh no, let it be a secret between us.'

'All right, I shall go; but do not come with me,' she said. 'Stay outside the door with your dagger; if I cry out, come in and kill the painter.'

Thinking of nothing but his art, Poussin clasped Gillette in his arms.

'He no longer loves me!' thought Gillette when she was alone. She already regretted her decision. But very soon she fell prey to a terror more cruel than her regret, and she struggled to banish a terrible thought which rose in her heart. She felt that she already loved the painter less, suspecting him less worthy of admiration than before.

II
CATHERINE LESCAULT

THREE months after the meeting between Poussin and Porbus the latter went to visit Maître Frenhofer. At that time the old man was prey to one of those profound and spontaneous states of despondency whose cause, if we are to believe the calculations of medical men, lies in poor digestion, or hot or windy weather, or some thickening of the spleen;* and, according to spiritualist opinion, in the imperfection of our moral nature. The poor man was quite simply worn out from trying to finish his mysterious painting. He was slumped wearily in a huge carved-oak armchair covered in black leather; and, without relinquishing his melancholy expression, he threw Porbus a look of one resigned to his ennui.

'Well, Master,' Porbus asked, 'was the ultramarine that you went to Bruges to buy not to your liking, have you had trouble grinding your new white, is your oil dirty or are your brushes stiff?'

'Alas!' cried the old man, 'I thought for a moment that my work was done; but I am now sure that I have got some details wrong, and I shall not rest until I have cleared up my doubts. I have made up my mind to travel to Turkey, Greece, and Asia to find a model and compare my painting to various natural examples. Perhaps up there I have captured nature herself,' he continued, allowing himself a smile of contentment. 'Sometimes I'm almost afraid that a puff of air might awaken this woman and make her disappear.'

Then he suddenly got up, as if to leave.

'Hold on!' Porbus replied, 'I'm just in time to spare you the expense and fatigue of the journey.'

'How so?' asked Frenhofer in astonishment.

'The young Poussin is loved by a woman whose incomparable beauty is marred by no imperfection. But, my dear Master, if he consents to lend her to you, at least you will allow us to see your painting.'

The old man stood still in a state of absolute stupor.

'What!' he cried at last, in pain. 'Display my creature, my wife? Tear back the veil behind which I have chastely protected my happiness? But that would be a ghastly act of prostitution! I have lived with this woman for ten years, she is mine, and mine alone, she loves me. Does she not smile at me with every brushstroke I give her? She has a soul, the soul with which I have endowed her. She would blush if eyes other than mine lighted on her. Show her off! But what husband or lover would be so vile as to lead his wife into dishonour? When you paint for the Court, you don't invest your whole soul, you sell the courtiers only coloured puppets! My painting is not a painting, it's a feeling, a passion! She was born in my studio, and here she must remain a virgin, and may leave only when clothed. Poetry and women reveal themselves naked only to their lovers. May we possess Raphael's model, Ariosto's Angelica,* Dante's Beatrice?* No! We see them only as forms. Well, then, the work which I have locked away up there is an exception to our art. It is not a piece of canvas, it is a woman! A woman with whom I weep, I laugh, I converse and think. Would you want me to simply cast aside ten years of happiness as we throw off an overcoat? To cease at a stroke to be father, lover, and god? This woman is not a creature, she is a creation. Let your young man come, I shall give him my treasures, I'll give him paintings by Correggio, by Michelangelo,* by Titian, I shall kiss his footprints on my dusty floor: but let him be my rival? Shame on me! Oh, no! I am even more of a lover than a painter. Yes, I shall have the strength to burn my Belle Noiseuse* with my dying breath; but let her submit to the gaze of another man, of a young man, of a painter? No, no! I would kill on the morrow any man who defiled her with his gaze! I would kill you on the spot, you, my friend, if you did not fall on your knees before her! Now you want me to submit my idol to the cold eyes and clumsy criticism of fools! Ah! love is a mystery, it lives only in the depths of the heart, and all is lost when a man says, even to his friend: "Look, here is the woman I love!"'

The old man seemed to have grown young again: his eyes sparkled with life; his pale cheeks were touched with bright red, and his hands were trembling. Porbus, astonished by the passionate violence of these words, did not know how to reply to such new and profound sentiments. Was Frenhofer rational or insane? Had he fallen victim to an artist's fantasy, or were the ideas which he had expressed the fruit of that unspeakable fanaticism produced by the long gestation of a great work? Could one ever hope to come to terms with this strange passion?

Tortured by all these thoughts, Porbus asked the old man: 'But isn't it woman for woman? Would not Poussin deliver his mistress up for your eyes?'

'What mistress?' replied Frenhofer. 'She will betray him sooner or later. Mine will always be faithful!'

'Very well,' Porbus rejoined, 'let us speak of it no more. But before you find a woman as perfect and beautiful as the one I have mentioned, even in Asia, you may well die without finishing your painting.'

'Oh! It is finished,' said Frenhofer. 'Anyone who viewed it would notice a woman reclining on a velvet couch, behind a curtain. Beside her a golden tripod exhales incense. You would be tempted to pull the cord retaining the curtains,* and you would imagine the breast of Catherine Lescault, a beautiful courtesan known as La Belle Noiseuse,* rise and fall with her breathing. And yet, I would like to be certain...'

'Well, then, go to Asia,' replied Porbus, noticing a kind of hesitation in Frenhofer's eyes.

And Porbus took a few steps towards the door.

At that moment Gillette and Nicolas Poussin had arrived at Frenhofer's dwelling. Just as the girl was about to enter, she left the painter's arm and withdrew, as if seized by some sudden foreboding.

'But what am I doing here?' she asked her lover, in a low voice, and looking at him with a fixed stare.

'Gillette, I have left you mistress of your fate and intend to obey you in all things. You are my conscience and my pride and joy. Come back home, and I shall be happier, perhaps, than if you...'

'Am I mistress of myself when you speak to me in those terms? Oh, no, I am just a child! Come on,' she added, appearing to make a violent effort, 'if our love perishes and I allow regret to take hold of my heart, will your fame not be the price of my subservience?

Let us go in, I might still have a life, if only as a memory on your palette.'

As they opened the door the two lovers encountered Porbus who, surprised by the beauty of Gillette, whose eyes were still brimming with tears, took hold of her as she trembled and led her before the old man:

'Look, is she not worth all the masterpieces in the world?'

Frenhofer shuddered. Gillette was there, in the naive and simple attitude of a frightened young Georgian woman, ravished by brigands and offered to some slave-dealer. A modest blush coloured her face, she lowered her eyes, her hands hung by her sides, her strength seemed to abandon her, and her tears bore witness to the outrage done to her modesty. At that moment Poussin, in despair at having taken this treasure out of his attic, cursed himself. He became more lover than artist, and a thousand scruples tortured his heart when he saw the old man's rejuvenated eyes as, from the habit of the painter, he undressed the girl, so to speak, guessed at the secrets of her most intimate contours. Poussin then reverted to the fierce jealousy of true love.

'Gillette, come away!' he cried.

Hearing his cry, in such tones, his mistress joyfully raised her eyes to him, saw him, and ran to his arms.

'Ah! You do love me!' she answered, breaking into tears.

Having had the energy to suppress her suffering, she lacked the strength to hide her happiness.

'Oh! Leave her with me for a moment,' said the old painter, 'and you shall compare her to my Catherine. Yes, I consent.'

There was still love in Frenhofer's plea. He seemed to be flirting with his imitation woman, and enjoying in advance the idea that his virgin's beauty would triumph over that of the real girl.

'Don't let him go back on his word,' cried Porbus, clapping Poussin on the shoulder. 'The fruits of love pass quickly, those of art are immortal.'

'For him,' replied Gillette, watching Poussin and Porbus closely, 'am I then no more than a woman?' She raised her head proudly; but when, having flashed a glance at Frenhofer, she saw her lover busy re-examining the portrait which he had previously taken for a Giorgione, she said: 'Ah! Let's go upstairs! He has never looked at me like that.'

'Old man,' Poussin went on, roused from his thoughts by Gillette's voice, 'you see this sword—I shall plunge it into your heart at the first complaint uttered by this girl, I shall set fire to your house, and no one will come out alive. Do you understand?'

Nicolas Poussin looked grim, and his words sounded terrible. This attitude and, above all, the gestures of the young painter consoled Gillette, who almost forgave him for sacrificing her to his future fame. Porbus and Poussin remained at the door of the studio, looking at each other in silence. If at first the painter of the Egyptian Mary spontaneously exclaimed: 'Ah! she's getting undressed, he's asking her to step into the light! He's comparing her!', soon Porbus fell silent on seeing that Poussin's face was profoundly sad; and, although such an old painter no longer observed these petty scruples in the presence of art, he still respected their innocence and beauty. The young man had his hand on the pommel of his dagger and his ear almost glued to the door. The two men standing in the shadows thus resembled two conspirators awaiting the hour to strike down a tyrant.

'Come in, come in,' said the old man, radiant with happiness. 'My work is perfect, and now I may show her with pride. No painter, no brushes, no colours or canvas or light will ever rival Catherine Lescault, the beautiful courtesan.'* Burning with curiosity, Porbus and Poussin rushed into the middle of a vast studio covered in dust, where everything was in disorder and where they saw paintings hanging on the walls here and there. They stopped first in front of a life-size, half-naked figure of a woman, which fired their admiration.

'Oh! Take no notice of that,' said Frenhofer, 'that's a canvas I daubed to study a pose, the painting is worthless. These are my mistakes,' he continued, showing them delightful compositions hanging on the walls around them.

At these words, Porbus and Poussin, stupefied by this contempt for such great works, looked for the promised portrait, without being able to detect it.

'Well! Here it is!' the old man announced, his hair tangled, his face flushed, and his eyes on fire with supernatural excitement, breathless like a young man intoxicated with love. 'Ah! Ah! You did not expect such perfection. You are confronted with a woman when you were looking for a painting. There is so much depth in this canvas, its air is so real that you can no longer distinguish it from the air that surrounds it. Where is art? Lost, vanished! These are the very contours of a young woman. Have I not captured her colour, and the very life of the line which seems to enclose the body? Is it not the same phenomenon which makes objects in the air appear to us like fish in water? Admire the way the contours stand out from the background. Don't you feel that you could run your hand down her back? Thus, for seven years I studied the effects of the interplay between daylight and objects. And is not that hair flooded with light?... But she did just breathe, surely!... Look at that breast! Ah! Who would not fall down and worship her! Her flesh is pulsing with life. She is about to stand up, just wait.'

'Do you see anything?' Poussin asked Porbus.

'No. And you?'

'Nothing.'

The two painters left the old man to his ecstasy, and tried to see whether the light falling full on the canvas that he showed them might not be interfering with all of its effects. They then examined the painting, placing themselves to the right, to the left, and in front, bending down and standing up in turn.

'Yes, yes, it is a canvas,' said Frenhofer, misunderstanding the aim of their careful scrutiny. 'Look, here are the frame, the easel, and even my paints and brushes.'

And he picked up a brush, which he held out with a naive gesture.

'The old trooper is playing games with us,' said Poussin, turning round to confront his so-called painting. 'All I can see in it is a confused mass of colour inside a multitude of weird lines, making a wall of paint.'

'We must be mistaken, look!...' continued Porbus.

Drawing closer, they noticed, in one corner of the canvas, part of a naked foot emerging from a chaos of colours and indistinct tones and hues, a sort of formless fog; but a delicious foot, a living foot! They stood petrified with admiration, faced with this fragment which had escaped the extraordinary process of slow but inexorable destruction. The foot emerged, like the torso of some Venus in Parian marble, from amid the rubble of a burnt-out city.

'There is a woman underneath all that!' cried Porbus, showing Poussin the layers of colour that the old painter had successively superimposed, believing that he was perfecting his painting.

The two painters turned spontaneously to face Frenhofer, as they began, confusedly, to understand the ecstasy that possessed him.

'He speaks in good faith!' said Porbus.

'Yes, my friend,' replied the old man, coming to his senses, 'you need faith, faith in art, and you need to live a long time with your work to accomplish such a creation. Some of these shadows cost me painful labour. Look, there on her cheek, below the eyes, there is a pale shadow which, if observed in nature, would seem to you almost untranslatable. Well, then! Don't you think that it cost me untold efforts to reproduce it? But also, my dear Porbus, look carefully at my work, and you will better understand what I told you about ways of treating modelling and contour. Look at the light on the breast, and see how, with a series of heavy impasto strokes and highlights, I have succeeded in capturing the real light and combining it with the shining whiteness of the lighter tones; and how, in contrast, by toning down the raised edges and the texture of the paint, I have managed to remove any notion of artificial drawing and technique, by caressing the contours of my figure, which I have left drowned in half-tones, endowing her with the fully rounded appearance of nature. Come closer, you will see the craftsmanship better. Go back, and it disappears. You understand? It is, I believe, quite remarkable just there.'

And with the tip of his brush he pointed out a thick patch of clear, bright colour. Porbus clapped the old man on the shoulder and turned to Poussin: 'You know that we see him as a truly great painter, don't you?'

'He's an even greater poet than he is a painter,' replied Poussin gravely.

'Here endeth', said Porbus, touching the canvas, 'our art on this Earth.'

'And thence', said Poussin, 'it ascendeth unto Heaven.'

'How filled with bliss is this piece of canvas!' exclaimed Porbus.

The old man, lost in his thoughts, was not listening to them. He was smiling at his imaginary woman.

'But sooner or later he'll see that there is nothing on his canvas!' cried Poussin.

'Nothing on my canvas?' said Frenhofer, looking from painter to painter and at his so-called painting.

'What have you done?' said Porbus to Poussin.

The old man grasped the young man's arm forcefully and said: 'You see nothing, do you, you beggarly, doltish, lily-livered whoreson!* Why did you come up here? My good Porbus,' he continued, turning to the other painter, 'might you too be playing games with me? Answer me! I am your friend, tell me, could it be that I have spoiled my painting?'

Porbus hesitated, not daring to speak; but the anxiety which blanched the features of the old man was so cruel that he pointed at the canvas, saying:

'Look!'

Frenhofer contemplated his painting for a moment, and staggered back. 'Nothing, nothing! After ten years of work!'

He sat down and wept.

'So I am a fool, a madman! So I have neither talent nor skill, I am no better than a man of means, whose idea of progress has amounted only to walking on the spot. So I have created nothing!' Gazing at his painting through his tears, he suddenly stood up proudly, and looked fiercely at the two painters.

'By the blood, the body, and the head of Christ, you are jealous and you want me to think that she has been spoiled so that you can steal her from me! But I can see her!' he cried. 'She is marvellously beautiful'.

At that moment Poussin heard Gillette, forgotten, weeping in a corner of the room.

'What is the matter, my angel?' asked the painter, suddenly in love again.

'Kill me!' she replied. 'I would be ashamed to love you still, for I despise you. I admire you, and you disgust me. I love you, but I believe that I already hate you.' While Poussin was listening to Gillette, Frenhofer covered his Catherine with a green baize cloth, with the studied calm of a jeweller locking his drawers, believing himself to be in the company of professional thieves. He cast a profoundly sullen look, full of contempt and suspicion, at the two painters, and with silent but urgent haste showed them to the door of his studio. As they left he said: 'Farewell, my young friends.'

This farewell chilled the two painters. The next day Porbus returned anxiously to visit Frenhofer, and learned that he had died during the night, having burnt his paintings.

*Paris, February 1832**

THE GIRL WITH THE GOLDEN EYES

*To Eugène Delacroix, painter**

ONE of life's most terrifying spectacles is surely the general appearance of the population of Paris, a people ghastly to behold, gaunt, jaundiced, and leathery. Is Paris not a vast prairie constantly swept by turbulent storms of self-interest, harvesting its crop of men, whom death reaps here more frequently than elsewhere, but who rise again in ever more serried ranks? Their twisted, contorted faces exude from every pore the thoughts, desires, and poisons which bloat their minds; indeed, these are not faces but masks, masks of weakness or strength, masks of misery, joy, or hypocrisy, each one drained and marked with the indelible signs of breathless greed. What do they want? Gold, or pleasure?

A few remarks on the Parisian soul may explain the causes of its cadaverous physiognomy, which knows only two ages, either youth or dotage: youth, pale and haggard, dotage painted to look young. When foreigners, who have no reason to think more deeply on the matter, see these living dead, they immediately recoil in disgust from this capital city, this vast pleasure factory, from which they too will soon be unable to escape, and, having taken the decision to stay, will willingly become deformed in their turn. A few words will suffice to explain in physiological terms the almost hellishly tinted faces of the Parisian, for it is not merely in jest that Paris has been called Hell. The term must be taken literally. Here smoke billows, fires roar, everything flashes, boils, burns, and evaporates, everything is extinguished and rekindled, everything sparkles, glitters, and is itself consumed. In no other country has life ever been more ardent, more scorching. In its constant fission and fusion, after each completed stage this social organism seems to be saying: 'On to the next!' as does Nature herself. Like Nature, this social creature is concerned with tiny insects and flowers that bloom for a day, with fireflies and will-o'-the-wisps, and yet it also belches smoke and spews flame from its everlasting crater. Perhaps before we analyse what it is that creates a physiognomy specific to each of the tribes which constitute this intelligent and energetic nation, we should indicate the underlying reasons for the more or less discoloured, haggard, bruised, and leathery appearance of each individual.

By dint of being interested in everything, the Parisian ends up being interested in nothing. Since his face, with the wear and tear of constant contact, expresses no dominant feeling, it becomes as grey as the plaster on the houses which are covered in all kinds of dust and smoke. Indifferent one day to what will thrill him the next, the Parisian lives like a child, no matter what his age. He grumbles about everything, gets over everything, he laughs at everything, forgets everything, he wants everything, tries a taste of everything; he takes everything with passion and leaves it without a care, whether his kings, his conquests, his fame, or his idols, be they cast in bronze or blown in glass: he takes them up or discards them as easily as his stockings, his hat, or his fortune. In Paris no feeling resists the flood of material things, and their tide provokes a struggle which weakens every passion: love is but desire, hatred a whim, there is no family but the thousand-franc note, there is no friend but the pawnshop. This universal carelessness has its consequences, and in the salons as in the streets, nobody is superfluous, nobody is absolutely necessary or absolutely detrimental, whether they be fools and rogues or men of wit and honest citizens. All is tolerated, the government and the guillotine, religion and cholera. There is always a place for you in this world, but no one will notice your absence. What holds sway over this country without morals, beliefs, or feelings? What is the source and what the goal of all feelings, beliefs, and morals? Gold and pleasure. Take these two words as if they were a lantern leading us through this great prison of plaster, through this hive of black runnels, and let us follow the twists and turns of the one driving thought which sets the whole thing in motion, making it heave and strain. Let us see. Let us first explore the world of those who have nothing.

The workman, or proletarian, is the man who uses his feet, his hands, his tongue, his back, his right arm, and all of his fingers in order to survive: he of all people should husband his vital resources, but instead constantly drains his energy; he shackles his wife to one machine and exploits his child by chaining him to another. The factory manager is the middleman, whose activity sets the workmen in motion: dirtying their hands to mould and gild porcelain, sew suits and dresses, hammer iron, plane wood, plait steel cables, spin hemp and thread, burnish bronze, engrave crystal, copy flowers, embroider wool, train horses, braid harnesses and officers' epaulettes, beat copper, paint carriages, bend old elm staves, steam-dye cotton, dry out tulle, cut diamonds, polish metal, turn marble into leaves, lick stones into shape, illustrate thought and colour, bleach and blacken everything. So, into this world of sweat and willpower, of study and patience, this middleman arises, promising extravagant wages, either in the name of the passing whims of the city or in the name of that monster called Speculation. So these four-handed creatures stay awake all night, suffer, work, swear, go without meals, march to and fro night and day; all of them driven beyond their limits in the search for the gold which enthralls them. Then on Mondays,* lords for a day, with no care for the future, avid for pleasure, flexing their muscles, as a painter lavishes paint on canvas, so they splash money about in the bars which form a muddy girdle round the city, the haunt of the most shameless of Venuses, constantly fastened and loosened, where the momentary wealth of this populace, as frenzied in pleasure as it is peaceful at work, is lost as surely as the gambler's stake. For five days in the week there is no rest for these active Parisians. The labours they undertake make them twisted and pale, too fat or too thin, or cause them to burst into a thousand sparks of creative energy. After this their pleasure and relaxation leave a debilitating trail of debauchery, with sunburnt skin, black eyes, wan-faced hangovers or jaundiced indigestion, lasting only two days, but robbing them of the bread for the morrow and the soup for the week, dresses for their wives and clean clothes for their ragged infants.

These men, doubtless born to be beautiful, for all creatures have their own kind of relative beauty, are from infancy press-ganged by superior forces, and made to live under the rule of hammer, chisel, and loom, and have rapidly become vulcanized. Is Vulcan,* with his ugliness and strength, not the emblem of this ugly and strong nation, with its sublime mechanical intelligence: patient when need be, terrible for one day per century, inflammable as gunpowder, and preparing for revolutionary conflagration by drinking brandy, in the end quick-witted enough to ignite at the sound of a specious phrase as long as it means one thing: gold and pleasure! Including all those who hold out their hands for alms, for legitimate salaries, or for the five francs paid in Paris for all forms of prostitution, that is to say, for all money well- or ill-gotten, this populace counts three-hundred thousand individuals. Without the bars, would the government not be overthrown every Tuesday? Luckily, on Tuesdays the people are dull-witted, and, nursing their hangovers, return to work and bread and water, penniless and stimulated by the need for material production, which becomes for them a matter of habit. Nonetheless, this people has its virtuous specimens, its whole men, its unknown Napoleons,* who embody the strengths of their race in its highest degree, and sum up its social significance, in a life which combines thought and action, less to spread joy than to control the effects of suffering.

Chance has created the industrious worker, chance has granted him ideas, he has thoughts for the future, he meets a woman, becomes a father, and after some years of severe privation he rents some premises and sets up a small haberdashery. If neither illness nor vice stop him in his tracks, if he has prospered, here is a sketch of his daily life.

First of all, let us salute this king of Parisian activity, who has subjugated time and space. Yes, let us salute this creature made of saltpetre and gas, who peoples France with children during his nights of toil, and diversifies his roles by day for the service, glory, and pleasure of his fellow citizens. This man solves the problem of pleasing at once an amiable wife, their household, the *Constitutionnel*,* his office, the National Guard,* the Opéra, and God; but he does this by converting the *Constitutionnel*, the office, the Opéra, the National Guard, and the wife into hard cash. In other words, let us salute an accomplished jack-of-all-trades.

Rising each morning at five, he flies like a bird from his home to the Rue Montmartre. Come hell or high water, rain or snow, he is at the *Constitutionnel*'s office, the delivery of whose newspapers he has commandeered. He greedily grasps this political manna, takes it away, and distributes it. At nine o'clock he is back at hearth and home, cracking a joke with his wife, stealing a smacking kiss, sipping a cup of coffee, or scolding his children. At a quarter to ten he turns up at the town hall. There, on the edge of his stool like a parrot on its perch, warmed by the city of Paris, he spends until four o'clock without the trace of a tear or a hint of a smile, recording all the births and deaths of a whole borough. The happiness and sorrows of the entire neighbourhood pass through the nib of his pen, just as the thoughts of *Le Constitutionnel* were previously borne on his shoulders. Nothing gets him down! He keeps looking straight ahead, finds his patriotism pre-packaged in the paper, contradicts nobody, condemns or applauds along with everyone else, and flits about like a swallow. He lives close enough to his parish church to be able to leave his duties to a substitute in the case of an important ceremony, and sing a requiem from a stall in the church, where, on Sundays and holy days, he is its chief ornament, its most imposing voice, as he energetically wraps his wide mouth round a sonorous and joyful Amen. He is the cantor.

Free from his official duties after four o'clock, he turns up at the most famous shop in the city to spread joy and gaiety. His wife is happy, he has no time to be jealous, he is a man of action rather than of feeling. So, as soon as he arrives, he teases the sales-girls, whose bright eyes attract plenty of gallant customers; he wallows amid the jewellery, the shawls, and the muslin made by these skilful working-girls; or, even more often, before dinner, he serves a customer, copies up a page of his logbook, or delivers some overdue bill to the bailiffs. Every other day, at six o'clock, he is faithfully installed as a regular baritone in the chorus of the Opéra, ready to become a soldier, an Arab, a prisoner, a savage, a peasant, a ghost, the rear end of a camel, a lion, a demon, a genie of the lamp, a slave, a black or white eunuch, always practised at expressing joy or suffering, pity or astonishment, with endless, heart-rending cries, or to fall silent, to hunt, to fight for Rome or Egypt, but always, in his heart of hearts, a haberdasher. At midnight we rediscover him as the good husband, man, and kind father, slipping between the conjugal sheets with his imagination still excited by the elusive forms of operatic nymphs, and thus diverting the depravities of the world and the seductive glimpses of Taglioni's* thighs towards the harmonies of conjugal love. At last, if he falls asleep, he sleeps briefly, and despatches his sleep as he despatches his life.

Is this man not pure motion, space personified, is he not a Proteus* of civilization, the sum of all things: history, literature, politics, government, religion, and the arts of war? Is he not a living encyclopedia, a grotesque atlas, ceaselessly in motion like Paris, which never sleeps? He is all legs. No physiognomy could remain pure among such labours. Perhaps the workman who dies of old age at thirty, his stomach lined with increasing doses of spirits, will be found by some well-heeled philosophers to be happier than the haberdasher. The one dies all at once, the other by degrees. Through his eight occupations, his shoulders, his throat, his hands, his wife, and his business, our haberdasher—like a landowner with so many farms—provides himself with a few thousand francs and a number of children, and earns the most hard-won happiness that ever heart of man invented. This wealth and these children, who are the goal of all his efforts, are offered up to a superior world, where he takes his cash and his daughter, or his son educated in a private school, and who, better educated than his father, casts his ambitious eyes higher. Often the youngest son of a small shopkeeper wants to become someone in the civil service.

This ambition turns our thoughts to the second of the Parisian spheres. Go up a floor and look at the next level, or come down from the attic and stay on the fourth floor; that is, enter the world of those who have something: there, the result is the same. The wholesalers, shop-assistants, and lads that they employ, the small-time bankers with their staunch probity, the financial swindlers, the condemned souls, the chief and junior clerks, the assistant bailiffs, barristers and solicitors, in short, the active, thinking, speculating members of the petty bourgeoisie who manipulate the interests of Paris and mete out its daily bread, pocket the rent and stock up the goods produced by the proletariat, devour fruit from the south, fish from the sea, and wine from every sun-kissed hillside; who stretch their hands out to the East, pick up shawls spurned by the Turks and the Russians; even prospect as far as India, lie in wait for sales, lust after profit, discount bills, roll over and rake in the shares, wrap up and deliver the whole of Paris piece by piece, second-guess children's dreams, spy on the whims and vices of adults, bleed the sick; in short, without downing spirits like the workman, or wallowing in the low life at the city limits, each of them exceeds his strength; they stretch their minds and bodies beyond their limits, each at war with the other; exhaust their desires and wear themselves out in the endless race. Their strenuous efforts are governed by the crack of the whip of interest, as the scourge of ambition torments the upper circles of this monstrous city, as the world of the proletariat is under the cruel sway of the material schemes unceasingly required by the despotism of the 'I want' of the aristocrats.

So there, too, to obey this universal master, be it pleasure or gold, time must be devoured and harried, more than twenty-four hours must be extracted from day and night, you need to be angry, self-destructive, and sacrifice three decades of old age in exchange for two years of miserable decline. But the working-man dies in the workhouse, when the very last stages of decrepitude are reached, whereas the petty bourgeois still insists on living on, but as a cretin: you will know his worn, thin old features, with no light in his eyes and no strength in his legs, wandering listlessly along a boulevard, that girdle of his Venus, his beloved city. What was the bourgeois seeking? The sabre of the National Guard, a reliable dish of stew, a decent plot at the Père Lachaise cemetery,* and for his old age, a small, honestly earned pot of gold. For him, his Monday is like Sunday; his leisure is a promenade in a hired carriage, a country picnic, during which wife and children cheerfully ingest the dust or roast in the sun; his ideal wild night out is spent at restaurants whose dinners are renowned but inedible, or some family ball where you suffocate until midnight.

Some fools are surprised by the St Vitus's dance which affects the organisms detected by a miscroscope in a drop of water, but what would that sublimely audacious but misunderstood figure, that giant, Rabelais's Gargantua,* say if he tumbled down from his celestial spheres, if he entertained himself by contemplating the frantic movement of this second circle of Parisian life, of which this is one example? Have you seen those little stalls, cold in summertime and heated only by a small stove in winter, situated under the vast copper dome which covers the corn exchange? Madame arrives early in the morning, she is a sales agent in the market and this trade brings in, so they say, twelve thousand francs a year. Monsieur, when Madame rises, makes his way into a dingy office, where he lends small sums of money to the traders of his neighbourhood a week at a time. At nine o'clock he takes up his position at the passport office, where he is one of the minor officials.

In the evening you can find him at the box-office of the Théâtre-Italien, or any other theatre you may care to mention. Their children are put out to nurse and only come home when they are ready to be placed in a fee-paying or boarding school. Monsieur and Madame live on the third floor, their only servant is their cook, and they hold their dances in a drawing-room measuring twelve feet by eight, lit by carriage lanterns; but they endow their daughter with a hundred and fifty thousand francs, and retire at the age of fifty, when they start to appear in the third circle at the Opéra, or in a carriage at Longchamp,* or in faded finery on sunny days on the boulevards, where all these investments come to fruition. Esteemed in his neighbourhood, favoured by the government, and linked to the upper bourgeoisie, Monsieur at sixty-five is awarded the cross of the Légion d'Honneur,* and his son-in-law's father, the mayor of a borough, invites him to his receptions. Such lifelong labour thus tends to benefit the children of this petty bourgeoisie and inevitably raise them to the ranks of the upper bourgeoisie. So, each circle casts all its spawn into the next higher circle. The son of the rich grocer becomes a solicitor, the son of the timber merchant becomes a magistrate. Not a single cog misses its groove in the wheel, and everything contributes to the upward movement of money.

Which brings us to the third circle of this Hell, which one day will perhaps find its Dante.* In this third circle, which is, so to speak, the belly of Paris, where the interests of the city are decided and where they coagulate into the form of *business*, we find the bitter, splenetic, intestinal motion and agitation of the crowd of doctors, solicitors, barristers, businessmen, bankers, wholesale traders, speculators, and magistrates. There we may find even more causes of physical and moral destruction than anywhere else. Almost all of these people are housed in vile chambers, unhealthy halls, or mean offices; trapped behind bars, they spend their days bowed under the weight of business, rise at dawn to avoid being robbed, whether to win all or avoid losing all, to arrest a man or confiscate his money, to undertake or dissolve a transaction, to take advantage of some fleeting circumstance or to have a man hanged or acquitted. They take it out on their horses, whose legs, like their own, they run to ruin before their time. Time is their tyrant; they waste it, it escapes them, and they can neither expand nor contract it. What soul could remain great, pure, morally generous, and, in short, what person could remain noble in the depraved exercise of a profession which forces them to bear the weight of social misery, to analyse, calculate, and measure it out? Where do such people deposit their hearts, where? I know not, but, should they have one, they do leave it somewhere, before they go each morning to plumb the depths of suffering which afflict the family. For them there are no mysteries; they see the underside of society, they are its confessors, and they despise it. Yet, whatever they do, the more they face corruption the more it disgusts and horrifies them: or alternatively, from lassitude or from secret compromise they espouse it, and finally and inevitably those very people, whom men, laws, and institutions send swooping like vultures onto corpses not yet cold, become numb to all feeling.

At every moment the man of money weighs the living, the man of contracts weighs the dead, the man of law weighs their conscience. Obliged to talk incessantly, they all replace ideas with words, emotions by phrases, and their souls by their vocal chords. They become exhausted and demoralized. Neither the great merchant, nor the judge, nor the barrister preserves his sense of justice: they lose all feeling, they apply rules which individual cases render unjust. Borne along by the sweeping torrents of life, they are no longer husbands, fathers, or lovers; they skate over the surface of life, and live every moment driven by the affairs of the great city. When they get home they are obliged to go to a ball, to the opera, to receptions where they may solicit clients, acquaintances, patrons. They all over-eat grossly, gamble, and stay up all night, until their faces fill out, redden, then sag. Confronted by such a terrible expense of intellectual effort, and such multiple moral contradictions, they plump not for pleasure, which is too bland to provide any contrast, but debauchery, secret and terrifying, for they can summon and dismiss at will anyone and anything, and regulate the morals of society. Their actual stupidity is disguised by their specialist knowledge. They know their profession, but they know nothing beyond it. So, to protect their self-esteem, they call everything into question, criticize left, right, and centre; seem sceptical, but are in fact gullible, fuddling their wits in endless discussions. Nearly all of them find it helpful to adopt social, literary, and political commonplaces to avoid having to form an opinion, just as they shelter their consciences behind the statutes, or the Chamber of Commerce.

Given a head start as remarkable men, they become mediocre and crawl around the foothills of social greatness. Thus, their faces present that gaunt pallor, that false colour, those faded, wrinkled eyes, those sensual, gossipy mouths where the observer recognizes the symptoms of the degeneration of thought as it spins like a top within the circus of a special interest which kills all the creative faculties of the brain: the gift of taking the longer view, of making comparisons, of drawing conclusions. They nearly all shrivel up in the furnace of business. Thus, no man who has let himself be caught up in or ground down by the cogs of these huge machines can achieve greatness. If he is a doctor, either he has practised little medicine, or he is an exception, a Bichat* who dies young. If he is a great merchant with sufficient staying-power, he is almost Jacques Coeur.* Did Robespierre ever practise his profession? Even Danton was a passive man who waited for things to happen. Moreover, has anyone ever envied the figures of Danton and Robespierre,* however magnificent they seem?

Our supremely busy and active men of affairs attract money and hoard it in order to create alliances with aristocratic families. If the ambition of the workman is similar to that of the petty bourgeois, here too the same passions reign. In Paris all passions are reducible to vanity. The model of this class would be either the ambitious bourgeois, who, after a life of relentless anxiety and scheming, slips into the State Council as an ant creeps through a crack; or perhaps some newspaper editor, riddled with intrigues, created peer of the realm by the king, perhaps to take revenge on the nobility; or maybe some solicitor becomes mayor of his borough: all died-in-the-wool businessmen, should they reach their goal, would be *dead on arrival*. In France our habit is to worship the wig. Only Napoleon, Louis XIV,* and the great kings insisted on having young men to execute their plans.

From here we step up into the circle of the artist. There too, however, the faces, stamped with the seal of originality, are nobly ravaged, but ravaged nevertheless, tired and haggard. Exasperated by a desire to produce, overwhelmed by their costly whims, hungry for pleasure, the Parisian artists all want to compensate through excessive labour what they have lost through their laziness, and they seek in vain to reconcile polite society with artistic fame, money with art. When he starts out, the artist is constantly harassed by his creditors, his needs generate debts, and his debts lead to nights of sleepless toil. After work, pleasure. The actor performs until midnight, learns his part in the morning, rehearses over lunch; the sculptor buckles beneath his statue; the journalist is a thinker on the run like a soldier in wartime; the fashionable painter is overwhelmed with commissions, while the unknown painter eats his heart out if he feels he is a man of genius. Competition, rivalry, and slander destroy their talents. Some, desperate, wallow in the troughs of vice, others die young and remain unknown, for having counted too soon on their future. Few of these initially sublime figures retain their charm. At all events, the flamboyant beauty of their features is never appreciated. An artist's face is always extravagant, it always finds itself above or below the conventional line of what imbeciles call ideal beauty. What is the power that destroys them? Passion. All passion in Paris seems to be reduced to these two terms: gold and pleasure.

And now, can you breathe at last? Do you not feel that space and air have become purified? Here toil and travail are no more. The soaring spirals of gold have reached the summits. From basement vents where it begins to trickle forth, and from the back of shops where it is still restricted by gutters, from the belly of the counting-houses and the great laboratories where it consents to be cast into ingots, gold, in the shape of dowries or inheritances passing through the fingers of maidens or the hands of bony old men, streams up towards the aristocracy, who will let it glitter, spread, and flow. But before we leave the four terrains upon which the great property of Paris is based, should we not, having cited the aforementioned moral causes, deduce its physical causes and draw attention to what we might call an underlying plague which constantly eats away at the faces of the doorkeeper, the shopkeeper, and the workman? Should we not point out a deleterious influence whose corruption is equal to that of the Parisian administrators who so complacently allow it to persist! If the air of the houses where most of the bourgeoisie live is infected, if the atmosphere of the streets spews forth cruel stews into the back rooms starved of oxygen, remember that apart from this pestilence, the forty thousand houses of this great city steep their roots in disgusting filth; the powers that be have not tried seriously enough to build walls of concrete strong enough to prevent the most putrid mud from filtering up through the ground, poisoning the wells and continuing to justify the famous and ancient name of 'Lutetia'.* A good half of Paris lies floating in stinking vapours, whether from yards, streets, or underground works.

But let us approach the great, airy, gilded salons, the mansions with private gardens, the rich, idle, happy society of private means. Here people's faces are lined and scarred by vanity. Nothing here is real. Is to seek pleasure not to find ennui? People in high society soon corrupt their own nature. Being concerned only with procuring their pleasure, they prematurely abuse their senses, as the workman abuses cheap spirits. Pleasure is like certain medical substances; to maintain the same effect you have to keep doubling the dose, which leads to death or stupefaction. All the classes beneath the rich crawl to them and envy their tastes, looking to turn them into vices they can exploit for their own gain. How to resist the seductive temptations which underpin our country? Thus, Paris has its *theriakis*,* for whom gambling, gastronomy, or whoring are their opium. Thus, you see early on in such people the development of tastes rather than passions, of romantic fantasies and half-hearted love affairs. Here impotence rules, here ideas cease; like energy, they have been exhausted in the counterfeits of the boudoir, in feminine wiles. There are ignorant youths aged forty, learned scholars aged sixteen. The rich may find in Paris ready-made wit, pre-digested knowledge, and regurgitated opinions which excuse them from the need to have wit, knowledge, or opinions of their own. In these social circles there is little difference between weakness and libertinism. Wasting time makes them greedy for more time. No need to look for affection there, any more than ideas. Their embraces disguise a profound indifference, and their etiquette a systematic contempt. They never love anyone but themselves. Shallow witticisms, much indiscretion and gossip, and universal commonplaces; these form the basis of their language, but these wretched happy few claim that they do not come together in an attempt to reformulate and re-enact La Rochefoucauld's maxims;* as if the eighteenth century had never found a middle way between the superfluous and the totally vacuous. If one or two worthy men strike a note of subtle and refined witticism, it is misunderstood; and, soon tired of giving without receiving, they prefer to stay at home and allow the fools to reign supreme. This hollow life, this continual expectation of pleasure which never materializes, this permanent ennui, this vacuity of spirit, of heart, and of brain, this lassitude of fashionable Parisian routs is reproduced in all their features, and creates cardboard cut-out faces, premature wrinkles, that physiognomy of the rich in which gold flickers, impotence lurks, and from which intelligence has fled.

This view of the moral life of Paris proves that the physical Paris could not be other than what it is. This crowned city is a perpetually pregnant queen, driven by insatiable and furious desires. Paris heads the world, it is a brain bursting with genius and a guide for human civilization, a great man, a constantly creative artist, a politician with second sight who must necessarily harbour the convoluted grey matter and the flaws of the great man, the imaginings of the artist, and the detachment of the politician. Its physiognomy traces the birth of good and evil, of struggle and victory; the moral war waged in 1789* whose trumpets still resound in the four corners of the earth, and also the downfall of 1814.* This city can therefore never be more moral, more inviting, nor cleaner than is the boiler-house of those magnificent fire-breathing monsters which you see slicing through the waves! Is Paris not a sublime vessel laden with intelligence? Yes, her coat of arms is like an oracle which destiny sometimes deigns to grant. The *City of Paris** has its own mast of solid bronze, carved with victories, and Napoleon for lookout.* This vessel is, of course, subject to pitch and toss; but it ploughs its furrow across the globe, spouts fire from its hundred mouths, tills the seas of science, sails with full canvas, crying from the top of its crow's nests through the voices of its scientists and artists: 'Onward march! Follow me!' She carries a vast crew which loves to fly fresh flags. There are cabin boys and lads laughing in the rigging, a heavy ballast of the bourgeoisie; tar-stained workmen and sailors; reclining in its cabins are the idle passengers; elegant midshipmen lean over the bulwarks, smoking their cigars; then, on the upper deck, there are its soldiers, whether pioneers or adventurers, ready to disembark on any unknown shore, hoping to spread enlightenment at the same time as they seek the fame that would fulfil their happiness or the love that can be bought and sold for gold.

Thus the extraordinary activity of the proletariat, the corrupt interests which torment the two conflicting classes of the bourgeoisie, thus the cruelty of artistic thought, and the excesses of pleasure incessantly sought by the great, explain the general ugliness of the Parisian physiognomy. Only in the Orient does the human race present an imposing bust; but this is the effect of the unwavering calm displayed by their profound philosophers with long pipes, stout bodies, and short legs, who despise and revile movement; while in Paris the Small, the Middling, and the Great run, jump, and caper, whipped on by that pitiless goddess, Need: need for money, for glory, for amusement. Thus the occasional serene, relaxed, graceful, and genuinely youthful face is the most extraordinary exception. It is rarely encountered. If you do see one, it most assuredly belongs to a young and zealous cleric, or some mild, forty-year-old vicar with a triple chin; a young lady of impeccable morals, as we may find in certain bourgeois families; a twenty-year-old mother, still imbued with illusions and suckling her firstborn, or a young man freshly arrived from the provinces and lodged with a pious dowager who keeps him penniless. Such a face might belong to a shop-assistant, who goes to bed at midnight, tired out from folding and unfolding rolls of calico, who has to rise at seven in the morning to set out his shelf; or often to a man of science or poetry, living monastically and happily in the embrace of a beautiful idea, staying sober, patient, and chaste; or some well-satisfied fool, bursting with health and always practising his smiles in the mirror, or the happy, passive species of *flâneurs*,* the only truly happy inhabitants of Paris, who taste its fleeting pleasures from moment to moment.

Nonetheless, Paris does contain its quota of privileged beings who benefit from this extraordinary activity of manufacture, interest, commerce, arts, and gold. These are its women. Although they have a thousand secret concerns, which in their case more than others tend to ruin their appearance, you can find in the world of women some small colonies living happily in oriental fashion, who preserve their beauty; but these women rarely venture out on foot in the streets, but lie hidden, like those rare plants which open their petals only at certain times, and are a genuinely exotic rarity.

And yet Paris is also essentially a land of contrasts. If true sentiment is rare, you may also encounter, there as elsewhere, noble friendship and unstinting devotion. On this battlefield of interest and passion, as in all those societies on the march, societies which we might liken to armies, where egoism triumphs and where it is up to every man to defend himself, it seems that a man prefers his feelings to be full-blown before he reveals them, and that they assume their most sublime expression only in contrast with others. So it is with faces. In Paris on occasion, in the upper aristocracy, we find at random here and there the handsome face of a young man, nurtured by an exceptional type of education and manners. The youthful beauty of English blood is allied with the strength of Mediterranean features, French wit, and a purity of form. Their sparkling eyes, the delicious redness of their lips, the lustrous jet of their flowing locks, their fair complexion and distinguished profile make them fine human specimens, flowering magnificently against the mass of other faded, ageing, twisted, grimacing features. Women will immediately admire such young men with the same avid pleasure that men take in viewing a pretty, decent, graceful young girl, endowed with all the maidenly perfection which illustrates our virginal ideal of the perfect woman.

If this rapid overview of the Parisian masses has helped us to realize how rare are such Raphaelesque figures* and what passionate admiration they must immediately inspire, the principal interest of our story will be justified. *Quod erat demonstrandum*, 'which was to be demonstrated', if we may be permitted to apply scholastic formulae to the science of human behaviour.

Now, on one of those fine spring mornings when the leaves have opened but are not yet green; when the sun sets light to the roofs, and the sky is blue; when the populace of Paris emerges from its cells and hums down the boulevards, slithering like a rainbow-hued serpent along the Rue de la Paix towards the Tuileries,* announcing the first rites of spring as they echo those of the countryside; on one of those joyful mornings, then, a young man, as handsome as that springtime morning, tasteful in dress and graceful in manner, and (we are obliged to admit) a child of love, the natural son of Lord Dudley and the famous Marquise de Vordac, was strolling down the Grande Avenue of the Tuileries. This Adonis, named Henri de Marsay, had been born in France, where Lord Dudley had come to marry off the young lady, who was already Henri's mother, to an aged gentleman called Monsieur de Marsay. This jaded and almost utterly faded butterfly recognized the child as his own, in return for a lifetime's interest on an income of a hundred thousand francs, due to revert eventually to his putative son; a folly which did not cost Lord Dudley a fortune: French government stock being worth at the time only seventeen francs, fifty centimes. The old gentleman died without having known his wife. Later Madame de Marsay married the Duc de Vordac; but, before becoming a marquise, she gave little thought to her son and to Lord Dudley. In the first place, the war between France and England* had separated the two lovers, and fidelity as such was rarely, and is hardly ever likely to be, fashionable in Paris. Then the success of this elegant, pretty, and universally adored Parisienne stifled her maternal instincts. Lord Dudley was no more concerned for his offspring than was the mother. The spontaneous infidelity of the girl he had ardently loved may have given him a kind of aversion to everything associated with her. Moreover, it may be that fathers love only those children whom they have got to know intimately; a social belief of the greatest importance for the peace of the family, and one that all bachelors must entertain, proving that paternity is a sentiment nurtured under glass by women, by custom, and by the law.

Our poor Henri de Marsay found a father only in the man who was not obliged to be one. Monsieur de Marsay's paternal role was significantly defective. In the natural order of things children know their father for only brief moments; and this gentleman followed the course of nature. Our man would not have traded in his name if he had had no vices. So he happily dined in gambling-dens and drank away in other places the termly revenue from his investment in the national debt. Then he turned the child over to an elderly sister, one Mademoiselle de Marsay, who took great care of him and, from the slim pension allocated by her brother, found him a private tutor, a penniless, threadbare priest, who took full measure of the young man's future and resolved to reward himself out of the hundred thousand pounds of income invested for the care of his pupil, toward whom he felt a growing affection. It happened that this tutor was a true cleric, one of those men of the cloth cut out to become a cardinal in France or a Borgia at the Vatican.* In three years he taught the child what would have taken ten years in school: then the worthy man, known as the Abbé de Maronis, completed the education of his pupil by making him study civilization in all its aspects: he gave him the benefit of his experience, wasted little time dragging him through churches, which anyway were closed in those days;* took him sometimes backstage, and more often to meet courtesans; he dissected the human passions for him one by one, educated him in politics, in the salons where in those days it simmered and fomented; he elaborated the machinery of government and attempted, out of friendship for a beautiful soul presently abandoned but rich in promise, to be a male substitute for the mother: is not the Church the mother of orphans? The pupil responded well to such solicitous treatment.

This dignified man died a bishop in 1812, with the satisfaction of leaving beneath the heavens a child of sixteen whose heart and mind were so well fashioned that he could run rings around a man of forty. Who could have expected to find a heart of bronze and a brain pickled in spirits behind the extremely seductive appearance that those ancient and naive painters gave to the serpent in the Garden of Eden? That is not all. This kind devil cloaked in purple had even introduced his favourite child to certain characters in Parisian high society who could, in the hands of the young man, be worth a further hundred thousand pounds of income. Finally, this priest, unprincipled but politic, unbelieving but scholarly, seeming frail but in fact equally energetic in mind as in body, was so genuinely useful to his pupil, so indulgent to his weaknesses, as devious as he was amiable, and so good at reckoning with different powers and judgements, so profound when he had to sum up some human problem, so lively at the dinner table, at Frascati's club,* well... almost anywhere, that by 1814, the grateful Henri de Marsay felt hardly any tenderness, except when looking on the portrait of his beloved bishop, the only worldly possession the prelate had been able to bequeath him; that admirable ideal of the kind of men who will save the Roman Catholic and Apostolic Church, presently compromised by the weakness of its recruits and the age of its pontiffs, but only if the Church is willing.

The continental war prevented the young de Marsay from making the acquaintance of his real father, whose name he probably did not even know. Having been abandoned as a child, he didn't know Madame de Marsay any better. Naturally, he had few regrets for his presumed father. As for Mademoiselle de Marsay, the only mother he knew, he had a very pretty little tomb built for her in the Père Lachaise cemetery when she died. Monseigneur de Maronis had guaranteed the old biddy one of the best places in Heaven, so that, seeing her happy to die, Henri shed a few selfish tears over her then began to grieve at his own loss. Seeing this suffering, the priest dried his pupil's tears, informing him that the old girl had been a messy snuff-taker, and had become so ugly, deaf, and tedious that he should be grateful for her death. The bishop had had his pupil freed from his ward in 1811. Then, when the mother of Monsieur de Marsay remarried, the priest at a family council meeting chose one of those innocent and brainless men carefully selected by him from the confessional, and charged him with administrating the fortune whose income he would, of course, distribute according to the needs of the community, but whose capital he would retain.

Thus, towards the end of 1814 Henri de Marsay had no sentimental obligations on earth and found himself as free as a bird on the wing. Although he was fully twenty-two years old, he looked only seventeen. In general, his most critical rivals considered him the handsomest young man in Paris. From his father, Lord Dudley, he had taken the most treacherously amorous blue eyes, from his mother the richest black, wavy hair; and from both their pure blood, a girlish complexion, a gentle and modest air, a slim aristocratic figure, and very fine hands. For a woman, to see him was to fall madly in love with him; which is, as we know, to entertain one of those desires that eats away at the heart, although it is forgotten when it becomes impossible to fulfil, since your average Parisian woman commonly lacks staying-power. Few of them are able to repeat, as men might, the motto of the House of Orange: *Je maintiendrai.**

Behind this sprightly freshness, and despite the limpid liquid of his eyes, Henri had the courage of a lion and the cunning of a monkey. He could put a bullet through the blade of a knife at ten paces, ride a horse as if embodying the myth of the centaur, drive a stylish four-in-hand and be as cheeky as Cherubino* or as mild as a lamb; but he could beat any man from the suburbs at the fearsome sports of *savate* or *combat de canne*,* fingered a piano well enough to become a professional if he fell on hard times, and had a voice which would have earned him fifty thousand francs a season from Barbaja.* Alas, all these fine qualities and appealing faults were tarnished by one appalling vice: he believed neither in men nor in women, neither in God nor the Devil. Nature, in her caprice, had initially lavished her gifts on him; a priest had brought them to fruition.

In order to make sense of this story, we have to add here that Lord Dudley naturally found many women disposed to make copies of such a delicious portrait. His second masterpiece in the genre was a girl called Euphémia, born of a Spanish lady, brought up in Havana enjoying ruinous colonial tastes, and then shipped back to Madrid, accompanied by a young Creole woman. However, she married well, to an old and extremely rich Spanish lord, Don Hijos, the Marquis de San-Réal, who, since the occupation of Spain* by French troops, had come to live in Paris and resided in the Rue Saint-Lazare. As much by negligence as by respect for their age of innocence, Lord Dudley gave no notice to his children of the relatives that he was everywhere providing them with. This is a mild inconvenience of civilized behaviour, that brings so many advantages that we should overlook its faults in favour of its many benefits. To finish Lord Dudley's story, he came to seek refuge in Paris in 1816, in order to escape pursuit by English law, which, in matters oriental, protects only merchandise. The itinerant lord, on seeing Henri, asked who the fine young man was. Then, when he heard him named, he exclaimed: 'Oh, he's my son! What a shame!'

This is the story behind the young man who, towards the middle of April 1815,* was strolling nonchalantly down the main alley of the Tuileries gardens, proceeding in peace and in majesty, like all creatures aware of their strength; the middle-class women turned round naively to watch him go by, while the other ladies did not turn their heads but waited for him on the way back, so that he would be etched in their memories for later reference as a refined figure who would not have disgraced the arm of the most beautiful among them.

'What are you doing here on a Sunday?' the Marquis de Ronquerolles asked Henri as they crossed paths.

'They are nibbling at the bait,' replied the young man.

This exchange of thoughts took place with two significant glances, without either de Ronquerolles or de Marsay appearing to know each other. The young man surveyed the Sunday strollers with that acuity of eye and ear peculiar to the Parisian, who seems at first glance to see and hear nothing, but who sees and hears everything.

At that moment a young man came up to him, took him casually by the arm, and said to him:

'How are you, de Marsay, my friend?'

'Very well, thank you,' replied de Marsay with that superficially affectionate air which between young Parisian men is of no significance, whether for the present or the future.

For indeed the young men of Paris are unlike those of any other town. They may be divided into two classes: the young man who has possessions and the young man who has nothing; or the young man who thinks and the young man who spends. But let it be understood that we mention here only those native Parisians who lead an elegant and delicious life there. There are, of course, other young men, but they are children who learn about Parisian life too late and never understand its duplicity. They do not speculate, they study; in the words of the other two groups, they work their fingers to the bone... And finally, you may still find some young men, rich or poor, who embrace a career and follow it wholeheartedly; rather like Rousseau's Émile,* they are grass-roots citizens, and never appear in polite society. Diplomatic people unkindly call them fools. Fools or not, they add to the number of mediocre people whose weight is crushing France. You find them everywhere, always ready to level affairs private and public with the flat spade of mediocrity, and they flaunt their impotence, which they call morality and probity. This kind of social 'top of the class' infests the civil service, the army, the judiciary, the two houses of parliament, and the court. They diminish and abase the country and constitute within the body politic a lymphatic humour, as it were, which clogs it up and makes it sluggish. These worthy people treat other, more talented men as immoral or crooked. If these latter knaves are paid for their services, at least they serve, while the former are worse than useless and are respected by the crowds; but luckily for France, our elegant youths dismiss them as old fools.

So, at first glance, it is natural to believe that both races of young men who live an elegant life, that amiable, genteel corporate body which counts Henri de Marsay among its number, are quite distinct. But the observer who sees below the surface of things is soon convinced that the differences are purely moral, and that nothing is more deceptive than that pretty shell. Nonetheless, they all elbow their fellow men aside and speak at the drop of a hat with utter disrespect of persons and topics, of literature and art; they are always ready to discuss each year's new crop of suspected enemy spies in the pay of Pitt and Coburg,* and interrupt a conversation with a quip; they make fun of science and scholars, despise everything that they are ignorant or fearful of, then place themselves above everyone else, appointing themselves supreme judges of everything. They all led their fathers up the garden path, and would be ready to cry crocodile tears in their mothers' arms; but generally they believe in nothing, and speak ill of women; or pretending modesty, they in fact serve some wily courtesan or some elderly lady. They are all equally rotten to the core through self-interest, depravity, or a ruthless desire to succeed, and if they are in danger of turning into stone, if you plumbed their depths you would find stone not in their kidneys but in every one of their hearts.

In their normal state they have the finest appearance, bring friendship into play on every occasion, are unfailingly charming. The same ironic tone accompanies their ever-changing slang; they seek extravagance in their dress, are proud of repeating the stupidities of whatever actor is in vogue, and make a show of their contempt or impertinence as soon as they meet anyone, in order to win, as it were, the first round of the game; but woe betide anyone who doesn't know how to lose one eye for the sake of putting out both of his rival's. They seem equally indifferent to the misfortunes of their country, and its running sores. To sum up, they all resemble the lovely white foam that crowns the waves of a stormy sea. They dress up, dine, dance, and amuse themselves on the day of the Battle of Waterloo, in times of cholera,* or during a revolution. What is more, they all have the same expenses, but from here the two strains diverge.

In terms of wealth, which fluctuates but is so pleasing to squander, one group owns the capital and the other waits upon it; they share the same tailor, but the bills of the latter group have still to be settled. Then, if some, like sieves, are open to all sorts of ideas but retain none, the others compare them and claim all the best as their own. If the first, who think they know something, yet know nothing while understanding everything, lend everything to those who need nothing and offer nothing to those who need something, the second secretly study the thoughts of others, and invest their money as well as their follies at high rates of interest. The first no longer have reliable impressions, because their souls, like a mirror tarnished with use, no longer reflect any image; the others are economical with their senses and their life while giving the impression that they are throwing them out of the window, as the first group do. The first group, in the belief of some future inheritance, devote themselves without conviction to a system which has the wind behind it as it sails upstream, but they jump ship onto a different political vessel as soon as the first one starts to drift; the second fathoms the future, plumbs its depths, and sees in political loyalty what the English see in commercial probity, an element of success. But where the young man of property makes a pun or a witticism at the drop of a hat on the fluctuating fates of the monarchy, the man who has nothing takes an overt risk or makes a secret compromise and makes his way by a series of handshakes with his friends. The first never believe in the talent of others, consider all their own ideas to be original, as if the world were born yesterday; they have unlimited confidence in themselves and are in fact their own worst enemies. But the others are armed with a constant suspicion of others, whom they judge at their true worth, and are acute enough to keep one move ahead of the friends that they exploit; so at night, with their heads on the pillow, they weigh their fellow men as a miser weighs his gold coins. The first are annoyed by some insignificant slight and are liable to be mocked by the diplomatic, who make them dance like puppets before the public by pulling on their main string, which is self-interest; while the others gain respect by choosing both their victims and their patrons. Then there comes a time when those who had nothing have acquired something; and those who had something have nothing. The latter then look on their comrades, who have made a place for themselves, as devious, disloyal, but also strong. 'He is really a capable man!' is the greatest praise reserved for those who have succeeded, *quibuscum viis*,* in politics, love or fortune. Among them we find certain young men who are already in debt when they start to play; and naturally they are more dangerous than those who enter the game with nothing to their name.

The young man who called himself a friend of Henri de Marsay was a scatterbrained provincial lad, learning from his modish young companions how to thoroughly blow an inheritance, while he still had a last treat in store in the country: an estate which was his due. He was, quite simply, an heir suddenly promoted from his meagre hundred francs a month to the whole paternal fortune, and who, even if he had not wit enough to realize that he was a figure of fun, knew enough arithmetic to use up no more than two-thirds of his capital. In Paris he had recently discovered, for only a few thousand franc notes, the exact price of a harness and the art of not taking too much care of one's gloves; he listened to sophisticated arguments on what wages to pay your servants, and found out the lowest annual retainer which could be most advantageously offered to them; he thought it most important to be able to speak knowingly of his horses and his Pyrenean mountain dog, to recognize a woman's social class by her dress, her way of walking, and her lace-up boots; he learned how to play *écarté*,* how to quote some fashionable phrases, and to gain, through his stay in Parisian society, the authority necessary to carry off, later in the provinces, a taste for English tea and English silverware, and to assume the right to look down on all around him for the rest of his days. De Marsay had cultivated his friendship in order to make use of him in society, as a bold speculator takes a broker into his confidence. De Marsay's friendship, true or false, provided a social foothold for Paul de Manerville, who, for his part, felt the stronger for exploiting his close friend as best he could. He lived in the shadow of his friend, sheltered under his umbrella, trod in his footsteps, glowed in his reflected light. Striking a pose beside Henri, or even walking at his side, he seemed to say: 'Do not insult us, we are tigers when we are roused.' Often he allowed himself to drop an aside: 'If I asked Henri such and such a favour, he is friend enough to oblige.' But he took care never to ask a favour. He feared him, and his fear, although hardly perceptible, had an effect on others and was useful to de Marsay.

'De Marsay is a proud man,' said Paul. 'Ah! You will see, he will become whatever he wants. I would not be surprised to find him Foreign Minister one day. Nothing is beyond him.'

Then he treated de Marsay as Corporal Trim did his cap,* as a perpetual point of reference. 'Ask de Marsay, and you'll see!'

Or he might say: 'The other day, I was out hunting with de Marsay. He found it hard to believe, but I cleared a hedge without rising in the saddle.'

Or perhaps: 'De Marsay and I were in the company of women, and upon my word of honour, I..., etc.'

Thus, Paul de Manerville could be classed only among the great, illustrious, and powerful family of brainless *arrivistes*. He was likely to become a member of parliament one day, although for the moment he was hardly a full-grown man. His friend de Marsay defined him in these terms. 'You ask me what Paul de Manerville really is. Paul?... well, he is Paul de Manerville.'

'I am surprised, my good fellow,' he said to de Marsay, 'to see you here on a Sunday.'

'I was about to say the same thing to you.'

'An intrigue?'

'Perhaps...'

'Well?'

'I can admit it to you without compromising my true feelings. Besides, a woman who visits the Tuileries on a Sunday has no value, in aristocratic terms.'

'Ah ha!'

'Be quiet then, or I shall tell you nothing. You are laughing too loud, people will think that we have had too much wine for lunch.

Last Thursday, here, on the Terrasse des Feuillants, I was strolling along with not a thought in my head. But as I arrived at the gate to the Rue de Castiglione where I was heading, I found myself face to face with a woman, or rather with a young lady, who, if she did not throw herself in my arms, was restrained less by a sense of human dignity than by one of those profound shocks which paralyses your arms, runs down your spine, cuts your legs from under you, and roots your feet to the ground. I have often had this kind of effect, it's a sort of animal magnetism* which becomes very powerful when the attraction is mutual. But my good fellow, she was not a common whore, nor was she drugged out of her mind. Figuratively speaking, her expression seemed to say: "Well, there you are, the ideal creature of my thoughts, of my night-time and daytime dreams. Is it really you? And why this morning? Why not yesterday? Take me, I am yours, etcetera!" "Well," I said to myself, "yet another!" I scrutinized her. Ah, my good fellow, in physical terms my passing stranger was the most beautifully formed woman that I have ever met. She belongs to that race of women which the Romans called *fulva*, *flava*, a woman of fire. And what struck me most in the first place, and what now still enchants me most, were her eyes, yellow as the eyes of a tiger, a shining yellow gold, living gold, thinking gold, loving gold, gold which yearns to pour straightway into your purse.'

'But no one is talking about anything else, my dear fellow!' cried Paul. 'She comes here from time to time, she's the Girl with the Golden Eyes. That's what we call her. She's a young lady of about twenty-two, and I saw her when the Bourbons were still here,* but with a woman a hundred-thousand times better than her.'

'Be quiet, Paul. No woman could possibly be superior to her. She is like a cat wanting to rub up against your legs, a girl with white skin and ash-blonde hair, seemingly delicate, but whose fingernails must be hidden by silky fur; and whose cheeks are dusted with a white down, visible only by the light of day, which starts at her ears and fades out at her neck.'

'Ah, but the other one, my dear de Marsay, she can show you black eyes that have never wept but which burn, black brows which meet and give her an air of severity contradicted by the subtle folds of her lips, which won't show the trace of a kiss, her fresh, ardent lips; a Moorish complexion where a man could bask as in sunlight, but, upon my word, she looks like you...'

'You flatter her.'

'A curvaceous waist, the slim waist of a corvette built for the chase, which races after its merchant prey with French bravado, tears into it, and sinks it in no time at all.'

'Come, my friend, what do I care for a woman I have never seen!' continued de Marsay. 'Since I started to study women, my passing stranger alone has the virgin breast and voluptuous and ardent figure of the only woman that I have ever dreamt of! She is the original of the fantastical painting entitled *Woman Embracing her Chimera*,* the most passionate and infernal inspiration of ancient genius; a sacred poem desecrated by those who copied it for frescos and mosaics; for the mass of the bourgeois see in that cameo only a trinket and hang it on their watch-chains, while she is the whole of womankind, an abyss of pleasure where one floats without end, an ideal woman who is seen occasionally in Spain or Italy, but hardly ever in France. Well, I saw that Girl with the Golden Eyes again, that woman embracing her chimera. I saw her again here on Friday. I guessed that the next day she would return at the same time. I was not wrong. I took pleasure in following her without her noticing, studying the nonchalant walk of the idle woman whose movements suggest a latent voluptuousness. But then she turned round, she saw me; she adored me again, trembled and shivered again. Then I noticed the veritable Spanish duenna guarding her; a hyena disguised as a woman by a jealous lover, a female devil well paid to protect that beautiful creature... Oh! Then the duenna made me feel even more amorous, I became intrigued. Saturday, no one. So here I am today, waiting for the girl like her chimera, and asking nothing better than to play the part of the monster in the fresco.'

'There she is,' said Paul, 'everyone is turning round to look at her.'

The stranger blushed, her eyes sparkled as she noticed Henri. She lowered her eyes and passed on.

'You say that she notices you?' cried Paul de Manerville, ironically.

The duenna stared intensely at the two young men. When the mysterious young lady passed Henri again, she brushed against him, and clasped the young man's hand in hers. Then she turned round and gave him a passionate smile; but the duenna hurried her away towards the gate leading to the Rue de Castiglione. The two friends followed the girl, admiring the magnificent turn of her neck where it met her head in a series of powerful curves, and on which nestled the first tight curls of her hair. The Girl with the Golden Eyes walked with a firm step, showing slim, shapely ankles, which offered infinite attraction to the hungry imagination. Not to mention her elegant shoes and her short skirt. As she walked, she turned around from time to time to look at Henri, and seemed to regret following the old woman, to whom she reacted both as mistress and slave: she could have her beaten, but she could not have her dismissed. This was perfectly evident.

The two friends arrived at the gate. Two valets in livery let down the step of a fashionable coupé, embellished with a coat of arms. The Girl with the Golden Eyes was the first to mount, and sat on the side where she would be seen when the carriage turned the corner; she placed her hand on the ledge and waved her handkerchief, out of sight of the duenna, careless of what idle bystanders might think, as if saying in public to Henri with every wave of her handkerchief: 'Follow me.'

'Have you ever seen anyone wave a handkerchief like that?' said Henri to Paul de Manerville.

Then, catching sight of a cab which was about to leave after its clients had dismounted, he hailed the coachman to wait.

'Follow that coupé, watch the street it enters and the house where it stops, and you will earn ten francs—Farewell, Paul.'

The cab followed the coupé. It went up the Rue Saint-Lazare and turned in at one of the finest mansions of the neighbourhood.

De Marsay had a sensible head on his shoulders. Many other young men would have yielded to the immediate desire to find out more about this girl who embodied so perfectly the most luminous ideas expressed about women in oriental poetry; but he was clever enough to avoid compromising his future chances, he told his coachman to continue along the Rue Saint-Lazare and to drive him home. The next day his valet, Laurent, a smart lad, like Frontin in Marivaux's comedy,* lurked in the shadows of the stranger's house at the time when the post would be delivered. In order to spy more easily and prowl around the mansion, he had followed the example of police informers who love disguise and bought the costume of an Auvergnat,* and he tried to look and act like one. When the postman who happened to be delivering to the Rue Saint-Lazare that morning went by, Laurent pretended to be an errand-boy having trouble remembering the name of someone he had to deliver a package to, and consulted the postman. Taken in by first appearances, this most picturesque representative of Parisian civilization told him that the mansion inhabited by the Girl with the Golden Eyes belonged to Don Hijos, Marquis de San-Réal, a Spanish grandee. Naturally, it was not the Marquis whom our Auvergnat was looking for.

'My package', he said, 'is for the Marquise.'

'She is away,' replied the postman. 'Her letters are forwarded to London.'

'So the Marquise is not a certain young lady who…'

'Ah!' said the postman interrupting the manservant and looking him up and down. 'If you are an errand boy, I am a ballet dancer.'

Laurent proffered a few gold coins to the civil dignitary armed with a clapper,* who began to smile.

'Here you are, this is the name of the bird you are stalking,' he said, taking from his leather satchel a letter bearing a London postmark and the following address, written in a fine, sloping script which betrayed a feminine hand:

> To Mademoiselle
> PAQUITA VALDÈS
> Rue Saint-Lazare, Hôtel de San-Réal,
> PARIS.

'Might you fancy a bottle of Chablis and a few dozen oysters, followed by braised fillet steak and mushrooms?' asked Laurent, who wanted to win the valuable friendship of the postman.

'At half-past nine, after I finish work. Where?'

'At the corner of the Rue de la Chaussée d'Antin and the Rue Neuve-des-Mathurins, at the *Puits sans vin*,* said Laurent.

'Listen, my friend,' said the postman when he met our manservant an hour later, 'if your master is in love with that girl, he'll have one hell of a task. I doubt if you'll manage to catch sight of her. I've been a postman in Paris for ten years, and I've made quite a study of its doorways! But I can tell you straight, with no fear of contradiction from any of my mates, that there is no door more mysterious than that of Monsieur de San-Réal. Nobody can enter the place without some password or other, and look how they chose a house situated between a courtyard and a garden to avoid any access from the other houses. The porter is an old Spaniard who speaks not a word of French, but who looks right through you, as Vidocq* would, to see if you're a thief. And even if this first gatekeeper is fooled by a lover or a thief or even by you, if you pardon the comparison, well then, in the entrance hall, which is closed round with doors with glass panels, you will meet a butler surrounded by an army of valets who is an even more grotesque and monstrous old thug than the porter. If anyone slips through the service door, our butler arrives and catches you under the porch and gives you a real grilling, as if you're a downright criminal caught in the act. It happened to me, and I'm just the postman. He took me for a discreet agent* in disguise,' he said, laughing at the joke. 'As for the servants, don't hope to get nothing out of them, I think they are all deaf mutes, nobody in the neighbourhood can get a word out of them. I don't know how much they pay them not to talk and not to drink; the fact is, you can't get near them. Either they are afraid of getting shot, or they would lose a great deal of money if they let something slip. And if your master loves Mademoiselle Paquita Valdès enough to jump over all of these obstacles, he certainly won't get past Doña Concha Marialva, the duenna who chaperones her and who would stuff her under her skirts rather than let her out of her sight. Those two women seem to be sewn together.'

'What you are telling me, my fine friend,' said Laurent after tasting the wine, 'confirms what I have just learnt. Upon my honour as an honest man, I thought that people were making fun of me. The greengrocer's wife across the way told me that at night they send out the dogs into the gardens, where their food is tied up on stakes so that they can't reach it. These damned animals then think that anyone trying to enter the grounds is trying to get at their food, and they would tear them to pieces. You might think that you could throw them chunks of meat, but it seems that they have been trained not to eat anything the porter hasn't given them.'

'In fact the porter at Monsieur le Baron de Nucingen's* house, whose grounds border on the San-Réal garden, has told me as much,' said the postman.

'Yes, my master knows him,' thought Laurent.

'Do you know', he said, looking slyly at the postman, 'that I am employed by a master who is a proud man, and if he suddenly wanted to kiss the feet of an empress, she would have to allow it. If he needed your services, which I rather hope, for your sake, since he is a generous man, may we count on you?'

'Oh gawd, Monsieur Laurent, my name is Moinot. M-o-i-n-o-t, en-oh-tee, Moinot, just like a sparrer in our native French.'*

'Quite so,' said Laurent.

'I live at number 11, Rue des Trois-Frères, fifth floor,' said Moinot, 'I have a wife and four children. If what you require of me does not go beyond the limits of my conscience and my administrative duties, you understand, I am all yours!'

'You are a good man,' said Laurent, shaking his hand.

'Paquita Valdès must be the mistress of the Marquis de San-Réal, the friend of King Ferdinand.* Only a decrepit, eighty-year-old Spanish walking bag of bones could take such precautions,' reasoned Henri, when his manservant had delivered the results of his research.

'Monsieur,' said Laurent, 'nobody can enter that place unless they fly in by balloon.'

'What a fool you are! Do I need to enter the house in order to have Paquita, since she is free to leave?'

'But, sir, what about the duenna?'

'We'll lock her up in her room for a few days, this duenna of yours.'

'Well then, we'll have our Paquita!' said Laurent, rubbing his hands.

'You may well laugh,' replied Henri. 'I shall force you to have Doña Concha if you are insolent enough to speak in such terms of a woman that I have not yet had. Now help me get dressed, I have to go out.'

Henri remained silent for a moment, plunged in joyful contemplation. Let us say this to the credit of women, that whichever of them he deigned to desire, he would then possess. And what might one think of a woman who has no lover, but is able to resist a young man endowed with beauty, that spiritual essence of the body, possessed of wit, that finest expression of the soul, and of moral courage and wealth, which are the only two forces that really matter? But de Marsay was bound to tire of such facile success, so for the past two years he had become very bored. The more he plumbed the depths of sensual pleasure, the more he emerged with grit rather than pearls. Thus, like many a monarch, he had come to that pass where at the drop of a hat he pleaded with fate for some obstacle to overcome, some enterprise which would require him to galvanize all of his dormant physical and moral strength. Although Paquita Valdès was, in his mind, a wondrously perfect whole, of which he had previously glimpsed only isolated fragments, the lure of passion hardly affected him. Repeated satisfaction had dulled all feeling of love in his heart; like old men and libertines, he could only respond to the lure of the risqué, the ruinous fantasies of depravity, none of which, once he had experienced them, left him with a single happy memory. For young men, love is the most wonderful feeling. It makes the soul burst into life, its sun-like warmth engenders its finest inspiration and its greatest thoughts: the anticipation of anything is always delicious. In mature men love turns to passion, strength leads to abuse; in old men love leads to vice, impotence leads to excess. Henri was old, mature, and young at the same time. In order to feel the rapture of true love he needed, like Lovelace, a

Clarissa Harlowe.* Without the magical lustre of that elusive pearl, he was reduced to feeling only fleeting emotions teased by Parisian vanity, or accepting a challenge to lead a particular woman to a certain depth of depravity, or embarking on an adventure that aroused his curiosity. The information provided by his valet Laurent had intervened to set the highest possible price on the Girl with the Golden Eyes. He would have to take up arms against some secret adversary, apparently both dangerous and skilful. In order to win, Henri could not leave any of his multiple resources untapped. He was going to participate in that age-old but evergreen play whose characters are: an old man, a young woman, and a lover, such as Don Hijos, Paquita, de Marsay. For all that Laurent was a match for Figaro,* yet the duenna remained seemingly incorruptible. The real-life drama was in this way more closely determined by fortune than in any play ever written. But is fortune not also a form of genius?

'We are going to have to play our cards close to our chest,' said Henri to himself.

'Well,' said Paul de Manerville, as he came in, 'how are you getting on? I have come to have dinner with you.'

'Good,' said Henri. 'You won't mind if I get washed and dressed in front of you?'

'How very amusing!' said Paul.

'We are adopting so many of those English habits that we are likely to become as hypocritical and prudish as they,' said Henri.

Laurent had laid out for his master so many attractive utensils, in so many decorative trays and cases, that Paul could not help saying, 'But won't it take you nearly two hours?'

'No, two and a half!'

'Well, since we are alone, and we can be quite frank, tell me why a man of your superior class, for you are indeed superior, needs to put on such a fatuous, affected appearance, which cannot be your true nature. Why spend two and a half hours preening yourself, when fifteen minutes in a bath, a quick brush and comb, and a change of clothes is quite enough. So, what's it all about?'

'If we weren't such good friends, you lovable oaf, I would never entrust you with such lofty thoughts,' said the young man who at that moment was having his feet gently lathered with a brush dipped in English soap.

'But I have always been sincerely devoted to you,' replied Paul, 'and I love you the more for being better than me...'

'You must have noticed, assuming that you are capable of psychological insight, that women love a fop,' continued de Marsay, responding to Paul's declaration with no more than a glance. 'And do you know why they love a fop? My friend, fops are the only men who take care of themselves. So isn't taking extra care of oneself actually looking after someone else's prized possession? The man who does not belong to himself is the very one who whets women's appetite. Cupid is essentially a thief.

'I don't have to tell you about women's obsession with absolute cleanliness. Can you think of any woman conceiving a passion for a slovenly man, however remarkable he might be? If such a thing had ever happened, we would have to put it down to the cravings of pregnancy or the sort of crazy whim that anyone may fall prey to. On the contrary, I have seen the most remarkable men rejected out of hand because of their self-neglect. A fop looking after his own person is devoting himself to foolish, petty matters. But what is woman? A foolish, petty creature. A chance remark or two will give her something to think about for hours on end. She can rely on the fop to look after her, because he has no graver concerns. She will never be neglected in favour of glory, ambition, politics, or art, those notorious whores that she sees as her rivals. So the fop brave enough to make himself a laughing-stock in order to please a woman is amply rewarded by her heart for his ridiculous love. In the end, a fop can only be a fop if he has some reason to be one. And it is women who raise us to that station. The fop is the colonel of love, he is fortune's favourite, he has a whole company of women at his command!

'My dear friend, in Paris everyone is in the know, and no man can be a fop for free. You, who have only one woman, and who may be right to have only one, could you act the fop? You would not even be ridiculous, you would be completely dead. You would be a walking cliché, sentenced without appeal to endlessly repeat the same act. You would stand for utter stupidity as Monsieur de

La Fayette stands for America, Monsieur de Talleyrand for diplomacy, Désaugiers for song and Monsieur de Ségur* for romance. If they act out of type, no one will give them credit for what they do. That is what we are like in France, always supremely unjust. Monsieur de Talleyrand might well be a great banker, Monsieur de La Fayette a despot, and Désaugiers an administrator. You could have forty mistresses next year, society would not credit you with a single one. And thus, my dear friend, foppishness is the sign of an incontestable conquest of the female race. A man who is loved by a number of women is thought to possess superior qualities; and so it's every woman for herself, let him beware, poor man! But is it nothing in your eyes to have the right to walk into a salon and look down at everyone from behind your cravat or down through your monocle, and feel able to despise the most superior man because he happens to be wearing last season's waistcoat? Laurent, you're hurting me. After lunch, Paul, we shall go to the Tuileries to see the lovely Girl with the Golden Eyes.'

After an excellent meal the two young men walked up and down the Terrasse des Feuillants and the main avenue of the Tuileries, but failed to find the sublime Paquita Valdès on whose account fifty of the most elegant young men in Paris had gathered, with their scent, their high cravats, their boots and spurs, swishing their whips as they walked along, talking and laughing, sending everyone to the devil.

'We've drawn a blank,' said Henri, 'but I've just had the most brilliant idea. That girl gets letters from London. We must bribe the postman or get him drunk, open a letter, read it of course, slip in a little billet-doux, and seal it up again. The old tyrant, *crudelo tiranno*, must obviously know who it is who sends letters from London, and no longer feels suspicious about them.'

The next day de Marsay returned to walk in the sun on the Terrasse des Feuillants and saw Paquita Valdès: his passion had already added to her beauty. He was driven almost to distraction by her eyes, whose gaze seemed like sunbeams and whose intensity announced the absolute delight of her perfect body. De Marsay was burning with the urge to brush up against her dress when their paths crossed. His attempts were in vain. At one point, when he had overtaken the duenna and Paquita in order to find himself beside the Girl with the Golden Eyes when he passed them again, Paquita, no less impatient, took a quick step forward, and de Marsay felt her squeeze his hand so quickly, but with such passionate meaning, that it was as if he had received an electric shock. In a flash, all the emotions of his youth welled up in his heart. As the two lovers looked at each other Paquita seemed to feel ashamed, lowered her eyes in order not to look into Henri's again, but her gaze drifted downwards towards the feet and the figure of the man who, before the Revolution, a woman would have called her 'conqueror'.

'I shall definitely make her my mistress,' said Henri to himself.

Following her to the end of the terrace which gave on to the Place Louis XV, he caught sight of the aged Marquis de San-Réal, who was leaning on the arm of his valet as he moved forward with the tentative steps of a doddery old man afflicted with gout. Doña Concha, who was suspicious of Henri, made Paquita walk between her and the old man.

'Oh, as for you,' said Henri to himself, casting a contemptuous eye on the duenna, 'if you refuse to yield, a bit of opium will send you to sleep. We know our mythology and the story of Argus.'*

Before getting into her carriage, the Girl with the Golden Eyes exchanged glances with her lover. Her expression left no room for doubt, and Henri was entranced. But the duenna intercepted one such glance and spoke a few sharp words to Paquita, who threw herself into the coupé with an air of despair. Paquita did not return to the Tuileries for some days. Laurent, who followed his master's instructions to keep watch on her residence, learned from the neighbours that neither the two women nor the aged Marquis had left the house since the day on which the duenna had intercepted a look exchanged between the young lady entrusted to her care and Henri. The tenuous bond which had united the two lovers was thus already broken.

A few days later, though no one knew by what means, de Marsay had achieved his aim. He had a seal and wax identical to the seal and wax used on the letters sent from London to Mademoiselle Valdès, some paper identical to that used by her correspondent, in addition to all the apparatus needed to stamp the letter with the English and French postmarks. He had written the following letter, which gave every appearance of having been sent from London:

'Dear Paquita,

I shall not try to paint in words the passion which you have aroused in me. If, by good fortune, you share this passion, let me tell you that I have found a way of corresponding with you. My name is Adolphe de Gouges and I live at 54, Rue de l'Université. If you are too closely watched to write to me, if you have neither paper nor pen, your silence will tell. So, if tomorrow between eight in the morning and ten at night you have not thrown a letter over the wall dividing your garden from Baron Nucingen's, where someone will be waiting all day, a man entirely devoted to me will throw two flasks tied to the end of a ropc over the wall at ten o'clock on the following day. Be sure to take your walk there at that time. One of the two flasks will contain opium to send your Argus to sleep, six drops will be enough; the other contains ink. The ink is in the cut-glass flask, and the opium in the smooth one. Both of them are slim enough to slip into your corset. Everything I have already done to be able to correspond with you should tell you how much I love you. If you doubt me, I swear that I would give my life to spend just one hour in your company.'

'And they believe it, the poor creatures!' said de Marsay to himself, 'but they are right to do so. What would we think of a woman who did not allow herself to be seduced by a love-letter supported by such convincing evidence?'

The letter was delivered to the doorkeeper of the San-Réal residence by the estimable Moinot, postman, at about eight o'clock on the following morning.

In order to move closer to the battlefield, de Marsay had come to lunch with Paul, who lived in the Rue de la Pépinière. At two o'clock, just when the two friends were laughing over the story of the discomfiture of a young man who had wished to lead an elegant life without the secure funds to back it, and while they were still trying to think of the way his story might end, Henri's coachman came knocking at Paul's very door in search of his master, and had with him a mysterious character who absolutely insisted on talking to Henri in person. This character was a mulatto, who would certainly have inspired Talma in his portrayal of Othello,* had he met him. Never did an African face express such haughty vengefulness and swift suspicion, such alacrity in putting thought into action, with all the force and childish impetuousness of the Moor. His black eyes were as unflinching as those of a bird of prey, and, like those of a vulture, they were set within blueish lids with no lashes. His narrow, low forehead had something threatening about it. The man was clearly labouring under the weight of a single notion. His muscular arm seemed independent of his will.

He was followed by a man whom everyone, whether they shivered in Greenland or sweated in New England, would describe in the same way: *he was a miserable wretch.* By this description everyone will imagine him and what he looked like according to the particular notions of their own country. But who could picture his lined and livid face, his red nose and ears, his long beard, his tie of yellowish string, his greasy shirt collar, his frayed hat, his shabby green frock-coat, his wretched trousers, his crumpled waistcoat, his imitation gold tiepin, and his filthy shoes, whose laces had been dragged through the mud? Who could comprehend the whole depth of his misery present and past? Who else but a Parisian? The miserable Parisian wretch is the supremely abject man, for he can still find extra pleasure in knowing how unhappy he is.

The mulatto seemed like one of Louis XI's executioners* waiting to hang a man.

'Wherever did this odd couple come from?' said Henri.

'Heavens above! One of them gives me the shivers,' replied Paul.

'Who are you?' Henri asked, looking at the man of misery. 'You have more of a Christian air about you.'

The mulatto kept his eyes fixed on the two young men, as one who understands nothing and was trying nevertheless to glean some sense from their gestures and the movements of their lips.

'I am a public scribe and interpreter. I work for the law-courts. My name is Poincet.'

'Very well. And what about him?' said Henri, pointing to the mulatto.

'I don't know. He speaks only some Spanish dialect, and he brought me here so as to be able to talk to you.'

The mulatto took the letter that Henri had written to Paquita from his pocket and returned it to him. Henri threw it on the fire.

'Well now, things are starting to happen,' Henri thought. 'Paul, leave us alone for a moment.'

When they were alone, the interpreter continued, 'I translated that letter for him, and when I had finished he went off somewhere. Then he came back to fetch me and bring me here, with the offer of two louis d'or.'

'What have you to say to me, Chinaman?' asked Henri.

'I left out the word "Chinaman",' said the interpreter, waiting for the mulatto to answer.

Then, having heard the stranger's reply, he went on, 'He says, sir, that you must be on the Boulevard Montmartre in front of the café at half-past ten tomorrow night. There you will see a carriage, which you will enter, on saying to the person standing in readiness at the door the word *cortejo*, a Spanish word which means *lover*,' added Poincet, looking admiringly at Henri.

'Very well!'

The mulatto wanted to give Poincet two louis, but de Marsay would have none of it and rewarded the interpreter himself. While he was paying him, the mulatto spoke a few words.

'What is he saying?'

'He is warning me', replied the unfortunate man, 'that if I commit the slightest indiscretion, he will strangle me. He's a man of his word, and he looks perfectly capable of it.'

'I have no doubt', said Henri, 'that he would do exactly as he says.'

'He adds', the interpreter continued, 'that the person who sent him begs you, for your sake and hers, to proceed with the utmost caution, or the daggers held over your heads will be plunged into your hearts, and no human hand would be able to stay them.'

'He said that! All the better, that makes it more amusing. It's all right, Paul, you can come in,' he called to his friend.

The mulatto, whose hypnotic gaze had not strayed from Paquita Valdès's lover for a second, left the room, followed by the interpreter.

'At last, an adventure worthy of a novel,' thought Henri, as Paul returned. 'I've been involved in quite a few, but at last I've encountered in this Paris of ours an intrigue with all the trappings of dangerous circumstances and deadly perils. Oh, how devilishly brazen danger makes a woman! If you corner a woman and try to tie her down, are you not giving her the right and the courage to scale in a moment hurdles which she would otherwise take years to climb over? Sweet creature, go on, leap. Death and daggers? My poor child, what female fantasies! They all feel the need to have their little joke taken seriously. All right, we'll play along with that, Paquita, we'll play your game, young lady! The devil take me, now that I know that this beautiful girl, this masterpiece of nature, is mine, the adventure has lost most of its charm.'

Despite this frivolous talk, Henri became his young self again. In order to get through to the following day without too much suffering, he resorted to extravagant pleasures: he gambled, dined and supped with his friends, drank like a trooper, ate like a horse, and pocketed ten or twelve thousand francs. He left the *Rocher de Cancale** at two o'clock in the morning, slept like a baby, woke later that morning fresh as a daisy, and dressed to go to the Tuileries, with the idea, after having seen Paquita, of going for a ride to work up an appetite and enjoy his dinner, all in order to make time fly.

At the appointed hour Henri was on the boulevard and saw the carriage. He gave the password to someone who he thought must be the mulatto. When he heard the word, the man opened the door and quickly let down the step. Henri was driven through Paris at such speed, and he was so absorbed in his thoughts, that he was barely able to notice the streets through which he passed, so that he couldn't tell where the carriage drew up. The mulatto led him into a house where the carriage entrance gave on to a staircase as gloomy as the landing, where Henri was forced to wait during the time it took for the mulatto to open the door of a dark, damp, and evil-smelling apartment, whose rooms, barely lit by the candle found by his guide in the antechamber, seemed empty and poorly furnished, like those of a house whose owners have left on a journey. He recognized the feeling he experienced when reading one of Ann Radcliffe's novels* in which the hero walks through cold, gloomy, lifeless rooms in some sad and lonely dwelling. At last the mulatto opened the door of a drawing-room. The state of the old furniture and faded drapery with which the room was decorated made it look like the reception-room in a house of ill repute. There was the same failed attempt at elegance and the same assortment of tasteless, dusty, and grimy furnishings. On a divan upholstered in red Utrecht velvet, sitting by a smokey fireside whose flames were smothered by the ashes, was an old lady, rather shabbily dressed and wearing one of those turbans which English ladies tend to adopt when they reach a certain age, and which would have achieved astounding success in China, where artists believe that ideal beauty is to be found in the grotesque. This drawing-room, this old woman, and this cold hearth would have chilled his ardour, if Paquita had not been seated there on a small sofa, wearing a seductive negligée, free to dart golden, burning glances, free to display the curve of her foot and her flowing movements.

This first meeting was like all initial encounters between people who, passionately in love, have quickly overcome distance and who desire each other ardently, even though they do not know each other. There are bound to be some disturbing moments of discord at first in such a situation, until the two souls have found the same key. If desire makes a man bold and unscrupulous, his mistress, unless she renounces her womanhood, however extreme her passion, is dismayed at finding herself suddenly so near to her goal and confronted with the need to yield, which for many women is like falling into an abyss at the bottom of which they know not what they may find. The unintentional coldness of such a woman contrasts with the passion she has admitted, and inevitably has consequences for even the most ardent lover. These thoughts, which often cling like a mist around the lovers' souls, infect them with a sort of passing sickness. When lovers undertake their sweet journey through the beautiful regions of love, this moment is like a moor to be crossed, a wasteland with no heather, now hot, now humid, now covered with scorching sand, now criss-crossed with marshes, leading to laughing groves decked in roses where Cupid and his amorous train disport themselves on luscious lawns. Often a man of wit finds himself afflicted with a foolish laugh as his response to everything; his intelligence being numbed by the icy grip of his desire. It would not be impossible for two equally beautiful, intelligent, and passionate people to begin by exchanging the most banal commonplaces, until by chance a word, the flicker of a certain look, or the exchange of some electric spark allows them to make that happy transition which leads them onto the flowery path where they float onwards, but still without leaving these high plains.

Such a state of mind always arises in proportion to the strength of their feelings. Two people who are only mildly in love never experience this. The effect of such a crisis can also be compared to that produced by the burning light of a cloudless sky. At first glance, nature appears to be covered with a gauze veil, the blue of the heavens appears black, the intensity of the light looks like darkness. Both Henri and the Spanish girl felt the same violent passion, and that law of mechanics whereby two equal and opposite forces cancel each other out when they meet might also hold true in the psychological world. Moreover, the confusion of this moment was peculiarly heightened by the presence of the mummified old hag. Love can find fear or fun in anything, everything has a meaning and is either a good or bad omen. This decrepit woman prefigured one possible ending to their story, and represented the horrible fish's tail with which the ancient Greeks, with their genius for symbols, terminated their chimeras and sirens, so seductive above the waist at first glance, yet, like all nascent passion, so disappointing below. Although Henri was not 'single minded', a term which we tend to use ironically, but a man of extraordinary strength, as great as a man with no beliefs can be, the overall impression of these details struck him with force.

Besides, the stronger the man, the more impressionable he is by nature, and hence the more superstitious, if by superstition we mean those instinctive first reactions which are no doubt an insight into a set of circumstances not even visible to other people's eyes.

The Spanish girl took advantage of his momentary stupor to allow herself to give way to the kind of unbounded, ecstatic adoration which takes possession of a woman's heart when she is truly in love and finds herself in the presence of her desperately desired idol. Her sparkling eyes were filled with joy and happiness. She was bewitched and fearlessly intoxicated by the bliss she had dreamt of for so long. Thus, to Henri, she seemed so miraculously beautiful that the whole nightmare of rags, old age, the worn-out red drapery and the greenish mats in front of the armchairs, the badly scrubbed red-tile floor, the whole dilapidated, ailing luxury—all vanished instantly. The drawing-room was lit up, he saw the horrible harpy as through a mist, where she sat motionless and silent on her red divan, the expression in her yellow eyes betraying the kind of servility that is engendered by misfortune, or by enslavement to a vice which tyrannizes its victims, brutalizing them with its despotic whip. Her eyes had the cold gleam of a caged tiger aware of its impotence and forced to choke back its destructive urges.

'Who is that woman?' enquired Henri of Paquita.

But she did not reply. She indicated that she did not understand French and asked Henri if he spoke English. De Marsay repeated his question in English.

'She is the only woman in whom I can place my trust, although she has sold me once already,' Paquita said calmly. 'Adolphe, my dear, she is my mother, a slave bought in Georgia* for her exceptional beauty—of which little now remains. She speaks only her mother tongue.'

The young man suddenly understood the woman's attitude and her desire to guess through her daughter's and Henri's movements what was happening between the two, and this understanding put him at ease.

'Paquita, will we then never be free?' he asked her.

'Never!' she said sadly. 'In fact, we have but a few days left.'

She lowered her eyes and looked at her hand, counting with her right hand the fingers of her left, thereby revealing to Henri the most beautiful hands he had ever seen.

'One, two, three...'

She counted to twelve.

'Yes,' she said, 'we have twelve days.'

'And then?'

'And then,' she said, still absorbed in thought, as though she were a frail woman facing the executioner's axe, one who has already been killed by fear and stripped of the magnificent energy which nature appeared to have accorded her, with the sole aim of enhancing her voluptuous attractions and transforming the most vulgar pleasures into endless poetry. 'And then,' she repeated. Her eyes glazed over; she seemed to be looking at something far away, something threatening. 'I don't know,' she said.

'This girl is mad,' Henri said to himself, immersed in strange thoughts of his own.

It seemed to him that Paquita was preoccupied with something other than him, like a woman torn equally between remorse and passion. Perhaps another passion beat in her heart, which she in turn forgot and remembered. Henri was assailed by a thousand contradictory thoughts. This girl was becoming a mystery to him, and yet, when considering her from the point of view of a knowledgeable man of the world who is hungry for new sensual pleasures, like an oriental king continually demanding fresh distractions to assuage the terrible thirst which plagues great souls, Henri discovered in Paquita the most sumptuous harmony that nature had ever succeeded in composing for the purpose of love. Imagining just the workings of this mechanism, without even involving the soul, would have terrified any lesser man than de Marsay: yet he was fascinated by this bounteous harvest of promised pleasures, by these unending variations on happiness which are every man's dream and the aim of every woman in love. He was driven wild by the idea of holding infinity in his hands, and his fantasy transported him to the realms of the utmost pleasure another being can offer. He saw all of this more clearly in the young girl than ever before, for she basked in his gaze, happy to be admired. De Marsay's admiration became a secret, devouring obsession, but his gaze revealed it completely. The Spanish woman's eyes told him that she understood; she was used to being looked at in that way.

'If you are not to be mine alone I will kill you,' he cried.

On hearing this, Paquita hid her face in her hands and exclaimed naively: 'Mother of God, what have I got myself into?'

She got up, threw herself upon the red divan, and buried her head in the rags which covered her mother's bosom: there she wept. The old woman accepted her daughter without moving, without showing any reaction. Her mother commanded to the highest degree the gravity of savage races, the impassivity of statues which confound all scrutiny. Did she or did she not love her daughter? It was impossible to tell. Every human emotion, good and bad, simmered beneath her mask, and this creature was capable of anything. Her gaze travelled slowly from the lovely hair which veiled her daughter's head like a mantilla to Henri's face, which she watched with an indefinable curiosity. She seemed to be wondering by what magic means he had come to be there, and what fluke of nature had fashioned such an attractive man.

'These women are making fun of me,' thought Henri.

At that moment Paquita lifted her head, threw him a look which penetrated his very soul and set it on fire. She seemed so lovely that he swore he would make that beautiful treasure his own.

'My Paquita, be mine!'

'Do you want to kill me?' she asked, frightened and trembling, disturbed yet drawn to him by an inexplicable attraction.

'Me, kill you?' he said smiling.

Paquita screamed in terror, and said something to the old woman, who took hold of Henri's hand and her daughter's commandingly, looked at the two for a long time, then released their hands, nodding her head in a horribly significant way.

'Be mine tonight, this very moment, come with me, never leave me, it is my wish, Paquita. Do you love me? Then come!'

In the space of an instant he poured out a torrent of meaningless words, at such speed that it was like a cascade crashing from rock to rock and producing the same notes in endless variations.

'This is the same voice!' said Paquita sadly, though so softly that de Marsay could not hear her. 'And the same fervour,' she added.

'Well then, so be it,' she said, throwing everything to the winds in a passion for which there are no words. 'Yes, but not tonight. Tonight, Adolphe, I have not given Doña Concha enough opium, she might wake up and I would be lost. At this moment everyone in the house thinks I am asleep in my room. Be at the same place in two days' time, use the same password. The man you'll see is my foster-father, Christemio, who worships me and would die under torture rather than say a word against me. Farewell,' she said, grasping Henri to her and wrapping her body about him like a serpent.

She folded him in her arms, nestled her head under his chin, offered him her lips for a kiss which made both of them so dizzy that de Marsay thought that the earth had opened beneath his feet, and made Paquita cry: 'Go away!' in tones which revealed clearly enough how little she was mistress of herself. She clung to him even as she cried, 'Go away!' and led him slowly to the staircase.

There, the mulatto, whose white eyes lit up at the sight of Paquita, took the torch from his adored mistress and brought Henri down to the street. He placed the torch under the archway, opened the coach-door, put Henri back into the carriage, and left him on the Boulevard des Italiens, all at amazing speed. The horses seemed to be driven by the devil himself.

To de Marsay, these dramatic events were as a dream, but one of those dreams which, as it fades, leaves a feeling of such supernatural pleasure that a man will chase after it for the rest of his life. A single kiss had sufficed. Never had an assignation been conducted with more decency, more purity, more coldness perhaps, in a place littered with such horrible objects and facing an even more hideous idol; for her mother was imprinted on Henri's imagination as some hellish, squatting, cadaverous, immoral, ferocious, and savage beast, a creature which the imagination of painters and poets had yet to conjure up. Indeed, no previous assignation had so inflamed his senses, or hinted at bolder pleasures, or caused so much love to flow from his heart until it seemed to surround him like a cloud. It was darkly mysterious, sweet and tender, both stifling and invigorating, a marriage of the horrific and the heavenly, paradise and hell, and intoxicating to de Marsay. He was no longer himself, but he was still man enough not to allow himself to be swept uncontrollably along by pleasure.

In order to understand his behaviour towards the end of this story, we shall have to explain how his personality had developed at an age when most young men limit their horizons either by dallying with women or becoming too preoccupied with one of them. As he grew up, a combination of mysterious circumstances had endowed him with enormous hidden powers. This young man held in his hand a sceptre more powerful than that wielded by recent monarchs, constrained as they are in their simplest wishes by the law. De Marsay exercised the autocratic power of an oriental despot. But this power, so clumsily applied in Asia by brutish men, was multiplied ten times over by the European intellect, by the French mind, the liveliest and sharpest of all intellectual instruments. Henri could do as he liked in pursuit of pleasure and ambition. The imperceptible effect of this on society had made him into a man of true majesty, albeit in secret, without any of its outward trappings and known only to himself. He saw himself not even as Louis XIV did, but rather as the proudest caliphs, pharaohs, and Xerxes* of this world believed they belonged to a divine race when they copied God by veiling their faces in the presence of their subjects, assuming they would be killed by looking on them.

Thus, feeling no remorse at being both judge and jury, de Marsay coldly condemned to death any man or woman who had gravely offended him. Although often pronounced lightly, the sentence was irrevocable. Any mistake he might make was simply an unfortunate incident, as when lightning strikes a Parisian lady travelling happily in a carriage instead of destroying the old coachman driving her to her assignation. Moreover, the profound and bitter mockery which marked de Marsay's conversation generally made his listeners frightened; no one wished to challenge him. Women fall head over heels in love with men who proclaim themselves to be pashas. Such men seem to be flanked by lions and henchmen, and to live and breathe all the trappings of terror. As a result, they are confident in their actions and certain of their power, with a proud bearing and a leonine sense of self which personifies for all women the kind of force they dream of. De Marsay was just such a man.

Happy at what the future held for him, he became once more that young man who was open to experience, and as he went to bed his thoughts were only of love. He dreamt of the Girl with the Golden Eyes in the way that passionate young men do. His dreams were full of monstrous images and inexplicable aberrations, flooding hitherto unknown worlds with their light, yet in visions which remained fragmentary, as if a veil had intervened to alter the conditions of perception. He disappeared for the next two days without letting anyone know of his whereabouts. He could only retain his powers if certain conditions were met and, luckily for him, during those two days he became simply a soldier in the service of the demon who granted him his charmed existence. But that evening, at the appointed hour, he awaited the carriage, which was exactly on time. The mulatto approached Henri and addressed him in French, with a phrase he had clearly learnt by heart: 'If you wish to come, she told me, you must agree to be blindfolded.'

And Christemio showed him a white silk scarf.

'No!' said Henri, whose innate sense of superiority suddenly rebelled at the idea. As he was about to enter the carriage, the mulatto gave a sign and the coachman drove off.

'All right!' shouted de Marsay, furious at having to forgo the pleasure he had anticipated. Yet how could he possibly yield to a slave whose blind obedience was like that of an executioner? And what would be the purpose in making such a passive instrument the object of his anger?

The mulatto whistled, and the carriage returned. Henri jumped in quickly. Already a few onlookers had gathered on the boulevard to gape. Henri was a strong man, and thought he might get the better of the mulatto. When the carriage started off at a fast pace, Henri seized the hands of his guard, in order to force him into submission and to concentrate his wits on working out where he was going. The attempt was in vain. The mulatto's eyes flashed in the darkness. He cried out, choking with fury, he wrenched himself free, flung de Marsay away with an arm of steel, and nailed him, so to speak, to the back of the carriage; then, with his free hand, he pulled out a triangular dagger and whistled to the coachman, who heard him and stopped. Henri was unarmed, he was forced to yield, and offered his head for the blindfold. This act of submission appeased Christemio, who tied the scarf over his eyes with a careful respect which expressed a kind of veneration for the person of this man whom his idol loved, but before taking these precautions he had defiantly put his dagger in his side pocket and buttoned up his coat to the chin.

'This Chinaman might have killed me!' said de Marsay to himself.

The carriage had started rolling swiftly forward again. There was one last resort left to a young man who knew Paris as well as Henri did. To know where he was going, he needed only to concentrate, as long as the carriage continued straight ahead, on counting the number of gutters* they crossed as they passed each street giving on to the boulevards. He would then be able to recognize which turn the carriage took, whether towards the Seine or towards the heights of Montmartre, and thus to guess either the name or the location of the street where his guide would stop the carriage.

But the violent shock caused by the struggle, his anger at the offence to his dignity, the thoughts of vengeance to which he gave way, his conjectures as to why this mysterious girl had gone to such lengths to bring him to her, all this prevented him from enjoying the heightened perception that a blind man would need in order to focus his intellect and sharpen the perfect accuracy of his memory. The journey took half an hour. When the carriage stopped it was no longer on the cobbles. The coachman and the mulatto took hold of Henri, lifted him up and put him on a kind of litter, and carried him through a garden, where he could smell the flowers and the various scents of the trees and shrubbery. The silence which reigned there was so profound that he could make out the sound of some raindrops falling from the wet leaves. The two men carried him up a staircase, set him back on his feet, guided him through a number of rooms, leading him by the hands, and left him in a chamber where the air was perfumed and he could feel a thick carpet beneath his feet. A woman's hand pushed him onto a divan and untied his blindfold. Henri saw Paquita in front of him, but it was Paquita in all her voluptuous feminine glory.

The part of the boudoir where Henri found himself traced the graceful curve of a soft semicircle, which contrasted with the perfect square of the other half, in the middle of which gleamed a white-and-gold marble mantelpiece. He had come in by a side door, hidden behind a rich tapestry curtain, opposite which was a window. The horsehoe-shaped alcove displayed a genuine Turkish divan, that is, a mattress, flat on the floor. The divan was the widest of beds, measuring fifty feet round, covered in white cashmere embroidered with bows of black and poppy-red silk, sewn in diamond patterns. The head of this immense bed rose several inches higher than the profusion of cushions which adorned it with tasteful effect.

The walls of the boudoir were hung with red material, over which some Indian muslin was draped, fluted like Corinthian columns with alternating grooves and piping, gathered together at top and bottom by a scarlet sash embroidered with black arabesques. Behind the muslin the poppy-red became pink, the colour of love, which was echoed at the window by the curtains of Indian muslin, which were lined with pink taffeta and decorated with tassles mingling the poppy and the black. Six silver-gilt candelabras, each holding two candles, projected from the wall, illuminating the divan at equal intervals. The ceiling, from the middle of which hung a chandelier of unburnished silver-gilt, was dazzlingly white, and the cornice was picked out in gold. The carpet looked like an oriental shawl and displayed designs alluding to the poetry of Persia, where it had been fashioned by the hands of slaves. The furniture was upholstered in white cashmere, set off with flecks of black and poppy. The clock and the candelabras were all in white marble and gold. The solitary table in the room was covered by a cashmere cloth. Elegant flowerpots contained roses of every variety, with white or red blooms. Every last detail seemed to have been accorded loving attention. Never had wealth been so charmingly disguised to suggest elegance, express grace, and inspire pleasure. The entire scene would have inflamed the coldest heart. The shimmering wall-coverings changed colour, depending on the angle from which they were seen, becoming either pure white or pink, and reflected the play of light filtering through the diaphanous fluting of the muslin, creating misty visions. The soul is somehow attracted to white, love delights in red, and gold encourages our desire, as it has the power to make its dreams come true. And hence all the vague and mysterious feelings in a man, all those inexplicable affinities, are enhanced by the caress of their silent, mutual understanding. This perfect harmony of colours created a concert to which his soul responded with voluptuous, vague, elusive ideas.

It was amid this hazy atmosphere laden with exquisite scents that Paquita, dressed in a white negligée, bare-footed, with orange blossom in her black hair, appeared on her knees before Henri, worshipping him like a god in this temple where he had deigned to appear. Although he was used to seeing the most refined Parisian luxury, de Marsay was taken by surprise at the sight of this sea-shell, so like the birthplace of Venus. Whether it was the contrast between the dark shadows which he had left behind or the light which now bathed his soul, or whether it was the sudden comparison between this scene and their first encounter, he experienced one of those delicate sensations that we receive only from true poetry. As he saw such a masterpiece of creation arise and blossom at the wave of a fairy's wand in the middle of a magic enclave, this young woman with her warm-hued complexion, whose soft skin, gently gilded by the reflections of the reddish light and flushed with some hint of her love, glowed as though reflecting the lights and colours, all his anger, desire for vengeance, and hurt pride fell away. Like an eagle swooping down on its prey, he swept her up in his arms, sat her on his knees, and felt with inexpressible ecstasy the voluptuous pressure of the girl's beautiful, plump curves as they gently enfolded him.

'Come, Paquita!' he murmured softly.

'No need to whisper! Have no fear,' she said to him, 'this retreat has been designed for love, no sound can escape it, so strong was the desire to contain all the words and music of lovers' voices. However loud their cries, they would not be heard beyond these four walls. You could kill someone here, and his cries would no more be heard than if he were in the middle of the Great Desert.'

'Tell me who it is who has understood jealousy and its demands so well?'

'Never ask me that question again,' she replied, untying his neckcloth with a gesture of infinite tenderness, no doubt in order to get a better view of his neck.

'Oh, here is that neck that I so adore!' she said. 'Do you want to please me?'

This question, spoken in a tone that was almost lascivious, brought de Marsay's thoughts back from the speculation into which Paquita's peremptory response had thrown him, prohibiting any further enquiry into the mysterious being who hovered like a shadow over their heads.

'And what if I wanted to know who rules this kingdom?'

Paquita looked at him and trembled.

'So it isn't me,' he said, standing up and releasing himself from her grasp, so suddenly that she fell backwards. 'I want to be the only one, wherever I am.'

'Go ahead, hit me!' said the poor slave, gripped by terror.

'Who do you take me for? Will you answer me?'

Paquita rose slowly to her feet, took a dagger from one of the ebony chests, and held it out to Henri with a gesture of submission which would have softened the heart of a tiger.

'Treat me to a veritable feast of love,' she said, 'then while I am asleep, kill me, for then I shall not be able to defend myself. Listen: I am tethered to a stake like some poor beast; I am amazed that I was able to throw a bridge across the ravine that divides us. Intoxicate me, and then kill me.' Then, wringing her hands, she declared 'No, no! Don't kill me, I love life! Life is so beautiful to me! I may be a slave but I am also a queen. I could lead you astray with subtle words, tell you that I love only you, and prove it to you, make use of my brief reign to say, "Take me, as you would enjoy in passing the scent of a flower in a king's garden". Then, after using a woman's persuasive wiles and arousing your desire and soaring on the wings of pleasure that it inspires, having slaked my thirst, I could have you thrown into a pit where nobody would find you, a pit which had been dug to satisfy my vengeance without having to fear the repercussions of the law, a pit full of lime which would burn and consume you, leaving no trace of your being. You would live on in my heart, mine forever.'

Henri looked at the girl unwaveringly, and his fearless gaze filled her with joy.

'No, I shall not do it! You have not fallen into a trap, but into the heart of a woman who adores you, and it is I who shall be cast into a pit,' she said.

'All of this seems prodigiously droll,' said de Marsay, scrutinizing her. 'You seem to me to be well intentioned, yet a curious kind of girl; but you are, upon my word, a living charade whose meaning seems very difficult to guess.'

Paquita did not understand anything the young man was saying; she gazed at him softly, widening her eyes, with a look that could never seem stupid, since it revealed such intense desire.

'Well, my love,' she said, coming back to her first idea, 'do you want to please me?'

'I will do anything you want, and even things that you don't want,' de Marsay replied with a laugh, having rediscovered his former foppish manner now that he had decided to enjoy his good fortune without a backward or a forward glance. Then again, perhaps he was relying on his power and his skill as a man whom fate had favoured, to take possession of this girl in a few hours' time and learn all her secrets.

'So,' she said, 'let me dress you up according to my fancy.'

'Just as you choose,' said Henri,

Full of joy, Paquita took a red velvet dress from one of the chests, dressed de Marsay in it, then put a bonnet on his head and wrapped him in a shawl. And while giving herself up to this foolish game, played out with childish innocence, she was convulsed by gales of laughter, as free of care as a bird on the wing, and she saw nothing beyond the moment.

If it is impossible to describe the extraordinary delights experienced by these two beautiful creatures fashioned by heaven in one of its lighter moments, it is perhaps necessary to translate into metaphysical terms this young man's extraordinary and almost fantastical impressions. People who move in such social spheres as de Marsay and enjoy the same lifestyle recognize innocence in a young girl with the utmost ease. But strange as it may seem, if the Girl with the Golden Eyes was a virgin, she was certainly far from innocent. The strange marriage of the mysterious and the real, of light and shade, of the grotesque and the beautiful, of delight and danger, of paradise and inferno, which had already been encountered in the course of this adventure, continued to be expressed in the sublime but capricious creature with whom de Marsay was dallying. All the refinements of erotic pleasure, all that sensual poetry called love that Henri knew, was altogether insignificant in comparison with the treasures dispensed by this girl, whose luminous eyes never disappointed the promises they made. She was an oriental poem, radiant with the sunlight that Saadi and Hafiz* captured in their rapturous stanzas. Except that neither Saadi's nor Pindar's* rhythm could have expressed the ecstatic confusion and wonderment which seized that gorgeous girl, now that the iron hand which had for so long wrongly held her captive released its grip.

'Dead!' she said. 'I am dead. Adolphe, take me to the ends of the earth, to an island where we are completely unknown. Let us flee, leaving no trace! They will pursue us to the gates of Hell. My God! Dawn is breaking. Go. Will I ever see you again? Yes, tomorrow! I want to see you even if, for this pleasure, I have to kill all of my guards. Till tomorrow.'

She clasped him in her arms in an embrace full of mortal fear. She pulled a cord that must have been connected to a bell, and begged de Marsay to let himself be blindfolded.

'What if I no longer agreed, and what if I wanted to stay here?'

'You would hasten my death,' she said, 'for now I am certain that I shall die for you.'

Henri let her have her way. In a man who has gorged himself on pleasure we encounter a tendency to forget, a certain ingratitude, a wish to break free, an odd urge to take a breath of fresh air, a hint of contempt and perhaps distaste for his idol, that is to say, we encounter inexplicable feelings which render him despicable and base. The sure knowledge of this confusing but very real affliction of any soul which is not illuminated by the heavenly light nor scented with the holy balm which grant us insight into our feelings, is no doubt what led Rousseau to write the story of Lord Edward Bomston which concludes the letters of *La Nouvelle Héloïse*. Although Rousseau was obviously inspired by Richardson's fiction,* he departs from it in a thousand details which make this monumental work splendidly original. What has guaranteed its survival over the years are its grand ideas, which we tend to overlook when, in our youth, we read this book seeking a vivid depiction of our deepest sensual experience, whereas in fact we are unaware that philosophers and other serious writers resort to such imagery only when they can find no other way to express their deepest thoughts; and the experiences of Lord Edward represent indeed one of the most refined concepts in European fiction.

So Henri, under the sway of this confused emotion which is so alien to true love, needed somehow consciously to avoid making comparisons or yielding to the irresistible charm of memory in order to lead him back to a woman. True love reigns above all through remembrance. Can we ever love a woman who has not left her indelible imprint on our soul, either through excess of pleasure or intensity of feeling? Unknown to Henri, Paquita had established herself within him by both means. But for the moment he was so given over to the fatigue of happiness, that delicious melancholia of the body, that he was in no state to question his heart as he relived on his lips the taste of the most thrilling pleasures he had ever savoured. He found himself on the Boulevard Montmartre in the small hours, watched the horses and carriages in a daze as they sped away, drew two cigars from his pocket and lit one at the lantern of the good woman selling brandy and coffee to workmen, urchins, and street vendors, that whole Parisian populace which starts its day before dawn; he then went on his way, smoking his cigar and putting his hands in his trouser pockets in a shamefully casual fashion.

'What a fine thing a cigar is! That's truly something a man can never tire of,' said he to himself.

He spared hardly a thought for that Girl with the Golden Eyes who at the time had set the pulses of all the elegant young men in Paris racing. The notion of death lurking behind their pleasures, the fear of which had more than once darkened the brow of that lovely creature who was part Asian *houri** on her mother's side, part European through education, and part tropical by birth, seemed to him to be one of the tricks used by all women to make themselves interesting.

'She comes from Havana, from the most Spanish country of them all in the New World, so she chose to play the card of terror rather than woes or worries, coquetry or duty, as a Parisian woman would. Damn her golden eyes, I need to get some sleep.'

He saw a cabriolet for hire on the street corner outside Frascati's, waiting around for any gamblers to emerge. He roused the driver and had himself driven home, went to bed, and fell into the slumber of the wicked, which, though it has never been cited in a music-hall quip, is, strangely, just as deep as the slumber of the innocent. Which is perhaps an example of the proverbial saying, that extremes will tend to meet.

Towards midday de Marsay woke up, stretched, and felt as hungry as a wolf, with those pangs that any old soldier can remember feeling on the day after a victory. So he was glad to see Paul de Manerville standing in front of him, for nothing is more enjoyable than dining with friends.

'Well, well,' said his friend, 'we have all been imagining you closeted with the Girl with the Golden Eyes for the last ten days.'

'The Girl with the Golden Eyes! I haven't given her a second thought. Upon my word, I have plenty of other fish to fry.'

'Oh, so you are being discreet.'

'Why not?' said de Marsay laughing. 'My dear boy, discretion is often the better part of valour. Listen... but no, I won't say a word. You never take me into your confidence. I am not disposed to waste the secrets of my precious schemes on you. Life is a stream which turns the mill-wheels of commerce. By all that is holiest in this world, upon my cigars, I'm not here to teach social economics to an audience of nincompoops. Let's have lunch. It will cost me less to serve you fresh tuna in an omelette than to deliver up my brains.'

'Do you keep accounts with your friends?'

'My dear man,' said Henri, who hardly ever let an opportunity for sarcasm escape him, 'as you may well have an occasion to employ discretion—like any other man—and since I am fond of you, yes indeed, very fond, on my word of honour, if it needed only a thousand franc note to stop you from blowing your brains out here is where you would find it, for we are not yet in hock to the devil, are we, Paul? If you were to fight a duel tomorrow I would measure the paces and load the pistols, to make sure that you would be killed according to the rules and regulations. What is more, if someone other than I were to venture to speak ill of you behind your back, he would have to deal with the rough gentleman who dwells within me: that is what I mean by friendship, tried and tested. So then, when you do need discretion, my boy, remember that there are two kinds of discretion: positive and negative. Negative discretion is for fools who use silence, negation, and sulking behind closed doors, impotence personified! Positive discretion works through positive statements. So, if tonight at the club I were to say, "Upon my word as a gentleman, the Girl with the Golden Eyes is not worth the price I paid!" everyone, after I had left, would exclaim: "Did you hear that fop, de Marsay, trying to make us believe that he has already had the Girl with the Golden Eyes? Not a bad way of trying to shake off his rivals. Just how clumsy can you be?" But this ploy is both crude and risky, because however crassly stupid the remark we let slip, there will always be some idiots ready to believe it. The best kind of discretion is that employed by clever women when they want to deceive their husbands. It consists in compromising a woman that we don't care about, or are not in love with, or do not possess, in order to protect the honour of the woman whom we both love and respect. It's what I call a dummy mistress. Ah, here is Laurent. What do you have for us?'

'Oysters from Ostend, my Lord.'

'One day, Paul, you will understand how amusing it is to deceive society by disguising where your affections lie. I find it immensely gratifying to escape from the stupid jurisdiction of the crowd, who can never tell what they want, nor what they have been persuaded to want, who take the means for the ends, who by turns adore and curse, raise up and cast down everything! What a pleasure it is to dictate emotions to others, but refuse to receive any of theirs in return, to control them, and never obey them! If there is one thing that we can be proud of, is it not acquiring power on our own account, being both its cause and effect, its origin and outcome? Very well, no one knows whom I love nor what I want. Perhaps people will discover whom it was that I loved and what I would have loved and desired, as one learns the outcome of a play. But why should I let anyone see the cards I hold? That would be cowardly cheating. I have nothing but contempt for strength which allows itself to be outwitted by sleight-of-hand. I am learning, with utter lack of seriousness, the art of diplomacy, supposedly as difficult as learning how to live. I have my doubts about that. Are you ambitious? Do you want to make your mark?'

'But, Henri, you are making fun of me, as if I were not mediocre enough to succeed in anything I wanted to do.'

'Well done, Paul, if you carry on making fun of yourself, you will soon be able to make fun of the whole world.'

As the meal progressed, and de Marsay moved on to his cigar, he began to see the events of the previous night in a strange light. Like so many great minds, his intuition was not immediate, and he could not go straight to the heart of the matter. Like those gifted with the ability to live fully in the moment, to extract the very marrow and devour it, in order to arrive at a considered opinion, his mind needed a period of rest, before coming to terms with the explanation. Cardinal Richelieu* was similar in this respect, although this did not diminish the powers of foresight necessary for him to plan the greatest enterprises. De Marsay fulfilled all the same conditions, but at first he employed his talents purely in the service of enjoyment, and it was only after he had indulged to the point of satiety those pleasures which are uppermost in every young man's mind when he has money and power, that he would become one of the most thoughtful political men of our times. This is how a man hardens his heart: he makes use of women so that women cannot make use of him.

Thus it was only now that de Marsay realized that he had been deceived by the Girl with the Golden Eyes, when he considered the night as a whole, a night during which pleasure grew gradually from a gentle trickle to a raging torrent. Only now could he read the hidden meaning behind the dazzling surface of that page. Paquita's purely physical innocence, her cries of surprised pleasure, those words which escaped her in the throes of rapture, at first obscure but now crystal clear, were all proof that for her he was a replacement for somebody else. As de Marsay was perfectly acquainted with all forms of social immorality, and declared himself absolutely indifferent to every one of its forms and fancies, believing them justified by the very fact that they led to satisfaction, he was not afraid of vice, since it was as familiar to him as a friend, but he was upset to have been used as its fodder. If his suspicions were right, he had been most outrageously insulted in the core of his being. The mere thought of this filled him with fury. He let forth the roar of a tiger taunted by a gazelle, a tiger whose bestial force was allied to the intelligence of the devil.

'My goodness, what's the matter with you?' asked Paul.

'Nothing.'

'If someone were to ask you if you had anything to reproach me with, and you replied with a "nothing" like that, I should not like it at all, and we would have to fight a duel the next day, I'm sure.'

'I don't fight duels any more,' said de Marsay.

'That seems to me even more lamentable. So you would rather commit murder, would you?'

'You are twisting my words. I am an executioner.'

'My dear friend,' said Paul, 'your sense of humour is really very black this morning.'

'It can't be helped, the search for pleasure always leads to cruelty. Why that should be, I have no idea, and I am not that interested in finding out the reasons. (These cigars are excellent. Be a good fellow, will you, and pour me some tea?) Are you aware,

Paul, that I lead a brutish life? It's high time that I sorted out my destiny, used the strength I possess to some purpose that would make life worth living. Life is a strangely comic piece of theatre. The absurdity of our social order is appalling and risible. The government has any poor devil beheaded for killing a man, yet it licenses creatures who every winter put a dozen or so young men out of their misery, to use a medical term. Morality is powerless to deal with a dozen evils which are undermining society, but which can never be punished.—Another cup?—Upon my word, man is a clown dancing on the edge of a cliff. People talk about the immorality of *Dangerous Liaisons*, and some other book with a chambermaid's name for a title;* but there is a ghastly, filthy, disgusting book full of corruption always lying open for all to read, never to be shut: by that I mean the great book we call society; without mentioning another one, which is a thousand times more treacherous, and consists of all that men say to each other in whispers, or women share behind their fans in the evening at a ball.'

'Henri, something extraordinary must be affecting you, and it is quite obvious, despite your "positive discretion".'

'Indeed! I need to fritter away my time between now and this evening. Let's go and play cards. Perhaps I shall be lucky enough to lose.'

De Marsay rose, picked up a fistful of banknotes, stuffed them into his cigar-case, got dressed, and took advantage of Paul's carriage to go to the Salon des Étrangers,* where he used up the time until dinner on the thrilling alternatives of winning and losing, which are the last resort of a strong constitution when it is condemned to enforced inactivity. That evening he kept his appointment, and allowed himself uncomplainingly to be blindfolded. Then, concentrating his resolve in a way that only truly strong men can, he turned all his attention and applied all his intelligence to guessing through which streets the carriage was passing. He felt fairly certain that they had gone along the Rue Saint-Lazare and stopped in front of the side gate of the garden of the Hôtel San-Réal. As he passed through the entrance, he was lifted onto a litter, no doubt by the mulatto and the coachman, as had happened before. Hearing the sand crunching beneath their feet, he understood why they were taking such meticulous precautions. Had he been free, or able to walk, he might have been able to pluck a twig from a shrub, or note what kind of sand had stuck to his boots, whereas he was being transported, as it were, to a secret palace, for, once again, his happy fate was to remain as before in the land of dreams. Yet, to our eternal despair, none of our actions, whether for good or for ill, ever go exactly according to plan. All our physical and intellectual efforts are branded by the seal of destruction. There had been some light rain overnight, and the soil was still moist. At night-time certain plants have a much stronger scent than during the day, so that Henri was aware of the smell of sweet mignonette which lined the path along which they were carrying him. This was a clue that would help the enquiries he intended to make into finding the house where Paquita's boudoir was located. He paid the same attention to the twists and turns which his bearers took within the house, and thought he would be able to remember them.

As on the previous evening, he found himself on the divan, with Paquita standing in front of him undoing his blindfold, but she seemed pale and altered. She had been crying. Kneeling like an angel in prayer, but a sad and profoundly melancholy angel, the girl bore no resemblance to the lively, impatient, and exuberant creature who had swept de Marsay off his feet and transported him to love's seventh heaven. There was something so true about her despair, hidden behind a veil of enjoyment, that, even in his fury, de Marsay felt a certain admiration for this freshly minted masterpiece of nature, and forgot for the moment the main purpose of this assignation.

'So what is the matter, dear Paquita?'

'Dearest, take me away this very night, take me away somewhere where no one can catch sight of me and say "Look, that is Paquita"; and no one will reply, "That is the Girl with the Golden Eyes and the long hair". There I will afford you every pleasure you might ask of me. Then, when you cease to love me, and you leave me, I shall not complain, I shall not say a word, and you must not feel any remorse at having abandoned me, since one day spent with you close to me, one single day when I could feast my eyes upon you will be worth an entire lifetime to me. But if I stay here a moment longer, I am doomed.'

'I cannot leave Paris, my love,' replied Henri, 'I am not my own master. I have pledged an oath to a group of men who would give their lives for me, as I would for them. But I can find you a safe haven in Paris where no human hand can touch you.'

'No,' she said, 'you are forgetting the power of a woman.'

Never had a phrase spoken by a human voice expressed such utter terror.

'Who could possibly touch you, if I were there to defend you?'

'Poison,' she said. 'Doña Concha suspects you already. And', she continued, while tears flowed, glistening, down her cheeks, 'it is easy enough to see the change in me. Very well, if you wish to abandon me to the monster whose prey I am, then let your will be done. But come, let none of life's pleasures be excluded from our love. Be warned, I shall beg for mercy, I shall weep, I shall fight, I may run away.'

'Who will you call on for mercy?' he asked.

'Be quiet,' Paquita replied. 'If I am to be pardoned it will perhaps be because I have remained discreet.'

'Give me my dress,' said Henri, deviously.

'No, no,' she replied sharply, 'stay as you are, one of those angels that I was taught to hate, who seemed nothing but monsters, whereas you are one of the most beautiful creatures under heaven,' she said, stroking Henri's hair. 'Do you have any idea of my ignorance? I have no education. Since I was twelve I have been locked away and have spoken to no one. I cannot read or write, I speak only English and Spanish.'

'So why is it that they write to you from London?'

'My letters! Here, look at them,' she said, taking some papers out of a tall Japanese vase.

She held out to de Marsay letters where the young man was surprised to see strange characters like those of a pictogram, traced in blood, and illustrating notions charged with passion.

'But', he cried, as he admired these hieroglyphs skilfully crafted by a jealous hand, 'are you under the spell of some diabolical genie?'

'Diabolical,' she echoed.

'But how did you manage to escape...?'

'Ah! That is where I went astray. I forced Doña Concha to choose between the fear of instant death and the threat of some future revenge. I had a devilish curiosity, I wanted to break out of the iron railings which had been erected between nature and me, I wanted to discover what young men were like, for the only men that I knew were the Marquis and Christemio. Our coachman and the valet who waits on us are old men...'

'But you were not always confined? Your health must have...'

'Oh! We did go for walks,' she continued, 'but only by night, in the country, along the Seine, far from any people.'

'Are you not proud of the love which you inspire?'

'No, no longer! Although it was rich, my secret life was but shadow compared with the light of day.'

'What do you mean by the light of day?'

'You, my handsome Adolphe! You, for whom I would give my life. All the words of passion that I have heard and that I inspired, I feel for you! There were moments when I understood nothing of life, but now I know how we love one another, and that before this I was merely loved, without being in love myself. I would leave everything for you. Take me away! If you wish, treat me as your plaything, but keep me by your side until you break me.'

'Will you have no regrets?'

'No, never,' she said, opening her eyes for him to read their golden purity and clarity.

'Is it me she really prefers?' wondered Henri, who, if he surmised the truth, felt disposed to pardon the offence in favour of a love so naive. 'We shall see,' he thought.

Even though Paquita owed him no account of the past, the slightest act of remembrance became a crime in his eyes. He had therefore the unhappy task of mastering his own thoughts, of judging his mistress, of contemplating her while giving way to pleasures more celestial than any that might be bestowed on her beloved by a fairy queen descending from heaven. Paquita seemed to have been created for love, by a special favour of Nature. From one night to the next, her feminine genius had advanced in leaps and bounds. Whatever the powers of the young man, and his casual attitude to pleasure, and however sated he was from the previous night, he found in the Girl with the Golden Eyes that harem which a woman in love knows how to create and which no man will ever abandon. Paquita was the answer to the passion for the infinite which all truly great men feel, that mysterious passion so dramatically expressed in *Faust*, so poetically described in *Manfred*, and which drove Don Juan* to ransack the hearts of women, hoping to find there that limitless thought which so many people in pursuit of phantoms seek, which scholars think they glimpse in science, and which mystics believe resides only in God. The hope of having found the ideal being with whom the struggle might be constant, but never tiring, ravished de Marsay, who, for the first time in many years, opened up his heart. His nerves relaxed, his coldness melted, in the warmth of this burning soul; his doctrinaire opinions were cast to the winds, and his existence was bathed in a happiness coloured in the pink and white of her boudoir. Feeling the spur of a higher pleasure, he was drawn beyond the limits within which he had previously confined his passions. He did not wish to be surpassed by a girl whose love, although somewhat artificial, had been moulded in advance to suit the needs of his soul, and so, in the vanity which drives men to conquer all, he found the strength to tame the girl. Yet he had crossed the threshold beyond which the soul is no longer its own master, and lost himself in that delicious limbo which common people foolishly call the space of the imagination. He was tender, kind, and communicative. He made Paquita almost mad with love.

'Why couldn't we go to Sorrento, to Nice, to Chiavari, and spend all our lives like this? Would you like that?' he asked Paquita, urgently.

'Do you ever need to ask me "Would you like that?"' she cried. 'Do I have any will of my own? My only existence outside you is as an object of pleasure for you. If you want to find a refuge worthy of us, Asia is the only country where passion can unfurl its wings...'

'You are right,' replied Henri, 'let us go to India, the land of eternal spring, where the earth is always covered in flowers, where man can unleash his sovereign power without being subject to gossip, as in those foolish countries that want to fulfil the sorry fantasy of equality. Let us go to a land where we live surrounded by slaves, where the sun always shines on an all-white palace, where perfumes pervade the air, where the birds sing of love, and where we die only when we can no longer love...'

'And where we shall die together!' said Paquita. 'But let us not leave tomorrow, let us leave immediately and take Christemio with us.'

'In truth, pleasure is the finest goal in life. Let us go to Asia, but to be able to leave, my child, we need gold, and to be able to get our hands on it, we need to settle our affairs.'

She had no idea what he meant.

'There is gold here, this high!' she said, raising her hand.

'It doesn't belong to me.'

'What does that matter?' she replied. 'If we need it, let us take it.'

'It does not belong to you.'

'Belong!' she replied. 'Have you not taken possession of me? When we have taken it, it will belong to us.'

He laughed.

'Poor innocent girl! You know nothing of the ways of the world.'

'No, but here is something I do know,' she said, pulling Henri down on top of her.

At the very moment when de Marsay forgot everything, and formed the desire to make this creature his own forever, he was stabbed in the midst of his joy by a blow which pierced his mortified heart through and through for the first time. Paquita, who had suddenly thrust him away in order to gaze at him in admiration, had cried: 'Oh, Mariquita!'

'Mariquita!' thundered the young man. 'Now I know for certain something which I had always hoped was not true.'

He rushed to the cupboard which housed the long dagger. Luckily for her and for him, the cupboard was locked. This obstacle exacerbated his rage; but he recovered his calm, went to find his neckcloth, and marched towards her with such a significantly threatening air that, without knowing what crime she was guilty of, Paquita realized her life was in danger. So she made a bound towards the other end of the room to avoid the fatal noose that de Marsay had made for her neck. They fought. They were equally skilful, agile, and strong. As her last move, Paquita threw a cushion at her lover's legs, causing him to fall, and took advantage of the respite in order to pull on her alarm-bell. The mulatto arrived straight away. Christemio pounced on de Marsay, threw him to the ground, and placed one foot on his chest, with his heel at his throat. De Marsay realized that if he resisted he would be killed at a sign from Paquita.

'Why would you want to kill me, my love?' she asked him.

De Marsay made no reply.

'What did I do to offend you?' she asked. 'Tell me. Let me explain.'

Henri maintained the phlegmatic air of the strong man who knows that he has been beaten, his typically English cold and silent expression, demonstrating through his momentary resignation a self-conscious dignity. In fact, despite his fit of anger, he had already judged it imprudent to trifle with the law by killing this girl on the spot, without having prepared the murder in a way that would ensure his impunity.

'My love,' said Paquita, 'talk to me. Do not leave me without a lover's farewell! I do not wish to keep in my heart the terror with which you have filled it.—Will you not speak!' She stamped her foot in anger.

De Marsay's response was to flash her a look which so clearly said '*You shall die!*' that Paquita rushed at him.

'Well then, do you want to kill me? If my death will make you happy, kill me!'

She gestured to Christemio, who removed his foot from the young man's chest and left the room without betraying by his expression what he thought of Paquita's behaviour, good or bad.

'There's a real man!' said de Marsay, pointing at the mulatto with sinister intent. 'The only loyalty that counts is loyalty which follows friendship without judging it. In that man you have a true friend.'

'I'll give him to you if you want him,' she replied. 'He will serve you as loyally as he has served me if I ask him to do so.'

While waiting for his answer, she added tenderly: 'Adolphe, say something nice to me. Dawn is breaking.'

Henri did not reply. This young man had a dark side to his character, like many who tend to revere anything that resembles brute force, and thus often idolize excess. Henri was unable to forgive. Second thoughts, which are surely one of our spiritual graces, were meaningless for him. The ferocity of the men of the north, whose blood runs strongly through the veins of the English, had been passed on to him by his father. His sentiments, good or evil, were unshakeable. Paquita's exclamation was all the more horrible to him for spoiling the most triumphant moment of his masculine pride. Hope, love, and other emotions had inflamed his heart and his mind, but these sparks, kindled to light up his path through life, had been blown out by a cold wind. Paquita, stupefied with grief, had only the strength to tell him to leave.

'There's no point,' she said, throwing the blindfold away, 'if he doesn't love me, if he hates me, it's all over.'

She looked for a response in his eyes, found none, and fell in a dead faint. The mulatto shot Henri such a horribly significant look that the young man, for all his intrepid reputation, trembled with fear for the first time in his life.

'If you do not love her well, if you cause her the slightest harm, I shall kill you,' was the import of this flash of the eyes. De Marsay was led with almost obsequious concern down a dimly lit corridor, at the end of which he went out through a hidden door and down a secret staircase which led to the garden of the Hôtel San-Réal. The mulatto walked him cautiously along an alley of lime trees which ended at a small gate, opening onto a street which in those days was deserted. De Marsay took note of it all, and the carriage awaited him; this time the mulatto did not follow, and just as Henri leant out of the carriage window to catch sight of the gardens and the mansion, his eyes met the white eyes of Christemio and they exchanged glances. Each offered provocation, a challenge, suggestions of savage warfare, of a duel where ordinary rules were invalid, where treachery and treason would be legitimate means. Christemio knew that Henri had sworn to kill Paquita. Henri knew that Christemio wanted to kill him before he killed Paquita. They understood each other perfectly.

'The adventure becomes rather interestingly complicated.'

'Where would Monsieur like to go?' the coachman asked.

De Marsay asked to be driven to see Paul de Manerville.

For over a week Henri was absent from his home, letting nobody know what he was doing or where he was living. This absence saved him from the fury of the mulatto, and brought about the doom of the poor creature who had placed all her hopes in the man whom she had loved as nobody had loved anyone before on this earth. On the last day of this week, at about eleven o'clock in the evening, Henri came by carriage to the garden gate of the Hôtel San-Réal. He was accompanied by three men. The coachman was obviously also a friend of his, for he stood up by his seat like a watchman on guard listening for the slightest sound. Of the three others, one stood outside the gate, in the street; the second waited in the garden, leaning against the wall; and the third, holding a fistful of keys, accompanied de Marsay.

'Henri,' said de Marsay's companion, 'we are betrayed.'

'By whom, Ferragus, my friend?'

'They are not all asleep,' replied the leader of the Dévorants:* 'It is obvious that someone in the house has neither wined nor dined. Look, do you see that light?'

'We have a plan of the house. Where is the light coming from?'

'I don't need the plan to know,' replied Ferragus, 'it is the Marquise's bedroom.'

'Ah!' cried de Marsay. 'She must have arrived from London today. That woman will have stolen my revenge. But if she got there first, Gratien my friend, we will hand her over to the law.'

'Hark, now. The deed is done,' said Ferragus to Henri.

The two friends listened, and heard muffled cries which would have softened the heart of a tiger.

'Your Marquise didn't realize that the noise could be heard

coming out of the chimney-stack,' said the leader of the Dévorants, with the laugh of a critic delighted to find a flaw in a work of art.

'We alone know how to plan for all contingencies,' said Henri. 'Wait here, I am going to see what is happening up there, to find out how they deal with their domestic squabbles. In the name of God, I think that she must be roasting her over a slow fire.'

De Marsay swiftly mounted the familiar staircase and found his way to the boudoir. When he opened the door, he reacted with the instinctive shudder of any man, however determined, at the sight of great bloodshed. The scene that met his eyes gave him ample cause for astonishment. Like the woman she was, the Marquise had planned her revenge with the cunning perfidy that distinguishes the weaker animal. She had hidden her anger in order to ascertain the exact nature of the crime before proceeding to punish it.

'Too late, my beloved!' said Paquita, whose pale eyes turned towards de Marsay as she lay dying.

The Girl with the Golden Eyes was expiring, drowning in blood. The many lighted candles, the traces of delicate perfume that he could detect, a certain disorder which the eye of a man of experience would recognize as a sign of that excess common to all kinds of passion, showed that the Marquise had subjected the guilty party to some refined questioning. This white-painted apartment, where the blood showed up so brightly, revealed a prolonged struggle. Paquita's hands had left their prints all over the cushions. Everywhere she had clung to life, everywhere had defended herself, and everywhere she had been struck. Great shreds of the pleated tapestry had been torn away by her bloodstained hands, which had obviously held on as long as possible. Paquita must have tried to claw her way up towards the ceiling. Her naked footprints marked the divan along which she must have run. Her body, slashed by her executioner's dagger, bore witness to the ferocity with which she had fought for her life, which Henri had rendered so dear to her. She lay on the ground where, as she died, she had bitten right through the flesh to the muscles of Madame de San-Réal's instep. The Marquise's hand still clasped the bloodstained dagger; some of her hair had been ripped out, she was covered in bite-marks, some still bleeding, and her torn dress revealed her half-naked body, with scratches on her breasts. She looked sublime.

Her avid, furious face drowned in the smell of blood. Her mouth, still panting, was half open, and her distended nostrils were still struggling to inhale. Some animals, when goaded to a state of fury, pounce on their prey, slay it, and, reassured by their victory, seem to forget all about it. Others circle round their victim, holding it prisoner for fear that someone might cheat them of it, and then, like Homer's Achilles, drag their enemy by the feet nine times round the walls of Troy.* Such was the Marquise. She did not see Henri. At first she had felt sufficiently alone not to fear witnesses, then she had been so intoxicated by the warm blood, so excited, so exhilarated by the struggle that she would not have noticed if the entire population of Paris had been looking on. The house could have been struck by lightning without her noticing it. She had not even heard Paquita's dying gasp, and thought that the dead woman could still hear her.

'Die without confession!' she told her. 'Go to Hell, you monster of ingratitude, may you belong to no one but the Devil. For every drop of blood you have spilt for that man, you owe me all of yours! Die, die, die a thousand deaths! I was too kind, I took only a moment to kill you, I would have liked to make you feel all the pain that I am left with. As for me, I shall live on and shall suffer as long as I live. I shall be reduced to loving only God!'

She gazed at her. 'She's dead,' she said to herself, after a pause, with a violent shudder. 'Dead! Oh, I shall die of grief!'

The Marquise made as if to throw herself on the divan, overwhelmed with despair and robbed of speech, but as she did so she became aware of the presence of Henri de Marsay.

'Who are you?' she asked, as she ran at him with her dagger raised. Henri blocked her arm, and they stood staring at each other. A terrible shock made the blood run cold in their veins, and their legs trembled like those of two startled horses. Plautus's twins* could not have been more alike. Each spoke the same phrase at the same time: 'Surely, Lord Dudley must be your father?'

Each nodded in affirmation.

'At least she kept it in the family,' said Henri, pointing to Paquita.

'She was as guiltless as could be,' replied Marguerita-Euphemia Porrabéril, throwing herself upon the body of Paquita with a cry of despair. 'Poor girl! Oh, if only I could bring you back to life! I was wrong! Forgive me, Paquita! You are dead, and I am alive! I suffer more than you.'

At that moment the terrifying figure of Paquita's mother appeared.

'I know you will say that killing her was not a part of our bargain,' exclaimed the Marquise. 'I know what has brought you out of your den. I'll pay you double. Hold your tongue.'

She went and fetched a bag of gold from the ebony cabinet, and threw it contemptuously at the old woman's feet.

The clinking of the gold coins was enough to bring the trace of a smile to the stony features of the Georgian woman.

'I've come just in time, sister,' said Henri. 'You will have to answer to the law...'

'I shall answer no one,' replied the Marquise. 'There is only one person to whom I would have been answerable, but that is Christemio, who is dead.'

'And won't her mother', asked Henri, pointing to the old woman, 'still hold you to ransom?'

'She comes from a country where women are not people but things, you do whatever you want with them, they can be bought and sold, or killed, and in fact be used according to your fancy, as you use your furniture. What is more, she has one passion that overrules all others and would have destroyed her maternal love for her daughter, had she felt any. A passion...'

'A passion for what?' exclaimed Henri, interrupting his sister.

'For gambling,' replied the Marquise. 'May God protect you from it.'

'But', asked Henri, pointing to the Girl with the Golden Eyes, 'who will help you to remove these traces of your extravagance, which the law would never allow you to forget?'

'I have her mother,' replied the Marquise, pointing at the old Georgian woman and motioning her to stay.

'We shall meet again,' said Henri, who was thinking that his friends would be worried, and felt that it was time to leave.

'No, brother,' she said, 'we shall never meet again. I'm returning to Spain to enter the convent of Los Dolores.'

'You are still too young and too beautiful,' said Henri, taking her into his arms and giving her a kiss.

'Farewell,' she said, 'nothing can console us for losing what seemed infinite to us.'

A week later, Paul de Manerville encountered de Marsay at the Tuileries, on the Terrasse des Feuillants.

'Well, what has become of our beautiful Girl with Golden Eyes, you old rascal?'

'She died.'

'What of?'

'Something to do with the heart.'

Paris, March 1834–April 1835

EXPLANATORY NOTES

SARRASINE

3 *Charles de Bernard du Grail*: Charles de Bernard was an early admirer of Balzac's writings, and Balzac encouraged him to become a novelist himself. The dedication was added in 1844, when the story was republished in the collected edition of *La Comédie humaine*.

the Elysée-Bourbon Palace: the palace was purchased by Louis XVIII in 1816 as his royal residence. It is now the official residence of the President of the French Republic.

4 *Monsieur de Nucingen*: the fictional character of Monsieur de Nucingen, a wealthy banker, also features in Balzac's *Le Père Goriot* (1835) and *La Maison Nucingen* (1838).

5 *the magic lamp*: according to a story in *One Thousand and One Nights*, Aladdin finds a magic lamp which contains a powerful spirit who helps him to become rich and marry the Chinese emperor's daughter.

Malibran, Sontag, or Fodor: Maria Malibran (1808–36), Henrietta Sontag (1806–54), and La Fodor (1789–1870) were all famous singers of the time. Malibran was known for her vivacity and the dramatic power of her mezzo-soprano voice, Sontag for her charm and the clarity of her singing, and La Fodor was celebrated for her taste, elegance, and the natural quality of her singing voice.

Monsieur de Jaucourt: a similar anecdote featuring the Marquis de Jaucourt was recorded in Balzac's anonymous *Album historique et anecdotique* (1827).

6 *Antinous*: an effeminate favourite of the Roman emperor Hadrian, Antinous was proclaimed a god by Hadrian after his early death. Many statues and coins represent Antinous as the ideal example of youthful male beauty.

Metternich or Wellington: Prince Klemens von Metternich (1773–1858), an Austrian statesman who organized the Congress of Vienna (September 1814 to June 1815) and the convention of Berlin of 1833. Arthur Wellesley (1769–1852), first Duke of Wellington, who defeated Napoleon at the Battle of Waterloo of 1815.

Lord Byron: George Gordon, Lord Byron (1788–1824), Romantic poet and author of the narrative poems *Childe Harold's Pilgrimage* (1812) and *Don Juan* (1824).

Vespasian's axiom: Titus Flavius Vespasianus, known as Vespasian (AD 9–79), was Roman Emperor AD 69–79, and responsible for the rebuilding of Rome, including the beginning of the construction of the Coliseum. In France, public urinals are named *vespasiennes* after him, possibly in reference to the tax he placed on urine collection. In response to critics, he is reported to have said 'pecunia non olet' (money doesn't stink).

6 *Ann Radcliffe novel*: Ann Radcliffe (1764–1823), English novelist, author of *The Mysteries of Udolpho* (1794) and other Gothic novels associated with haunted castles, ancient ruins, and mysterious aristocratic families.

routs: a rout is a large evening party or reception that was popular in England in the eighteenth and early nineteenth century.

7 *vampire... Robin Hood*: 'The Vampyre' (1819) was a story by John William Polidori (1795–1821) and is believed by many to have been the first work of literature to feature a vampire. The idea of an artificial man derives from the novel *Frankenstein* (1818) by Mary Shelley (1797–1851). Faust is the scholar who makes a pact with the devil in Goethe's *Faust* (*Part I*, 1808 and *Part II* 1832). Robin Hood may have been familiar to French readers from his appearance in *Ivanhoe* (1819) by Sir Walter Scott, translated into French in 1820.

Prince of Mysore: Balzac's knowledge of the Prince of Mysore may have come from Sir Walter Scott's story 'The Surgeon's Daughter', which appeared in *The Keepsake Stories* (1828). Hyder Ali (1720–82) was the ruler of the Kingdom of Mysore in southern India and fought many successful battles against the British.

'*Genoese head*': in the Middle Ages the Italian city of Genoa was famous as a centre of wealth based on its shipbuilding and banking industries. A gold coin known as the 'génoïse' was minted there. Hence the idea of a rich patriarch, on whose life or death the whole family's fortunes depend.

Balsamo . . . Cagliostro: Count Alessandro di Cagliostro, also known as Giuseppe Balsamo (1743–95), was an Italian adventurer who practised alchemy and other occult sciences.

8 *Comte de Saint-Germain*: a famous adventurer (died 1784) of uncertain origin who spied for Louis XV, composed music in London, dabbled in alchemy and theosophy, and around whom swirled rumours of mysterious exploits in many different countries.

10 *Minerva . . . head*: according to classical myth, the goddess Minerva was born from her father Jupiter's head.

Tancredi: this opera by Gioacchino Rossini (1792–1868) enjoyed considerable success in Paris in the 1820s with Maria Malibran and Henrietta Sontag (see note to p. 5). Raphael, the hero of Balzac's *The Wild Ass's Skin*, whistles the same cavatina near the beginning of that novel.

11 *acute phthisis*: a progressive wasting disease; a form of consumption.

13 *chimera*: in Greek mythology, a monstrous fire-breathing monster made up of the parts of many animals. See also note to *The Girl with the Golden Eyes*, p. 93.

14 *Adonis*: in classical myth Adonis was a handsome youth who was gored by a wild boar in the hunt and died in the arms of his lover, the goddess Venus.

Vien: Joseph-Marie Vien (1716–1809), French painter who was appointed director of the School of France at Rome and was King Louis XVI's official painter.

15 *'Addio, addio!'*: 'Goodbye, goodbye!' (Italian).

17 *lily-gilded throne*: as a judge representing the Bourbon regime, the elder Sarrasine's throne was gilded with the 'fleur de lys', the Bourbon emblem.

prefect: in a French Jesuit school a prefect was one of the priests responsible for imposing discipline, not one of the pupils as in an English private school.

monitor: the monitor could be either a senior pupil helping his classmates to prepare their lessons or an auxiliary teacher.

tabernacle: the tabernacle in a Roman Catholic church is a small chest placed on the middle of the altar. It contains the ciborium, or gold-lined cup, in which the communion wafer is kept.

18 *Bouchardon*: Edmé Bouchardon (1698–1762), the most celebrated French sculptor of his time.

prize for sculpture: the 'Prix de Rome' was inaugurated by Louis XIV in 1663 and reinstated after the French Revolution by Napoleon. It gave painters and sculptors the opportunity to study art in Rome for three years.

Madame de Pompadour: Jeanne Antoinette Poisson (1721–64), known as Madame de Pompadour, the chief mistress of Louis XV.

Diderot: Denis Diderot (1713–84) was a French philosopher, art critic, and writer.

19 *Canova*: Antonio Canova (1757–1822), Venetian neoclassical sculptor whose works include *Psyche and Cupid* (1793) and the *Three Graces* (1814).

Comédie-Française: a famous Paris theatre that still exists today.

Madame Geoffrin's salon: Marie Thérèse Rodet Geoffrin (1699–1777) presided over a salon that became famous as a centre of Enlightenment thinking.

Sophie Arnould: (1740–1802), a soprano who was also famous for her witty conversation. Diderot refers to her in his *Lettres à Sophie Volland*.

Teatro d'Argentina: Rome's most important opera-house, opened in 1732.

"Jommelli": Niccolò Jommelli (1714–74), Italian composer who came to Rome to great acclaim in 1749.

Jean-Jacques Rousseau: philosopher and writer (1712–78) associated with the eighteenth-century Enlightenment movement. His work *The Social*

Contract (1762) had a decisive influence on the political ideas of the French Revolution.

20 *Baron d'Holbach's salon*: Paul-Henri Thiry, Baron d'Holbach (1723–89), French-German author, philosopher, and encyclopedist. He was a major figure in the French Enlightenment.

21 *Pygmalion*: in Ovid's *Metamorphoses* Pygmalion was a Greek sculptor who fell under the spell of the statue he had created and asked Aphrodite, goddess of love, to bring her to life.

24 *horses of the immortals depicted by Homer*: in Homer's *Odyssey* the horses of Helios or Apollo, god of the sun, cross the sky at lightning speed.

"Poverino!": 'Poor wretch!' (Italian).

26 *Madame du Barry*: Jeanne Bécu, known as Madame du Barry (1743–93), the mistress of Louis XV, was executed under the Terror during the French Revolution.

27 *Peralta wine and Pedro Ximenez sherry*: Peralta is a Tuscan wine and Pedro Ximenez is a rich, sweet sherry, still produced today.

28 *today is Friday*: Friday was a traditional day of abstinence for Roman Catholics.

Frascati: a town about 20 kilometres south-east of Rome.

Villa Ludovisi: the Villa Ludovisi was built in the seventeenth century by Cardinal Ludovisi (1767–1834), and is mentioned in Stendhal's *Promenades dans Rome* (1829).

phaeton: the phaeton, named after the rash son of Apollo who drove his father's steeds too fast and too near the sun, was a small open carriage, with two forward-facing seats and four large wheels. It was reputed to be fast, sporty, and dangerous.

31 *Sappho*: (*c*.630–570 BC), Greek lyric poetess whose poetry centres on passion for various characters of both genders, but particularly of her own sex, hence the dramatic irony of Sarrasine's words.

32 *berlin*: the 'berlin' was a covered carriage, with two or four inside seats, and a separate sheltered seat behind for a footman. La Zambinella is returning in a safe family carriage rather than in the more intimate phaeton.

Vien, Lauterbourg, and Allegrain: for Vien, see note to p. 14; the other two friends are fictional characters.

33 *Prince Chigi*: the Chigi family was a Roman princely family, also mentioned by Stendhal in *Promenades dans Rome* (1829).

35 *a divine harpy*: in Greek mythology a harpy was a winged, violent spirit of revenge, often depicted with a female face.

36 *Vien . . . Girodet . . . Endymion*: *The Sleep of Endymion* (1792) by Girodet (Anne-Louis Girodet de Roussy-Triosson, 1767–1824) was a painting much admired by the young Balzac, which now hangs in the Louvre

Museum in Paris. In an earlier version of the story it was Girodet, not Vien, who copied the statue of la Zambinella.

THE UNKNOWN MASTERPIECE

The dedication 'To a Lord' was added to the Furne edition (see Note on the Texts). The dedicatee is unknown, although it has been noted that '*A un lord*' is an anagram of 'Arnould'. The singer Sophie Arnould was a friend of Balzac's and is mentioned in his story 'Sarrasine', also published in 1831. The five lines of ellipsis are Balzac's. The opening chapter was entitled 'Maître Frenhofer' when the story was first published in *L'Artiste* in 1831. In later versions Balzac delays the revelation of Frenhofer's name. In 1847 'Gillette' appears, perhaps by oversight, as the title for the whole story.

39 *Towards the end of 1612*: the date of the action of *The Unknown Masterpiece* coincides with the career of Nicolas Poussin (1594–1665), who arrived in Paris at about the age of 18 to study painting, and who is named later in the story. Poussin went on to achieve fame in Rome before returning to Paris in 1640 to work for Richelieu and Louis XIII. His seventeenth-century classical style had a huge influence on French art.

Maître François Porbus: the French name for Frans Pourbus the younger (1570–1622), a Flemish painter who worked at the French court producing portraits of Henri IV and the young Louis XIII. A portrait of Henri IV (1553–1610) by Pourbus hangs in the Louvre.

Henri IV . . . Marie de Medici . . . Rubens: Marie de Medici (1573 1642) was the wife and queen of Henri IV (1553–1610; Protestant king of Navarre 1572–1610; king of France 1589–1610; converted to Catholicism in 1593), from 1600 until his assassination in 1610, then Regent during the childhood of their son Louis XIII until 1617. She chose the Flemish artist Peter Paul Rubens (1577–1660) as court painter in 1620, and commissioned from him the series of paintings known as the Marie de Medici cycle to decorate the newly restored Palais du Luxembourg.

41 *Rembrandt*: Rembrandt van Rijn (1606–69), the Dutch painter celebrated for his subtle interplay of light and shade.

three colours of crayon: the three-colour sketch, executed on tinted paper using white, sepia, and charcoal crayons, was already becoming rare by the seventeenth century.

42 *Saint Mary of Egypt*: no such painting by Porbus is known to exist, and Balzac's description does not resemble any other seventeenth-century painting of Saint Mary of Egypt. Mary was a young Alexandrian prostitute who travelled to Jerusalem in pursuit of her trade. Later, guided by a vision of the Virgin Mary, she reformed, and crossed the Jordan to live a life of pious hermitage in the desert. One version of the story has her paying the voyage out from Alexandria in kind rather than with money, and Balzac's imaginary painting seems to have been inspired by this episode.

42 *forced to sell it*: Marie de Medici was banished from France for conspiring against Cardinal Richelieu, and spent her last days in poverty in Cologne.

linear and aerial perspective: linear perspective was introduced in the Renaissance and, as formulated by Alberti, uses a vanishing-point to create the illusion of relative size and distance. Aerial perspective, whereby distance is indicated by the gradually increasing haziness of light and contour, was used by Dutch artists from the fifteenth century onwards and was championed by Leonardo da Vinci.

43 *Promethean torch . . . divine fire*: in Greek myth Prometheus stole fire, unknown to men, from Zeus, the king of the gods. With this fire he was able to create arts and crafts.

Hans Holbein and Titian, Albrecht Dürer and Paolo Veronese: Hans Holbein (1497–1543) was a German painter who illustrated Luther's translation of the Bible with woodcuts and portrayed leading Tudor dignitaries. Both he and Albrecht Dürer (1471–1528), a German painter and engraver, were dedicated to accurate draughtsmanship and realistic representation. Titian (1488–1576) and Paolo Veronese (1528–88) were Venetian painters who were celebrated for their sensuous and colourful art. Balzac hints at the debate between the nineteenth-century proponents of drawing (the supporters of Ingres) and those who promoted colour (the supporters of Delacroix).

44 *Proteus of myth*: in Greek myth Proteus was a sea-god who escaped his captors by changing form when charged with unwelcome questions.

Raphael: (1483–1520), Italian painter and architect of the High Renaissance.

45 *currus venustus . . . pulcher homo*: Latin for 'beautiful chariot' and 'handsome man'.

Mabuse: Jan Mabuse (1478–1532), also known as Jan Gassaert, was a Flemish painter who painted in England and Italy.

46 *Nicolas Poussin*: see note to p. 39.

47 *'O Filii' at Easter*: 'O Filii et Filiae' is a Catholic hymn, dating from the Middle Ages, that celebrates Christ's resurrection.

48 *my Belle Noiseuse*: a 'belle noiseuse' is a beautiful but nagging woman, along the lines of Shakespeare's Kate in *The Taming of the Shrew*. In 1847 Balzac changed the reference to 'my Catherine Lescault'. Lescault and her nickname, La Belle Noiseuse, are Balzac's invention.

the Norman's wretched jacket: Poussin came from Normandy.

Adam: an *Adam and Eve* by Mabuse can be seen at Hampton Court Palace.

49 *Giorgione*: (1478–1511), Venetian painter renowned, like Veronese, for his use of colour.

50 *the truth of it*: in this passage Frenhofer appears to anticipate developments in nineteenth-century painting.

51 *Pygmalion*: see note to *Sarrasine*, p. 21.

52 *Orpheus*: in Greek myth Orpheus descended into the Underworld to bring back his dead wife Eurydice, but disobeyed instructions not to look back at her, and so lost her forever.

old ruffian: in the original French Frenhofer is referred to as a *reître*, a mercenary medieval knight.

Charles Quint: Charles V (1500–58), king of the Spanish Empire (as King Carlos I of Spain) from 1516 and Holy Roman Emperor from 1519 until his abdication in 1556.

57 *thickening of the spleen*: the French term *hypochondrie* did not mean an imaginary illness in the nineteenth century, but an inflammation of the abdomen.

58 *Ariosto's Angelica*: Angelica is the heroine of *Orlando Furioso* (1532), the Renaissance epic poem by the Italian poet Ludovico Ariosto (1474–1533).

Dante's Beatrice: Beatrice di Folco Portinari (1266–90), with whom Dante (1265–1321) fell in love although he saw her only twice, and who appears in the *Divine Comedy*, written long after her death, to lead the poet-pilgrim from Purgatory into Heaven.

by Correggio, by Michelangelo: Antonio da Correggio (1489–1534) and Michelangelo (1475–1564) were Italian Renaissance painters. Michelangelo was also a sculptor, architect, poet, and engineer.

my Belle Noiseuse: changed in 1847 back to the 'my Catherine' of an earlier version.

59 *woman reclining . . . cord retaining the curtains*: the Oriental details of the painting recall *La Grande Odalisque* (1814) by the French painter Jean-Auguste-Dominique Ingres (1780–1867), first exhibited in Paris in the Salon of 1819.

Catherine Lescault . . . La Belle Noiseuse: abbreviated in 1847 to 'Catherine'.

61 *the beautiful courtesan*: in 1847, Balzac dropped these words, which had not appeared in the early versions of the text.

64 *beggarly . . . whoreson*: I have borrowed these seventeenth-century epithets from Kent's words to Oswald in Shakespeare's *King Lear*, II. ii.

65 *February 1832*: like the dedication, this date was added in the Furne edition. Since it corresponds neither to the period of first composition nor to that of the major revision, it no doubt refers to some personal event.

THE GIRL WITH THE GOLDEN EYES

67 *Eugène Delacroix, painter*: Delacroix (1798–1863) was an acquaintance of Balzac. He was known for his revolutionary and Romantic themes, with his *La Liberté guidant le peuple*, 1831, as well as his interest in the Oriental, in *Femmes d'Alger dans leur appartement*, 1834.

69 *Then on Mondays*: factories and workplaces were closed on Sundays for church and on Mondays for leisure.

70 *Vulcan*: the Roman god of fire, but also a blacksmith by trade.

Napoleons: Napoleon Bonaparte (1769–1821) became First Consul of the French Republic in 1799, Life Consul in 1802, and Emperor 1804–15. His name was a byword for egalitarian opportunity, since he had first arrived in France as an obscure Corsican immigrant and worked his way up through the ranks of the army by sheer talent and energy.

Le Constitutionnel: a newspaper founded as *L'Indépendant* during Napoleon's 'Hundred Days' (20 March 1815–22 June 1815), it became the main mouthpiece for liberal opposition under the Restoration (1815–30) and then under the July Monarchy (1830–48). It was in fact the principal bourgeois newspaper of the day.

National Guard: originally formed in 1791 from citizens' militias in each city and headed by Lafayette. It was disarmed by Napoleon in 1795 after it supported a royalist insurrection, and re-established after his abdication in 1814 by Louis XIV. Charles X dissolved it again in 1827. It was reinstated under Louis Philippe in 1831 after the July Revolution, with Lafayette once again in charge. All male citizens were obliged to undertake an annual period of service. Overall, this Paris reserve constabulary supported constitutional monarchy and was seen as a bastion of middle-class values.

72 *Taglioni's thighs*: Marie Taglioni joined the Opéra in 1827, and became their star ballerina with a celebrated performance in *La Sylphide*, 1832.

Proteus: see note to *The Unknown Masterpiece*, p. 44.

73 *Père Lachaise cemetery*: a Parisian cemetery, opened in 1804, which soon became the largest burial-ground in France.

74 *Rabelais's Gargantua*: in François Rabelais's *Gargantua* (1534) the exploits and opinions of his giant hero serve as a means to mock the pettiness of scholastic education and social conventions, among other things.

Longchamp: part of the Bois de Boulogne which was used for riding, but did not become an official racecourse until 1857.

Légion d'Honneur: an honour inaugurated by Napoleon on 19 May 1802 to reward outstanding military and public service. It is still awarded annually.

Dante: Dante Alighieri (1265–1321) whose *Divine Comedy*, comprising the *Inferno*, *Purgatory*, and *Paradise*, inspired Balzac's conception of his own *La Comédie humaine*.

76 *Bichat*: Xavier Bichat (1771–1802), a noted specialist in anatomy and physiology.

Jacques Coeur: businessman, merchant, trader, and banker (1395–1456), who served Charles VII as 'maître des monnaies' from 1436, 'argentier du roi' from 1439, and 'conseiller du roi' from 1442.

Danton and Robespierre: Georges-Jacques Danton (1759–94) was *avocat du conseil du roi* (Louis XV) from 1787 to 1791 and the new Republic's Minister of Justice from 1792. After protesting against the massacres of September 1792, and calling for an end to the Terror, he was ejected from the *Comité du salut public* in 1793 and executed. Balzac sees him as an opportunist. Maximilien de Robespierre (1758–94) was an advocate who turned Republican only after 1792. From 1793 he overthrew the Girondins and led the *Comité du salut public*, launching the Terror, but fell foul of his own extremists and was executed in July 1794; another opportunist, in Balzac's view.

77 *Louis XIV*: Louis XIV (1638–1715) concentrated the power of the monarchy to such an extent that his control over Church and State and all institutions earned him the title of 'le roi soleil'.

78 '*Lutetia*': 'Lutèce', the ancient name for Paris, was a Celtic word meaning 'swamp'.

79 *theriakis*: opium eaters or smokers.

La Rochefoucauld's maxims: François de la Rochefoucauld (1613–80) published his *Réflexions ou sentences et maximes morales* in 1665. These witty, cynical proverbs encapsulated an amoral, individualistic, detached view of human behaviour.

80 *1789*: the start of the French Revolution.

1814: the date of Napoleon's first abdication (4–6 April), and the restoration of the Bourbon monarchy under Louis XVIII.

City of Paris: the crest of the City of Paris, pictured as a galleon, bore, and still bears, the motto *fluctuat nec mergitur*, 'She is rocked by the waves but never sinks'.

Napoleon for lookout: probably a reference to the placing of a statue of Napoleon on top of the Colonne Vendôme by Louis-Philippe in July 1833.

81 *flâneurs*: Baudelaire later immortalized this figure of the idle dandy, strolling the boulevards merely to see and be seen, in his study of Constantin Guys, *Le Peintre de la vie moderne*, in 1863.

82 *Raphaelesque figures*: the paintings of Raphael were seen in the nineteenth century as embodying an ideal beauty.

Tuileries: the Tuileries palace had been Louis XV's royal residence in Paris (as opposed to the official court in Versailles). In 1793 it became the seat of the Republican *Convention nationale*. From the start of Napoleon's Empire (1804) it became the residence of the head of state (Napoleon, Louis XVIII, Napoleon, Louis XVIII, etc.)

83 *war between France and England*: George III's government declared war on the new French Republic after the Convention broke off relations with London in April 1793. Apart from a short-lived peace treaty in 1802–4 (which allowed Wordsworth briefly to meet the young French mother of

his love-child, conceived in Paris during the heady days of the Revolution), the so-called 'Continental War' lasted until 1815.

83 *a Borgia at the Vatican*: the Borgia family had produced popes in the fifteenth century (Alonso Borgia as Calixte III, 1455–8; Rodrigo Borgia as Alexander VI, 1492–1503). The family was also famed for its violence and corruption, as epitomized by Cesare and Lucrezia, the children of Alexander VI. Balzac suggests that corruption was an acceptable side-effect of ecclesiastic success, somehow stifled by Republican repression.

churches . . . closed in those days: after the initial rejection of religion by the French Revolution, in 1801 Napoleon as First Consul negotiated a first Concordat, or treaty, with Pope Pius VII. This established the supremacy of the French church over Rome, and of the French state over both. Stendhal's *Le Rouge et le Noir* remains the most witty and sarcastic fictional account of the struggle between the state and the church, whose schools remained closed until the 1830s.

84 *Frascati's club*: an elegant gambling club on the corner of the Rue de Richelieu and the Boulevard Montmartre.

85 *Je maintiendrai*: 'I will stand firm', motto of the Orange family, which had indeed showed staying-power. Guillaume le Grand, comte de Toulouse, was celebrated for his exploits against the Saracens in the twelfth-century *Chanson de Guillaume.* In the sixteenth century William the Silent was the hero of Dutch resistance against the Spanish occupying forces, leading to Dutch independence. William III of Orange became king of England in 1688, with his wife Mary as queen, after the 'Glorious Revolution' which deposed James II.

Cherubino: a naughty but charming young manservant to the Countess in Beaumarchais' play *Le Mariage de Figaro* (1784) and Mozart's opera *Le Nozze di Figaro* (1786).

savate or combat de canne: kick-boxing or stick-fighting. These sports (or self-defence martial arts) are still practised not only in the South-West of France but also in Britain.

86 *Barbaja*: Domenico Barbaja (1778–1841) was Rossini's impresario, who ran two opera-houses in Vienna, as well as La Scala in Milan.

occupation of Spain: known in England as the 'Peninsular War'. Napoleon installed his brother Joseph as ruler of Spain in 1808. Spanish guerillas and the allies entered into battle against Napoleon's 'Grande armée'. The Duke of Wellington—later to be victorious at Waterloo—finally won this bloody campaign in 1814.

April 1815: Henri de Marsay is walking through the Tuileries gardens during the 'hundred days' of Napoleon's return to power. Napoleon had escaped exile and taken up residence in the Tuileries palace on 20 March 1815; he was defeated at Waterloo on 18 June 1815.

87 *Rousseau's Émile*: Jean-Jacques Rousseau's work *Émile, or On Education*

(1762) won enormous fame for its depiction of the benefits of a natural, as opposed to repressive, education.

88 *Pitt and Coburg*: William Pitt (1759–1806) was British prime minister from 1783 until the victory at Trafalgar, 1805. Frederick-Joseph (1737–1815) was Duke of Saxe-Coburg, Austria, and commanded the allied coalition armies in the Netherlands from 1792. The 'Pitt and Coburg' faction denoted anyone with royalist tendencies, thought by the Convention to be supporting England and Austria against France.

89 *cholera*: cholera outbreaks were devastating and potentially revolutionary in the first half of the nineteenth century. In the spring of 1830 there was a cholera epidemic in Paris, and in 1831—soon after the 1830 'July Revolution'—the 'canuts', silk-workers of Lyons, rose in revolt, not just against their poor salaries but also their insanitary working and living conditions which they judged responsible for terrible outbreaks of the disease in the city. The insurgents were crushed.

90 *quibiscum viis*: Latin, 'by any means'.

écarté: a card game.

91 *Corporal Trim . . . cap*: in *Tristram Shandy* by Laurence Sterne (1713–68), Corporal Trim repeatedly says: 'I'll wager my Montero cap.'

92 *animal magnetism*: this notion had been popularized as part of the theory and therapy of 'hypnotism'—also known as 'mesmerism'—of Franz Anton Mesmer (1734–1815), a German doctor (*Mémoire sur la découverte du magnétisme animal*, 1779).

Bourbons were still here. Louis XVIII, placed on the throne by the allies in 1814, had fled to Belgium in March 1815 when Napoleon briefly stormed back into power.

93 *Woman Embracing her Chimera*: the chimera or *khimaera* was a fabulous beast in Greek mythology which had three heads, those of a lion and a goat on its neck, and that of a dragon at the end of its tail. In Henri de Latouche's *Fragoletta, ou Naples et Paris en 1799*, 1829, the fresco (not, *pace* Balzac, a 'cameo') discovered at Pompeii is described as it was seen on display at the museum of Naples. This version has the wings of a dove and the gills of a fish. Here Balzac refers loosely to the conjunction of the beautiful and the monstrous, as he does in another story in this collection, 'Sarrasine'. The chimera figure became increasingly popular later this century with a collection of verse by Gérard de Nerval, *Les Chimères* (1854), and a poem by Baudelaire, 'Chacun sa Chimère', in *Le Spleen de Paris* (1869). Balzac often uses the word in the sense of 'favourite fantasy'.

95 *Frontin . . . comedy*: the archetypal smart valet in sophisticated eighteenth-century comedy, for instance in Marivaux's *Les Serments indiscrets*, 1732.

costume of an Auvergnat: the Auvergne was an impoverished, mountainous, agricultural region in central France. In the nineteenth century many Auvergnat peasants emigrated to Paris looking for menial work. They were recognizable by their hats, long scarves, and clogs.

95 *armed with a clapper*: as there were no fixed collection or delivery times for post at this time, the postman would sound his clapper as he passed by a building so that the doorkeeper would know he was passing and come out to collect or send out letters.

96 *Puits sans vin*: the name is literally a 'wineless well', but probably more easily guessed as a 'bottomless pit'.

Vidocq: François Eugène Vidocq (1775–1857) was an escaped convict who was recruited by the police in 1809 as a 'secret agent', and became head of the security brigade in 1811. In 1827 he resigned to set up a paper factory, and published his memoirs in 1829. In 1832 he rejoined the police. Balzac immortalized him in fictional form as Vautrin in *Père Goriot* (1834), *Illusions perdues* (1843), and *Splendeurs et misères des courtisanes* (1847).

discreet agent: the postman says in French *hémisphère secret* ('secret hemisphere') instead of *émissaire secret* ('secret emissary'). The postman is laughing at the improbability of the attribution, rather than being aware of his own malapropism.

97 *Baron de Nucingen*: this great banker, an invention of Balzac's, is one of the recurrent characters of *La Comédie humaine*. He appears in *Père Goriot* (1834) and *La maison Nucingen* (1837). See also note to *Sarrasine*, p. 4.

sparrer . . . native French: I use the cockney spelling in English, because the correct French spelling for sparrow is 'moineau'.

King Ferdinand: Ferdinand VII (1784–1833) was briefly king of Spain in 1808 until Napoleon sent his brother Joseph to Madrid to rule there. Ferdinand was reinstated by the allies in 1814 after a long war, and continued to reign until 1833. His rule was bitterly contested from within for his abolition of Napoleon's relatively liberal constitution and his repression of dissent (see note to p. 86).

99 *Lovelace . . . Clarissa Harlowe*: the protagonists of *Clarissa, or the History of a Young Lady* (1748), by Samuel Richardson (1689–1761), are a dissolute man and a determinedly innocent girl (see note to p. 121).

Figaro: hero of Beaumarchais' and Mozart's *Marriage of Figaro* (see note to p. 85).

101 *La Fayette . . . Talleyrand . . . Désaugiers . . . Ségur*: the Marquis de Lafayette (1757–1834) fought against Britain in the American War of Independence and then helped to draft the Declaration of the Rights of Man for the French Revolution in 1789. But he was too moderate for the Jacobins. In 1818 he became a member of the French Restoration parliament, and leader of the radical opposition in 1825. During the 1830 Revolution he commanded the National Guard. Charles Maurice de Talleyrand (1754–1838) was president of the Assembly in 1790 but was exiled to London in 1792 by the Jacobin extremists, and left for the United States in 1794. Under the more moderate Directoire he returned to France as Foreign Minister, and in 1802 helped nominate Napoleon as Consul for life. He turned against Napoleon after his defeat in Russia (1812) and voted for his

deposition in 1814. He remained head of Foreign Affairs under Louis XVIII, and advised Louis-Philippe during the 1830 Revolution. Désaugiers (1772–1827) was a comic performer and vaudeville writer who founded the 'Caveau moderne' music-hall at the *Rocher de Cancale* (see note to p. 106). Alexandre-Joseph Ségur (1756–1805) and his brother Louis-Philippe (1753–1830) wrote comic operas and vaudeville sketches.

102 *Argus*: in Greek mythology Argus was a giant watchman with a hundred eyes. The goddess Hera had appointed him to watch over the nymph Io whom she had turned into a cow, but Hermes sent him to sleep by playing his flute, and then decapitated him.

104 *Talma . . . Othello*: François-Joseph Talma (1763–1826) was the best-known French tragic actor of his day, famous for playing the title-role in Shakespeare's *Othello* in 1825, and also for trying to use accurate period costume.

Louis XI's executioners: Louis XI (1423–83), king of France 1461–83. He fought against Charles the Bold, duc de Bourgogne, and was imprisoned in 1448. However, in 1477 he allied himself with Switzerland and Lorraine and managed to conquer Burgundy and kill Charles. He also annexed Anjou, Maine, and Provence to the kingdom of France. He supported the army and opposed the clergy. Balzac refers to him as an example of a ruthless, military-minded monarch who took no hostages.

106 *Rocher de Cancale*: a fashionable restaurant and cabaret (see note to p.101).

107 *Ann Radcliffe's novels*. see note to *Sarrasine*, p. 6.

109 *slave bought in Georgia*: in the first half of the nineteenth century Georgia was the centre of a trans-Caucasian slave trade.

113 *Xerxes*: Xerxes I, king of Persia 486–465 BC, destroyed Athens in 480 BC but was defeated by the Greeks at Salamis. He was famous throughout antiquity for his exploit in building a bridge of boats across the Hellespont to enable his army to invade Greece (484 BC).

115 *gutters*: before Baron Haussman's underground sewers were introduced to Paris in the 1860s, waste water ran through gutters down the side or the middle of each street. Henri's carriage, moving along the boulevards parallel to the Seine, would have rattled as it crossed each gutter running across the boulevard down a side-street from the hill of Montmartre to the Seine below.

120 *Saadi and Hafiz*: Saadi (1184–1292), Persian poet famous for his *Gulistan*, or 'rose garden'. Hafiz (1326–90), a later Persian lyric poet, celebrated wine, women, and flowers in his verse, with mystical overtones.

Pindar: Pindar, or Pindaros (*c.*518–*c.*438 BC), Greek lyric poet, the author of celebrated odes.

121 *Rousseau . . . Richardson's fiction*: Balzac refers to Rousseau's *Appendice à La Nouvelle Héloïse*, or *Les Amours de Milord Edouard Bomston*. Balzac is

suggesting that Rousseau's virtuous protagonist is modelled after Richardson's hero Grandison (*The History of Sir Charles Grandison*, 1754). See note to p. 99.

122 *houri*: one of the female virgin attendants of the blessed in the Muslim paradise.

124 *Cardinal Richelieu*: (1585–1642), Louis XIII's Minister for War and Foreign Affairs (1616), Minister of State (1624), and Chief Minister (1629). He suppressed the Huguenots, seized the Duchy of Lorraine, and was instrumental in winning the Thirty Years War against Spain. In addition to reforming French finance and law, he founded the Académie Française in 1635.

126 *Dangerous Liaisons . . . chambermaid's name for a title*: Balzac refers to two of the most scandalously erotic novels of the eighteenth century: *Les Liaisons dangereuses* (1782) by Choderlos de Laclos (1741–1803), and *Justine, ou les malheurs de la vertu* (1791) by the Marquis de Sade (1740–1814).

Salon des Étrangers: an aristocratic club, of which Talleyrand was a member.

130 *Faust . . . Manfred . . . Don Juan*: refers to the heroes of Goethe's *Faust* and Byron's *Manfred* (1817) and *Don Juan* (1819–24), seducers and conquerors, who are unafraid of God or the Devil.

134 *Ferragus . . . Dévorants*: Ferragus is the hero of Balzac's story of that name, the leader of an underworld fellowship known as 'Les Dévorants' ('The Devourers'), and member of the elite secret society of the Thirteen, to which de Marsay also belongs. The trilogy *L'Histoire des Treize* consists of *Ferragus*, *La Duchesse de Langeais*, and *La Fille aux yeux d'or*.

136 *Homer's Achilles . . . walls of Troy*: in Homer's *Iliad* the Greek hero Achilles drags the corpse of his Trojan enemy Hector behind his chariot around the walls of the besieged city of Troy to avenge the death of his own friend Patroclus.

Plautus's twins: *The Menaechmi* by the Roman comic playwright Plautus (*c.*254–*c.*184 BC) features two identical twins, separated in childhood and reunited later without recognizing each other, with comic repercussions. The play was one of the sources of Shakespeare's *Comedy of Errors* and Carlo Goldoni's *The Two Venetian Twins*.

The Oxford World's Classics Website

www.worldsclassics.co.uk

- Browse the full range of Oxford World's Classics online
- Sign up for our monthly e-alert to receive information on new titles
- Read extracts from the Introductions
- Listen to our editors and translators talk about the world's greatest literature with our Oxford World's Classics audio guides
- Join the conversation, follow us on Twitter at OWC_Oxford
- Teachers and lecturers can order inspection copies quickly and simply via our website

www.worldsclassics.co.uk

MORE ABOUT **OXFORD WORLD'S CLASSICS**

American Literature
British and Irish Literature
Children's Literature
Classics and Ancient Literature
Colonial Literature
Eastern Literature
European Literature
Gothic Literature
History
Medieval Literature
Oxford English Drama
Poetry
Philosophy
Politics
Religion
The Oxford Shakespeare

A SELECTION OF **OXFORD WORLD'S CLASSICS**

Ludovico Ariosto	**Orlando Furioso**
Giovanni Boccaccio	**The Decameron**
Luís Vaz de Camões	**The Lusíads**
Miguel de Cervantes	**Don Quixote de la Mancha** **Exemplary Stories**
Carlo Collodi	**The Adventures of Pinocchio**
Dante Alighieri	**The Divine Comedy** **Vita Nuova**
Lope de Vega	**Three Major Plays**
J. W. von Goethe	**Faust: Part One and Part Two**
Leonardo da Vinci	**Selections from the Notebooks**
Federico Garcia Lorca	**Four Major Plays**
Niccolò Machiavelli	**Discourses on Livy** **The Prince**
Michelangelo	**Life, Letters, and Poetry**
Petrarch	**Selections from the Canzoniere and Other Works**
Giorgio Vasari	**The Lives of the Artists**